D0807348

THE HOUSEWIFE ASSASSIN GETS LUCKY

JOSIE BROWN
DEBORAH COONTS

MLP
MACONDRAY
LANE PRESS

Library of Congress Cataloging-in-Publication Data is available upon request

Cover Design by Andrew Brown, ClickTwiceDesign.com

Formatting by Austin Brown, CheapEbookFormatting.com

Trade Paperback ISBN: 978-0-692-15092-4

V080718

Foreword

Some books are meant to happen, and some friendships are meant to be.

We've been friends since the day Josie picked up Deborah on the corner of Columbus and Bay streets in San Francisco. Other friends had picked her up (usually in a bar), so she has a habit of this. This time, however, was a bit more innocent: we were headed to a writer's meeting in Berkeley.

After being stuck on the Bay Bridge for an hour and a half on the return trip, we've been sisters-by-choice ever since.

Through the years, we've performed literary cross-pollination, introducing our respective readers to each other's books. We did so slowly at first, gauging reactions. With largely positive response, our efforts grew bolder, combining *The Housewife Assassin's Handbook* with *Wanna Get Lucky?* into a two-book bundle, both the first novels in our respective series. That too brought more readers and more fun.

So, the inevitable happened: folks started thinking it might be fun if Donna (Josie's housewife assassin) and Lucky (the star of Deborah's-series) finally met.

And *The Housewife Assassin Gets Lucky* was born...or at least conceived. The book-birthing thing took a bit longer.

We noodled on the idea for quite some time. Then, one day, we found ourselves sitting in the Milwaukee airport with time on our hands and mischief on our minds.

The result is what you see here...well, except for that pesky little police matter we are hoping to have expunged from our records.

We hope you enjoy this bit of merriment, but heed our warning —beware of what can happen when two authors get together and have time to kill.

Time, however, was not our intended victim.

Turn the page to find out who was....

—*Deborah Coonts* and *Josie Brown*

1

Lucky

y life imploded thirty seconds ago at 4:26 p.m. on a heretofore mundane Tuesday afternoon—well, mundane by Vegas standards. There was the dust-up with hookers trolling Delilah's Bar and the man who wanted his therapy horse to be allowed to watch him play the slots. And a bunch of young men had put a Vegas Knights hockey helmet on one of the statues, which I thought was an improvement, but unfortunately, nobody asked me. I let the kids go, said no to the horse and encouraged the hookers to move on down the Strip, but, like I said, fairly ho-hum Sin City shenanigans.

After that, I rushed back to my office to grab the one remaining suitcase. Yes, I am taking a vacation—I haven't had one in seventeen years, not a real one anyway. Two days in Reno didn't count. And my recent trip to Macau was business. Today will be all pleasure. I'm heading to Paris with my fiancé, Jean-Charles Bouclet—a French chef of world renown and a dish all on his own.

I'd promised. A promise that left me twitchy...for many reasons. First, I have an overblown sense of self-importance when it comes to my job. My name is Lucky O'Toole and I'm the go-to gal when the shit hits the fan at the Babylon, Vegas's most over-the-top playground. And, second, I have a near-pathological ability to screw up my personal life.

So, right now, straddling the fence of indecision, I didn't need complications. But one was standing in front of me blocking my exit.

My father.

I looked at him with one eye closed, as if sighting down the barrel of a gun. With his salt-and-pepper hair cut short, a strong jaw set at a defiant angle, and determination in his eyes, he'd come to get what he wanted. Today he wore his full battle dress: a light wool suit, diamond collar bar that secured an Hermès tie, Ferragamo loafers and no socks—the Vegas casino owner from Central Casting. A flash of gold at his wrist completed the look. Play to the crowd, he'd always told me. A dangerous thing in Las Vegas, a city that launched imaginations to the moon.

At six feet of solid woman, I had my father by several inches. And after recently taking a bullet to the chest, he had yet to find the flush of health. I could take him, but I didn't have the heart. "Say again? You need me to do what?"

His Adam's apple bobbed as he crooked a forefinger and ran it around the inside of his collar, pulling it away from his neck. "Make a quick detour to London on your way to Paris."

"You can't be serious." I'd mortgaged my soul and threatened death to anyone who screwed up this trip.

"Very." He looked it, too. Dammit.

I lowered my head. "Please?"

A tic worked in his cheek. "Lucky." His tone held a warning. He needn't have bothered—I was beyond caring. If he killed me, it would save Jean-Charles the trouble. Either way, one of them would. This dilemma had horns for sure.

I put down the suitcase I'd been holding, the last of three. The other two were already in the limo that waited at the front of the hotel. What did one take to meet the future in-laws? The chic and very Parisian future in-laws? A terrifying face-to-face that had me teetering on an emotional tightrope.

London would give me time to think. But that always got me into trouble.

I needed to get on that plane. If I didn't, somehow, I knew life would fray at the edges and eventually disintegrate. I summoned my most determined, grown-up voice—hard to do when giving my father the old push-back. "I can't. Jean-Charles has us on a tight schedule—parties in our honor, fancy dinners at restaurants that wouldn't accept a reservation from God herself. Send someone else."

"I can't." His push was stronger than mine, or perhaps just more practiced. "It has to be you. Sheik Mohammed Ben Halabi has a bee up his tight little ass and only my humblest apologies and grandest offerings will have a chance of making it right. I'd go myself but the doctors…" He trailed off.

No way would the docs clear him to fly to L.A. much less across the pond. He wasn't asking; we were negotiating.

What my father couldn't handle fell into my lap. My father, Albert Rothstein, a.k.a. the Big Boss, occupied the only rung on the corporate ladder above mine.

And the sheik—Ben to his friends—was our most important client. The amount of money he kept in play across many of our properties around the world exceeded the GDP of Switzerland. Okay, a bit of hyperbole, but not much. And, as one of my father's most ardent supporters, he'd invested in several of our properties in Macau and Singapore.

"You're offering me to Sheik Ben?"

"Of course not. But you are my family. And sending family will show him the matter is of utmost importance to me."

"I liked the days where a prize racehorse or a fast car would be sufficient." I felt myself caving. "So, what is this huge kerfuffle that has you offering to raise my salary and give me anything else I can think to ask for like unfettered use of the G 650 in order to get my compliance?" I'm a private jet whore, what can I say? I'd sell my mother to have the sleek jet at my disposal, but on the open market my mother Mona wouldn't bring enough to cover the hourly cost for a short hop to Palm Springs. London would cover it—not that I had a choice. But I did have a strong negotiating position and I wasn't above using it.

"I did not promise..." he stopped when he ran into my glare. Avoiding it, he selected a c-note from the slim wallet he'd extracted from his inside jacket pocket. He began to fold the bill, clean crisp folds he could do blindfolded. "Jesus," he muttered as a tiny figure began to take shape, "You're worse than your mother."

For once I didn't bristle at the comparison. My mother was the High Priestess of the Cult of Getting What You Want—a *quid pro quo* pro, if you will. I'd done a lot of giving people what they wanted—it was a character flaw that made me good at my job but made my personal life suck eggs. Now I was ready for a bit of take after all the give. "You going to tell me what you need handled in London, or do I need to order some tea leaves and rustle up a psychic?"

He blew a puff of disgust, then unfolded his tiny figure, smoothed the bill and began again. "Apparently the daughter of one of the highest-ranking members of the Royal family is working for us at the London Club."

"Really? Cool. A direct pipeline into the money pit. How'd we get her? That's quite a coup." This so did not seem to be the big goddammit he was making it out to be.

I had a hard time concentrating. Jean-Charles would be here any minute. I'd been running all day and must look a fright. I leaned around him where I could glimpse myself in the mirror hanging on the far wall. Light brown hair, blue eyes, cheekbones high and sharp enough to hold up my vanity. Even though my life was taking a hard right, I still looked like me, such as it was.

My father placed the tiny figure on my desk and raked a thumbnail down a crease. Then he held it up in the light. Satisfied, he began folding again. "You don't understand. The daughters from those families do not work. They consume. It is expected of them to display their father's wealth. Her working is an insult to the family. A very large insult."

"According to Sheik Ben." Like most of the world, I had little knowledge of the inner workings of the closed Saudi society.

4

"Yes. The girl, Aziza, is his niece. The family is most disgraced."

"According to Sheik Ben."

"Yes, according to Sheik Ben, but it's his opinion that matters. Lucky, this is right in your wheelhouse. With all your experience, with your deft touch and keen discernment, I can trust you to do it right, to smooth it over and avoid a huge diplomatic incident. God knows we don't want to land in the middle of something like that. Really, this is one day, max. Wine him, dine him, do your thing and you'll be on your way to Paris before you know it."

"Lathering it on a bit thick, don't you think? And no hip waders within easy reach."

"There!" My father admired his creation then pressed it into my hand with a smile. "For you."

A heart.

And mine melted. I never could say no to him. I pocketed the heart then gave him a hug. He didn't have to tell me how important this was—I could see it in every crease of his face. And he was right—this I could do with my eyes closed. "You owe me, big time."

"Thank you." He actually seemed to deflate in relief—so not like the pre-bullet version of my father. "I knew you'd go."

"Go where?" My French chef strode into my office, resplendent in creased jeans and an untucked, form-fitted cotton shirt in a pale blue that matched his eyes. He wore a scarf knotted around his neck, also blue but several shades darker. His brown hair curled slightly over his collar. Somehow, he had morphed into a Parisian when I wasn't looking. In his chef's whites—and out of them—he was just a man. A rather exquisite man, but a man. And I was a woman. Handy that. And now? Now he was French, I was a Vegas rat, and the differences took my breath. A frisson of fear slithered through me.

Opposites attract but likes stay together.

One of Miss P's platitudes that hit me right between the eyes.

Miss P is the head of my staff and my most trusted bellwether. She wasn't here, so I ignored her voice in my head and prepared to try to dazzle Jean-Charles with my best corporate soft-shoe. It wouldn't work—it never did. But it was all I had.

Jean-Charles grabbed my shoulders and leaned in. I met him more than halfway, putting everything I had into the kiss. God, he still made my toes curl. Did I do that to him? That's what I wanted —magic. Not just for me, but for both of us.

I felt a tug on my pants leg. A small voice said, "Lucky! What about me? Papa, let her go."

Both Jean-Charles and I started giggling which totally broke the spell. I reached down and grabbed Christophe, my rather insistent future stepson. His blonde curls mimicked his father's as did his blue eyes, although Christophe's were a few shades darker. At five years old, he still fit on my hip, but he was getting pretty heavy. It didn't help that he wiggled all over with excitement. In one hand he clutched a beautiful bouquet of hot pink tulips. "These are for you. I picked them out myself."

"Tulips are my favorite. How'd you know?" I made a big production of planting a noisy kiss on his cheek, which made him giggle. "Thank you."

His face turned serious...sort of. "We're going to Paris! Mémé and Papi will be there. And Tante Desiree." His face creased. "But no cows or pigs. That's right, Papa? And no chickens." He looked a bit distraught over the chickens.

"They must stay at the farm." Jean Charles fought a smile.

"He has no future in the restaurant business." What can I say, I have a flair for the obvious.

"But there will be cakes, and candies and pastries!" Christophe vibrated with the thought of it all. "We need to go, or we'll miss the plane. We can't miss the plane!"

"We won't." I took a quick glance at the clock. We'd make it, but it would be close.

With the limo idling at the curb and time-a-wastin', Paulo, our chief driver, would be getting antsy. The airport wasn't far, but Christophe was right, we needed to go. "I need to talk to your father for a minute, then we'll go."

I put him down and handed him off to my father. "Give us a few minutes, please."

It was the least he could do; we both knew it. He took Christophe's hand—I kept the tulips. I watched them until my office door closed behind them. Absent during my childhood, my father was getting a short course in parenting, not only from Christophe but from a set of unexpected twins born recently to him and my mother. As a former hooker, my mother would've been well aware that pregnancy can happen to a woman well into her forties. Guess she'd forgotten. Life had bitch-slapped that message home with a vengeance. Proof there is a God, if you ask me.

I buried my nose in the flowers.

"They don't have an odor." Jean-Charles sounded calm even though he had to have known he wouldn't like what I had to tell him.

I took that as a good sign. "I'm buying time."

"What is it your father needs?"

I gave him the *Cliff Notes* version.

"This man. This sheik. He is more important to your father than your happiness?" As an opening salvo that was a bit harsh.

"Probably." My honesty momentarily silenced him, giving me the opening I needed. "Look, my father wasn't my father for as long as I can remember. He and my mother just sprung all that on me recently, if you recall." There'd been a good reason they'd kept my heritage secret—my mother's subterfuge and a potential felony statutory rape conviction—but I still smarted from the years of wondering why my father hadn't wanted me. Ancient history that left me with thin scabs over old wounds. "I started working for him when I was fifteen, so our relationship still rests on a foundation of business as usual."

"You can change that." His jaw had turned to concrete, and he no longer smiled.

I had that effect on a lot of men. It's a gift. What can I say? A tool in my limited repertoire. "Working on that, but now is not the time for a major breakthrough. We haven't the time nor a skilled therapist on speed dial. I've got to go to London. I'm taking the Gulfstream. I won't be twenty-four hours behind you."

He didn't look convinced, but he was taking it as the *fait accomplis* that it was. "Friday night is my mother's big party. A party for you, if you recall."

"I recall." That reminded me of another party I could now check on—a prominent soirée for the third cousin to the Queen or something. "A big deal for our London Club. It wouldn't hurt to check over the preparations."

"She will not forgive you if you are not there because of your *job*."

Personally, I thought that sort of thinking a bit limited, but now was not the time to crack that nut. "I understand."

His shoulders rose and fell with a sigh. "Lucky, your job—"

"Is as important as yours."

"Of course." He tossed off the words as if they didn't hold my soul.

And there it was, the super big swamp pit separating us. He could say the words, but he wasn't so good at living them. If he couldn't make the leap, that would be a dealbreaker.

Teddie had understood that. *Teddie*. But he hadn't been able to live the truth either. And he'd broken my heart in the process. Now he was back, wanting me to trust him again.

Why did men put women to such choices?

I pushed all that aside. "Come. Let's get Christophe. We have to run."

"He will be so disappointed. He made me promise he could sit with you on the plane."

Guilt. Not the best thing to leave when parting from a loved one. "I'll make it up to him. And I'll be a day behind, no more."

I weighed the odds. If I were a betting gal, I'm not sure which side of that bet I'd put my future on.

2

Donna

A lacy shawl of snow drapes all of London. More is expected late this evening. And yet, be it rain, snow, sleet, or hail, the weather never seems to deter Londoners from getting on with their lives.

Even the posh set proves to be a hardy lot. They are out in droves for the latest Couture, Fashion, and Jewelry auction at Christeby's Auction House.

Already four items have been put on the block. Each has been auctioned off at a good 20 to 30 percent above the opening bid. The article I want—a rare cream and bronze Hermès Kelly handbag embellished with gold hardware— is estimated to go for between 10,000 and 20,000 Euros.

In any event, my employer, a CIA-contracted black-ops organization known as Acme Industries, has been instructed to offer whatever it takes to get the purse.

If you're wondering why the CIA is suddenly gaga over haute couture, let me assure you that it's a matter of national security. Somewhere deep in the handbag's lining is a tiny sliver of paper. Written on it is a password and ID to a secure cloud containing a list of the spies working for the MSS—China's Ministry of State Security—who are embedded in the United States. The handbag's seller is the wife of a Chinese defense minister. Her quid pro quo: to leap to the front of the United States' immigration line with an S-6 visa. Once stateside, she'll disappear into our Federal Witness Protection program.

The auction allows for a clean transaction. While the minister's wife gets a big payday, new identity—even a new face, the CIA rounds up a few bad guys and the cost is a pittance when compared to, say, a new war toy.

My cover is that of an American-based private buyer acting as the proxy purchaser for a wealthy Argentinian socialite. As such, I am unobtrusively chic. My long, brown hair is swept back and coiled at the nape of my neck. Although I don't need them, I wear glasses. I hold my numbered paddle in one hand and a small clutch and Christeby's catalog in the other. I'm dressed in a long-sleeved Roland Mouret black, gray, and white woven bouclé front-zip jacket with a nipped-waist peplum and a crew neck, paired with black crepe palazzo pants that easily hide the ceramic folding stiletto that is strapped to my calf. Odds are I won't need it, but having served as my youngest daughter, Trisha's, Daisy Scout leader in days gone by, I've learned to come prepared.

I'm here doing my bit for God and country when I should be coordinating the winter prom at the high school attended by my oldest two children, Mary and Jeff. The event is next weekend. In twenty-four hours I should be home. In the meantime, my aunt, Phyllis, has my proxy on the necessary decisions to be made—you know, the color of the balloons, if there should be a D.J. or a band, and whether sodas or punch should be served along with cupcakes or a healthier snack. Whenever Jack and I are away on missions, Aunt Phyllis covers our kids: not just Jeff and Mary, but also my youngest daughter, Trisha, who's now in the fifth grade. I have a ward too: Evan Martin. He's away at his first year of college, but officially he and Mary are a couple, and he's due back next weekend to take her to the prom.

So, yeah, the sooner I get home, the better.

The CIA isn't expecting too many bidders, and certainly, none who are foreign agents, but you never know. Acme's way of preparing for the unexpected is to equip me with a crackerjack mission team.

One of them, Abu Nagashahi, is waiting outside the auction house in a rented limousine. Even though on this mission he's acting as my chauffeur, in reality, he is a field agent who triples as surveillance, cleaner, and if need be, getaway driver.

The mission's tech operative, Arnie Locklear, is hunkered down in the back of the limo. He's already hacked into Christeby's surveillance cameras and has patched in our Communications Intel operative, Emma Honeycutt, who's based at Acme's headquarters in Los Angeles. She's now scanning the crowd to run their faces through Interpol's facial recognition network. That way, if there are any known diplomats, covert operatives, terrorists, or foreign actors among us, we'll know.

Another member of our team is Dominic Fleming. Silver-tongued and blazingly blond, this former MI6 agent is currently schmoozing with the auction's curator, Sharon Walker, the elegant woman who holds the keys to the kingdom: in this case, a short list of the bidders who have already expressed interest in the handbag.

The last member of my mission team, Jack Craig, stars in the public role of my paid bodyguard. In reality, this tall, dark, and eye-catchingly handsome man is also my husband, which means he always has my back. I'd put myself in front of a bullet to save him as well, so it works out.

Jack's third-row seat is the one closest to the center aisle. I'm in the chair beside him. As we converse quietly, we take turns looking behind each other's shoulder to scan the room. The entire ops team wears special lenses and earbuds that allow us to be each other's eyes and ears at all times. Arnie and Emma monitor all video and audio feeds.

I look over at the podium in time to see Sharon shoo Dominic away. Catching my eye, he shrugs, which tells me she was immune to his charms. But from the murmurs buzzing through this packed auditorium as the auctioneer is handed the Hermès handbag, there will, in fact, be many bidders.

Hopefully, none of them will feel the need to outbid the CIA.

While the auctioneer describes the highly-coveted accessory in a clipped tone, albeit in minute detail, I murmur, "Emma, any interesting bidders?"

"Thus far we've had just one Interpol match," she replies. "A Korean businessman named Park Sung Min. Last row, fourth chair from the left."

"Dammit, I guess the Chinese minister's wife invited him too," Jack mutters. "Let the bidding war begin."

"I've got him sighted." Dominic, who is leaning casually against the center of the far right wall, catches my eye and he nods in the direction of our Person of Interest. "Stylish fellow. Favors Gieves & Hawkes. Wears it well."

I look over. The man is scanning his catalog as if he doesn't have a care in the world.

Emma sighs. "It would help if we had today's VIP bidder list so that I could cross-reference any names that pop up."

This is Emma's broad hint to our tech op—her doting husband, Arnie—that he has to up his game, and fast.

"Christeby's client database has got a tight-ass firewall," Arnie grumbles. "Wait a sec...I'm IN, baby!"

"I'll alert the media," I mutter.

"Sending those bidders who have registered for today's auction now," Arnie assures us.

"Receiving," Emma says. "I'm matching them up now."

We can barely hear her over the auctioneer who declares, "And we'll start the bidding. Do I hear five thousand pounds?" He nods at someone.

"Was it Park?"

"No," Arnie says. "Some woman. Dark hair, brown pantsuit. The name is"—he pauses as he scans the database—"Nika Petrov. She has a Paris address. I've put all lenses on the auction room's feed."

"Nika is also on the Interpol list," Emma confirms.

"Ten thousand five hundred!" The auctioneer exclaims.

I start to raise my hand, but Jack stops me. "Wait until the auctioneer calls for the final bid," he suggests.

I nod. He's right. That way, we trump the others and fly under the radar for as long as possible.

Park raises his hand. So does some older gentleman sitting in the row in front of us. He's also on the aisle. He leans on a cane.

"Emma, can you ID the older man?" I whisper.

"Give me a second," She replies.

"Eleven thousand!" the auctioneer cries.

Again, paddles go up: Park, Nika, and the older man bid again.

Finally, Emma answers, "Christeby's has him listed as Chet Bakersfield, an American. Checks out. He's a buyer with a vintage shop in Manhattan."

"Eleven thousand five hundred," the auctioneer declares.

This time only Park's and Nika's paddles go up. Chet grimaces but keeps his paddle in his lap.

"Twelve thousand!" The auctioneer shouts.

Three paddles go up again: Park's, Nika's paddles rise, as well as one belonging to a plump woman in her twenties who wears jeans and a pea coat. Her red hair is buzzed into a flat top.

"B.J. Rosenthal," Arnie tells us. "Christeby's client card has her based in Los Angeles."

"Interpol IDs her as Mossad," Emma chimes in. "But, she lives in Santa Monica."

"Thirteen thousand!" the auctioneer shouts.

"Heck, I know B.J.—and not in a good way." I don't think now is the time to add that one of our industry trade magazines, *Femme Fatale*, ranks her at Number One with twice the number of exterminations than the next closest competitor.

Does it bother me I'm a distant fifth? Nah. I juggle three kids, a crazy aunt, and an attentive husband. B.J. only has to worry about a houseful of cats.

"Jeez! Russia, North Korea—and now Israel?" Jack grumbles. "Is there anyone who *isn't* bidding on this damn handbag?"

"Thirteen-five," the auctioneer exclaims. "Do I hear fourteen thousand?"

My cell phone rings. Instinctively, I look at the Caller ID. The name reads **TAKE THIS OR ELSE.**

I'm curious enough to play along. "Who is this?" I ask warily.

"Donna Stone Craig, where the hell are you?"

I can't recognize the voice because the auctioneer has just shouted, "Fourteen thousand!" At the same time, I hear my mission team acknowledging the bidders in furtive whispers.

"What?" I don't have time to play games. "Again, who the hell are you?"

"*Fifteen* thousand!"

"It's Penelope Bing," my caller huffs.

The meanest mommy in my gated community—Hilldale, California—is notorious for her bad timing.

The bids are now coming in fast and furiously. Over the auctioneer's shout "Twenty-three thousand!" I hiss, "Penelope, I'm in the middle of something now. I'll call you back—"

"Like hell, you will!" she snarls. "You're supposed to be heading up the Hilldale High School Winter Prom planning committee!"

"Twenty-five thousand!" The auctioneer yells, his tone rising.

"I sent my aunt in my stead! Isn't she there?"

I plug one ear with a finger so that I can drown out the auctioneer and hear myself think. "Granted, Aunt Phyllis is an acquired taste—"

"Is that how you'd describe her, 'an acquired taste'?" Penelope retorts. "I've got another term for it: Nuts! Did you know what she chose as the prom's theme?"

"Twenty-eight thousand! Do I hear thirty?" The auctioneer shouts.

"Surprise me," I mutter.

"'Game of Thrones'!" Penelope snaps.

"That sounds innocent enough," I reply just as the auctioneer shouts, "Do I hear thirty-five thousand?"

"Not if a pyrotechnical team is needed to build a fire-breathing dragon," Penelope retorts.

"I guess you have a point there," I admit.

"Do I hear forty thousand?" the auctioneer bellows.

"And do you know what your aunt wants to do for party games?"

"I'm afraid to ask," I reply.

"Use your imagination!" Penelope screeches.

"Yes, to the woman in the back. Do I now hear forty-five thousand?" the auctioneer exclaims.

"I give up!" I shout into the phone.

"Battle competitions," Penelope snickers. "With real swords, hatchets, and spiked clubs! She says she knows an antique dealer who'll lend them to her. Now I ask you: what if one kid accidentally murders another?"

"I guess we'd have some explaining to do," I admit.

"...For fifty-five thousand! Do I hear sixty?" the auctioneer shouts.

"And another thing—" Penelope says, but then she's interrupted by another call. The ID reads: **MARY**

Yikes.

"Penelope, I have to put you on hold!" To hell with waiting for a response. Instead, I tap onto Mary's call.

The auctioneer bellows, "Sixty-five thousand! Do I hear seventy?"

"Honey, I'm in the middle of something." My words are kind, but my tone is firm.

"I'm...I'm so sorry to bother you, Mom..." Mary is sobbing.

I shake off Jack's wide-eyed nod toward the auctioneer as I ask, "Mary...sweetie, what's wrong?"

"I just saw something on Evan's Facebook page that has me wrecked." Mary sighs deeply. "He took a selfie with some...some *girl*. And he—"

"Seventy thousand?...Yes?" The auctioneer sounds ecstatic "Do I hear seventy-five?"

Damn auctioneer! I can't hear Mary over him. "What did you say?" I hiss. "Evan did what again?"

"Eighty?... There, on the left again! Now, eighty-five, anyone?"

"I said *he had his arm around her waist*!" Mary chokes on her tears.

"Ninety? Anyone?...Final bid then..."

Jack nudges me. When I swat him away, he points to my paddle and hisses, "Now!"

Oh, yeah—*right!* I raise it high.

"Maybe Evan and this girl were just joking around!" I'm frantic to get off the phone, but I'll be darned if I hang up on my daughter at her lowest point.

"Do we have ninety-five thousand? Anyone?...The lovely lady in the back?" The auctioneer sounds relieved. "One hundred thousand, anyone?"

Jack elbows me in the waist.

I shoo him away with my paddle before waving it frantically.

"Woman Front and Center, thank you! How about one hundred and five?... Yes? Ah, there we go!"

"This girl looks so sophisticated—you know, very fashionista chic." Mary's anxiety comes in loud and clear, even in this room of gasping bid watchers. "How can I compete with that? I come off like a...*a silly teenager!*"

"One hundred and ten?" I feel the auctioneer looking directly at me now.

I nod frantically while waving my paddle as if calling over a search plane with a flashlight, all the while whispering frantically into the phone, "But you *are* a teenager—although, you're not silly."

Mary sighs. "You're lying. You tell me I am, all the time. And you're right! If I'm going to compete with college girls, I've got to up my game."

"What does that mean?" My mommy alert is clanging.

"One hundred and fifteen, anyone?" The auctioneer asks.

This time, when I lift the paddle again, Jack jerks my hand down to my side. "You're bidding against yourself!" he mutters. "I don't think our client would like that."

"I mean, I need to re-think what I'm wearing to the prom," Mary continues. "The dress I bought is much too young—so stupid! No, I'm stupid for thinking I could even compete with a...a college girl!" She bursts into tears.

"SOLD, to the Woman Front and Center!" The auctioneer points to me.

"Well, the client should be happy—sort of," Jack declares.

"Mom?...MOM! Are you listening?" Mary's grumbles indignantly.

Another call is coming in: It's Penelope again, dammit. I tap IGNORE.

"Honey, of course, I'm listening to you!" I reply.

"Bullshit! You hung up on me and didn't bother to call me back," Penelope snaps.

How did she get on the line? Did I hang up on Mary instead?

"Let me make something perfectly clear to you Donna Craig: you better put a leash on your aunt—before she ruins the dance—along with your reputation!"

The phone line goes dead.

I close my eyes and sigh. Suddenly, I could think of a few good uses for that knife strapped to my calf.

When I open my eyes again, Jack is already on his feet. Grinning down at me, he nods toward the purchase table. "Come on, Woman Front and Center. Let's claim your ill-gotten goods and get the heck out of London before Penelope Bing ends up murdering your aunt."

"Frankly, I'd bet on Aunt Phyllis. If she wanted to get someone whacked, she's got the right connections."

Jack shrugs because he knows I'm right. And since he and I have both had our own run-ins with Penelope, Aunt Phyllis would have to flip a coin as to who gets that honor.

As we walk over, it dawns on me that I've never held a purse that cost anywhere near one hundred and ten thousand Euros.

Once the intel is extracted, what would the CIA do with it, anyway? I guess it wouldn't hurt to ask if I could keep it as a souvenir.

"CONGRATULATIONS ON YOUR NEW ACQUISITION." SHARON WALKER

hands it over as soon as I put my John Hancock on the sales confirmation receipt.

Really, I write Johanna Hancock, but my scrawl is illegible, so it doesn't matter either way.

"Thank you," I reply with a pleased-as-punch smile.

Only the staff and final purchasers are allowed into the auction house's sales offices located behind the auction room. Considering all the hubbub currently keeping the sales associates busy with their bidding clients—not to mention a record-breaking sale—this department's lavatory should now be empty. Once I'm in there, I'll slice open the hidden compartment and take a picture of the minuscule piece of paper listing the cloud account and text it to Emma.

"Excuse me, can you point me to the ladies' room?" I ask.

"It's at the end of the hall," she replies. "I'll walk you out. I'm due back on the auction floor for the next items."

As we part ways in the hallway Sharon adds, "Again, thank your client for her patronage. Her participation made it a thoroughly thrilling auction!"

"I'll say," I murmur as she heads in the opposite direction.

I'm a few steps from the women's lavatory when the door to the men's lounge flies open. Park Sung Min stands there with a gun pointed at me. He nods at the handbag. "I'll take that."

"Sure. Catch." Instead, I throw my own purse at him.

It hits him in the face.

He's so surprised that he stumbles backward, through the door again. His gun goes off—

And the bullet hits flesh: Nika Petrov's, who somehow breached the sale corridor's security code and snuck up behind me.

Talk about lousy timing.

The bullet pierces her gut. As blood flows from the wound, she keels over, dead.

By now Park has smacked into a wall. I hold him there with my right forearm against his throat while my left hand slams the hand holding the gun against the wall until he drops it.

When he does, I punch him in the face a few times until he passes out, dropping to the floor.

And in the process I break a nail, *dammit!* Well, at least I never dropped the Hermès.

I'm breathing so heavy that I don't realize I'm not alone until I hear a woman's voice declare, "I'll take that handbag if you don't mind."

B.J. Rosenthal stands just inside the doorway. She has Park's gun pointed at me. "The Hermès this time, not the cheap Givenchy knock-off," she adds with a smirk.

Talk about rubbing it in.

"Do it *now*," she adds firmly. "I never thought I'd end up with the infamous Donna Stone Craig's scalp on my belt. But hey, when duty calls—"

At that second, the men's room door swings open again—

And into B.J., knocking her off balance and onto her knees. Her gun goes off—

But I've already taken a step to my right, just in time to dodge the bullet that catches Park in his left eye. Life leaves him with a jerk and a gasp.

Like me, B.J. turns around to see who walked through the door: Jack.

Though still on her knees, with both hands B.J. swings the gun in his direction.

But before she lines him up in her sights, I pull out my stiletto and plunge it between her fourth and fifth ribs, angled up to her heart.

B.J. gazes down, mesmerized by the slick, ruby red bloodstain now mushrooming on her shirt and coat. When she looks up again, her eyes meet mine. Finally, they roll back in her head, and she folds to the floor like a rag doll.

I reward Jack with a kiss. "I'm glad you came looking for me."

"When Arnie confirmed that none of the other high bidders left the building, he slipped me the security code, and I thought I'd come snooping," he replies. "Abu and Dominic are just down the hall. Arnie is looping the security footage to erase this killing party.

He's also put the sales offices in lockdown while they clean up this mess. In the meantime, we should get the hell out of here." He nods toward an alley exit door.

"I still haven't verified the intel," I point out.

"I suggest we take it with us to the Ritz and do it there." Jack grins. "That way, we're closer to some celebration bubbly."

I kiss his cheek. "You don't have to ask me twice."

"DESPITE HAVING PAID FOUR TIMES THE AMOUNT REQUISITIONED FOR the intel and having almost lost it in the process, the CIA deems the mission a success—especially since you kept it out of the hands of enemies that could have done us irreparable harm." Ryan's cheery declaration comes in over the speaker on Jack's cell phone in our Ritz Hotel suite. "In fact, you're to stay in London for another assignment."

Hearing this, I choke on a large swig of Charles Heidsieck Brut Reserve NV champagne. What if this means Jack and I will miss seeing the kids off for their prom?

As if reading my mind, Ryan assures us, "This assignment is a simple pick-up. Donna is to rendezvous with a CIA asset at the Babylon London, a private club in Mayfair."

Dominic exclaims, "By Jove, I happen to be a member of the Babylon! They hold a room for me on call."

Abu snorts, "Is there a club in this town you haven't joined?"

Dominic shrugs. "Can I help it if I'm a social animal?"

"You're half right," I mutter under my breath.

Dominic misses my slight because he's too busy preening in the sizable gilt mirror over the dresser.

To Ryan, I ask: "For just that reason, wouldn't it be simpler to send Dominic?"

"It has to be someone who has access to the club, but at the same time is not familiar to the club's employees or other guests. As it turns out, the club's guest quarters are booked up. However, as Dominic's companion, you'll certainly attain access."

The word 'companion' raises brows—Jack's and mine.

To make the situation even worse, Ryan adds, "Dominic can also provide a diversion if necessary."

"For that, we'll need to stay in my room." Dominic winks at me knowingly. From his smirk, I realize that he genuinely believes his own malarkey.

"Trust me, I won't be hanging around that long," I vow.

"But I have a reputation to uphold!" Dominic insists. "I get at least two front desk calls—sometimes three—about the alacrity in which my guests exclaim their joy."

Jack smothers a guffaw. "Seriously? *Joy?*"

Dominic shrugs. "As a matter of fact, my manhood has been bequeathed the nickname 'Joystick' by several satisfied damsels."

"You can invite other, more boisterous guests to your playpen when Donna is in the clear," Ryan proclaims. "Donna, you're to rendezvous with the asset—codename 'Hummingbird'—at 20:10, in the Royal Suite. You'll find it on the top floor of the club. Knock twice, pause, and then knock again."

"I assume the contact will be the only one there?"

"That's the plan," Ryan replies. "And since we don't know what form the intel takes, the face-to-face may need some instruction. Unfortunately, Hummingbird can't leave the club, so it has to take place there. And since every other room is taken for the evening and the handoff can't happen in any of the club's public spaces, the Royal Suite was suggested as the best location."

"Any discerning details about Hummingbird?" I ask.

"Female, and in her early twenties. Dark hair and eyes. Middle-Eastern descent. By the way, she'll be wearing a teardrop amulet around her neck," Ryan explains. "She'll need something to recognize you as well."

"I've got just the item," I purr. "The Hermès bag."

Ryan sighs. "At least, the CIA can't say it wasn't worth every penny you spent on its behalf."

All ears perk up at that. "The intel must be vital," Jack replies.

Ryan's pause is so long that I wonder if he's still on the line.

Finally, he murmurs, "It may mean peace will finally be achieved in the Middle East."

"Hot damn," Arnie murmurs.

"Donna, the key to this mission is discretion," Ryan warns. "You're to be as unobtrusive as possible."

"Got it. No one will even know I was there."

"Famous last words." Jack winks at me.

He says this because he only has eyes for me.

And, yes, I feel the same about him.

Now, that's true love.

DOMINIC DOESN'T MISS AN OPPORTUNITY TO PLAY THE LOTHARIO. THE moment a doorman ushers us through Babylon London's revolving door my colleague's hand slides to my waist, drawing me so close that I almost pass out from his pungent aftershave.

His way of doubling down on this Acme-sanctioned Me-Too moment is to nuzzle my cheek and whisper, "Let me do all the talking."

I giggle as if he's just told a scintillating aside. At the same time, I stifle the urge to drive my fist through his kidney. "You know, I've walked into more harrowing situations. I think I'll survive the scrutiny of your hoity-toity club's staff."

I nod toward the stuffy little man who stands beside the reception desk. While this slight, pale fellow's thin mustache practically bristles at the sight of us, two of the three comely receptionists—one raven-haired, the other auburn—perk up at the sight of Dominic to the point of licking their lips. In contrast, the third one, a slight, prim blonde, stiffens at the sight of him.

Smart girl.

Maybe it's because I made the stupid mistake of allowing Dominic to pick out my wardrobe, which he felt would "be up to snuff as it pertains to the club's code—and my own personal taste."

I'd have never said yes except for the fact that he agreed to put it on his own personal Harrods expense account.

So here I am, trussed up in a candy apple red leather dress suit that hugs every curve, along with matching red leather booties, gloves, and a full set of bright red Michael Kors luggage and a matching purse. A red silk scarf draped over my blond gamine wig, its ends crossed beneath my chin and then knotted behind my neck starlet-style, completes the look.

From the way Sir Stuffy's upper lip curdles, nothing I wear will offset Dominic's reputation for bedding screamers.

Sir Stuffy cringes when, in unison, the brunette and redhead receptionists sing out, "Good *evening*, Mr. Fleming!"

"Ah! Lavinia, Prunella, and"—he pauses as he leans in toward the third woman—"Julie. A pleasure to be in your quite capable hands again."

Whereas Lavinia and Prunella exchange sly glances, Julie winces.

Before the ladies can respond, Sir Stuffy sternly intones, "Your suite is ready, Mr. Fleming. However—"

Dominic shifts his gaze to the man. His eyes narrow, as if noticing him for the very first time. "Adderson, is it not?" He snaps his fingers. "No?...Give me a moment. It's on the tip of my tongue. Ackerman, then? Ableson?" He snaps his fingers. "Ah ha!—*Ahern!*" Pleased with himself, Dominic smiles supremely. "So kind of you to greet us."

Ahern's glare never wavers. "Yes, now, about your guest—"

Dominic interrupts with this cockeyed pronouncement: "You're right. A proper introduction is in order. Her Royal Majesty, Princess Maja, of Sweden, may I present Mr. Ahern—"

What the....

Now he tells me I'm playing a princess? How is this 'low profile'?

Ahern's eyes widen at the title.

Okay, yeah, maybe I should go along with this. I extend my right hand.

Bowing slightly over it, Ahern murmurs, "An honor, your Majesty."

Before I can answer in what would undoubtedly be the worst Swedish accent ever, Dominic interjects, "Alas, Ahern, my acquaintance doesn't speak English. And with all the inbreeding that went into making her the forty-fifth heir to the throne, I'm not sure she speaks Swedish with any fluency, either. To tell you the truth, Old Boy, I've never heard a peep out of her. For all I know, she's a mute."

Hearing this, the receptionists' faces mirror the same look: pity.

For that heaping pile of hogwash, he'll get an earful when we're alone in his room!

Lovingly, Dominic strokes my cheek. "However, in the language of love, she is quite fluent."

Dominic's hand is close enough to my mouth that I could easily bite through his pinky. Ever the team player, I stifle the urge. The mission comes first. I did note that the club has a back alley. When we're done here, Dominic may learn the hard way that he should never go there alone.

Certainly, not with a mute pseudo-Swede royal.

Ahern allows himself a stiff upper lip grimace. "I am somewhat relieved to hear—as I'm sure will be the case of guests with rooms adjacent to yours—that the usual 'gaiety' that invariably emanates from your suite will be...subdued." He taps the nearest bell to summon a man to help us with our luggage. "And as always, the baccarat table should provide additional diversions."

Like magic, a bellman appears at our side.

I guess I should be somewhat miffed that Dominic has taken it upon himself to slip each receptionist a personal calling card. When one of the women turns it over, I see that he's written in bold:

CALL ME LATER TONIGHT

At least one of them considers his invitation as disgusting as me: the youngest of the three, Julie.

As for the others, I'll be clearing out as soon as I possibly can. I've got just a half-hour to change out of this getup before heading up to the Royal Suite. Once the intel is in hand, Dominic can walk "Princess Maja" out the front door.

His penance for dissing me in front of the others: I'm keeping all my Harrods booty despite my promise to leave all tags attached so it can be returned.

THE ONLY ELEVATOR THAT GOES UP TO THE BABYLON LONDON'S ROYAL Suite—the club's penthouse—could easily pass for a small but well-appointed walk-in closet. Its walls are polished mahogany. A hand-knotted Persian rug lays on its parquet floor. A plush chaise placed there to accommodate those too weary to stand during its slow ride from the lobby to the fifth floor of this private club. The one tip of the hat to its Victorian past is the quaint metal grill that must be opened before one can step in or out of it. Although its placement is quite discreet, immediately I spot the elevator's security camera.

Princess Maja has disappeared. As per my mission directive, in keeping with my role as a club guest, I am dressed to impress—but this time my way, as opposed to Dominic's fantasy fangirl.

My cream tweed pencil-skirted Chanel suit's plunging vee jacket is embellished with all sorts of shiny gold and crystal bling, as are its cuffs, and pockets. A matching bucket hat sporting a gold brow-skimming veil is perched over my naturally brown hair, which is pinned into a French twist. My hands are clad in cream-toned Fendi gloves, and my feet are strapped in to-die-for textured gold Jennifer Chamandi stiletto pumps.

Needless to say, my favorite accessory is my newly acquired vintage Hermès Kelly purse.

An elegant elaborately carved double door graces the end of a hallway that runs almost the full length of this block-long building. I am just a minute late, so I take my time. Out of habit, I scan the hall's elaborate crown molding for security cameras. Yes, there are several.

Since I was told to knock twice and then once again, I'm

surprised to find the door slightly ajar. Because the club's security is as tight as a gnat's ass and the Hermès purse serves as my bonafide, I'm not so worried that some inquisitive guest may have wandered up here and Hummingbird may have passed him or her the intel by mistake. Still, I tap out the code.

Silence.

I do it again.

Still, no answer.

Odd.

Slowly, I open the door.

The lights are off, but the street lamps beyond a wall of intricately carved French doors cast eerie shadows on the heavy furnishings scattered throughout the large room. It is undoubtedly plusher and lusher than Dominic's digs, but to be expected for something called "the Royal Suite."

But I see no one.

The room has a hallway at each side. On the left is the dining room and I assume a kitchen is just beyond. I choose the one on the right, which faces the park.

There is only one room on this wing: the master suite. Its door, at the end of the short hall, is also open. My spidey-senses are tingling...

I see her: on the floor and on her back, legs and arms spread awkwardly, like a human hieroglyphic. Her hair is swept to one side. Something shines out from deep within the long and dark tendrils:

The amulet, still on the chain around her neck.

I see no blood or bullet wounds. I drop down to take her pulse.

There is none.

I scan the room. Nothing moves. Quickly, I walk through it. No one is in the large walk-in closet or the well-appointed bathroom.

I go back to Hummingbird. My eyes take her in, inch by inch. Dying is not an elegant endeavor. One's last breath is usually a quick gasp, an indignant gurgle, or a resigned sigh. We don't gracefully fall in repose; instead, we crumple to the ground.

In Hummingbird's case, her slim limbs look like playing cards that have somehow scattered, willy-nilly, from the rest of the deck.

Her legs are spread apart enough that her skirt has risen above her thighs. On the left one, a tattoo is visible: letters of some sort. Maybe symbols? I can't make them out, but on closer look, they resemble the characters on her amulet. I pull out my cell phone and take a photo of both.

If her hair hadn't been pushed to one side, I'd never notice the two tiny aligned holes on her neck. Odd.

I unclasp the amulet's chain. Gently I pull it out of her hair.

I then pat her down: back, sides and pockets. I find nothing other than her cell phone. I take it.

Hummingbird's left hand is palm down as if she attempted to push herself up. Her right hand clenches something: a tiny, exquisitely designed glazed ceramic vase, perhaps only seven inches in height. It is Chinese in provenance and an antique.

She grips it so tightly that she may have picked it up to use as a weapon. Still, in case it holds the intel, I pry it from her fingers and slip it into my purse.

Gently, I nudge her body to its side to see if she fell on something that might hold the intel we seek. She lies on a key ring with two room cards attached. I take it as well.

If what Ryan said is correct and there are no vacancies, she may have used the excuse of readying the room for the next guest to make our assignation. I don't know how long the rest of the club's staff anticipates she'll be up here. In any event, eventually, they'll come looking for her.

All the more reason I need to get out of here.

3

Lucky

*M*usty. That was it. Everything about London reeked of old and damp, despotic kings and unfortunate beheadings. All foreign to a visiting Colonist and diametric to my anything-goes Vegas vibe. Another Dorothy in Oz moment. And solving problems here made me more uncomfortable still. At home, with my staff around me and Detective Romeo of the local constabulary on speed dial, solving problems was a team effort.

Here, I danced alone.

But this would be a cakewalk. My father had said so. Twenty-four hours and I'd be free. Why then, did I feel the niggle of not-so-fast?

As if we were telepathic, or my father was GPS stalking me, a text rang through.

Are you keeping our partner happy? Utmost importance.

As if I hadn't already gotten the message. I ignored him.

My ride from London City Airport had been a conga line of traffic. Caught in the throes of winter, London had retreated to the anonymity of the mundane, brushed to a gloomy grey by bad weather and resignation. All of which did little to improve my jet-lagged, sorry-ass self, the only attendee at my pity party.

I could be in Paris.

I *should* be in Paris. Although, life had a way of directing you where you should go—I didn't have to like it, but simply pay attention. Which wasn't my strong suit.

The flight had not gone as planned. My *joie de vivre* that welled from satisfying a filial obligation had evaporated somewhere over Kansas. Then we stopped in Gander, Newfoundland. Some minor mechanical thing was fixed promptly but still set my teeth on edge, although I stocked up on real maple syrup. Once in London, the Neanderthal engaged by my Vegas office to fetch me had looked at me askance, asking me twice if I really had a room at the London Club and muttering something about my gender and my birth country. I let him live only because a justified homicide investigation would take not only a complicit attitude on my part, but lots of time, both of which were currently in short supply.

When we eased to a stop in front of the Babylon London Club, darkness was almost complete. The streetlights sparking on did little to hold back the gloom. The Club occupied a five-story, nondescript limestone building in a row of similar buildings across from a patch of park that lent the neighborhood a bit of Bourgeois flair—the perfect disguise for the luxury, the money, the wealth, and all that went with it, inside. Mayfair was that kind of neighborhood, basking in the noble glow of nearby Buckingham Palace —the epicenter of the über upper crust. The trees, flowers, and punting pond of nearby St. James Park softened the ostentation a tad.

Light streamed through the windows of the club, framing a glimpse into a world of rarified air. Liveried bellmen wearing cutaway jackets and pinstriped pants, their hands white-gloved, and young ladies attired in dresses designed for us by Alexander McQueen before he died, chokers of south sea pearls, perfectly-seamed silk stockings and Ferragamo kitten heels passed by like figurines turning in a department store Christmas display. Some carried trays of fluted glasses—Kir Royales, a *de rigeur* aperitif. My stomach roiled. Too much wine during the flight to hide too much worry. On the positive side, I'd found the one thing that killed my thirst for alcohol. A self-defeating Catch—22, of course. In naming me Lucky, my mother had made me a lightning rod for the opposite, turning me into a walking talking, real-life Joe Btfsplk.

The driver deposited my three suitcases at my feet. "Staying long, ma'am." It wasn't a question but rather an assumption.

"As long as it takes," I managed through gritted teeth. I turned up the collar of my Burberry against the misty drizzle and shook off a chill, and then I waved him away without even a perfunctory pleasantness.

The doorman rushed down the steps to greet me. "Madam O'Toole. Your father alerted us."

Great. Years of smoothing things over, as he called it, had taught me that flying under the radar was the best strategy. My father, long on strong-arm, short on subtlety torpedoed that. "You have a room for me then."

"Yes, ma'am. Third floor, one of the regular rooms as you like it."

At least he'd remembered I didn't like a big fuss—that should be reserved for the paying customers, the club members in this case. "Thank you." I motioned to my bags. "Would you have these sent up to my room, please. I have to attend to some business."

"Yes, ma'am, of course. Please see Julie at the front desk. She has some information for you." A coat clerk took my overcoat.

Julie wasn't hard to pick out. Of the three young ladies waiting behind a burled walnut reception desk that glowed from centuries of hand polishing, she was the only one who watched me like an expectant puppy.

"Hello Julie." I acted like I remembered her name.

My ruse intact, she beamed. "Miss O'Toole. The young lady you're looking for is in the Royal Suite, fifth floor. She has not been alerted you are looking for her. The sheik will be arriving any minute now. He's much earlier than expected." She passed a simple keycard across the desk. "It's been coded with your fingerprint. You must hold it with your thumb over the sensor for it to function. The elevators..." A light blush colored her cheeks. "I don't need to tell you where they are, do I?"

A bank of three new elevators hid around the corner, tucked out of sight. The permits alone had almost required a sign-off by the Queen herself. Then we'd had to engage a contractor with an expertise in historic buildings, who billed at twice the normal rate.

After all the headaches, I didn't much care for the new elevators, choosing the one old creaky one instead. A set of wooden double doors stood open revealing a golden grate—all that separated me from the elevator shaft. I pressed the button summoning the lift, as they say in these parts, feeling a bit of anxiety drift away. There was something calming about the British sense of decorum, the subtle but inescapable nod to civility. Here people spoke in hushed voices, the music was subtle, classical. No one hurried. No one yelled. No one groped. And for sure no one threw up in the potted plants. *No, Toto, we're not in Vegas anymore.*

Finally, after stretching my patience to the breaking point, the elevator cage slowly eased to a stop behind the latticework of gold metal, the inner doors sliding open to reveal a middle-aged couple, their arms hooked together. They smiled at me through the metal grate, which I grabbed and slid back. I felt a bit too American in my cherry-red Diane Von Furstenberg wrap dress and gold slingbacks. Apparently, I didn't get the brown tweed memo.

But the lady and I both had Birkins—a stupid-expensive Hermès bag that was often the calling card of those in-the-money. My father knew well my passion for vintage handbags. He'd gifted me one in brown leather that had been carried by Audrey Hepburn in the last decade of her life—something I thought both cool and creepy. All the rest of my meager collection, amassed over my lifetime, had disappeared when my apartment had been immolated. The guy responsible had died an ugly death—too small a price for what he'd done. I was feeling the need to replace at least a few pieces—hence my current fascination with fashion accessories.

The couple nodded in tandem as I stepped aside to let them by.

"Oh, Ms. O'Toole, I'm so glad we bumped into each other." The voice, frosty and clipped, belonged to the Babylon Club's fusty manager, Nigel Ahern. Thinning strawberry-blonde hair, a thin face, thin lips—well, thin everything, except for the caterpillar perched on his upper lip masquerading as a mustache. Adopting an unctuous air punctuated with a small bow, he motioned me to go in front of him.

With no gracious way to tell him to bugger off, I did as he suggested. "Which floor?" My hand hovered over the buttons.

"Third, please. A disgruntled heiress."

"That borders on redundant." I punched his button, then inserted my key in a small slot which granted me access to the top floor, the entirety of which comprised the Royal Suite.

Not even the hint of a smile moved the caterpillar. "Why wasn't I apprised of your coming?"

A bit cheeky. I owned the place—I could do damn well whatever I wanted...without Mr. Ahern's permission or complicity. "Do your job, Mr. Ahern. Leave me to do mine. When you need to know, you'll be...apprised."

He recoiled as if I'd raised a hand to slap him. "Very well." The doors opened, and he left me to finish the ride alone with my thoughts. To be honest, I was conflicted about my job at hand. Firing a young woman because the men in her family found her uppity went against everything I believed. In fact, it offended me on every level. But, nobody died and made me King, least of all the head of the Saudi royal family. Who was I to meddle? But how would change happen if I didn't? Why send her to Oxford if she was going to be relegated to the role of human mannequin? Why couldn't life make sense?

Untangling this Gordian knot and not hating myself afterward would take a level of championship social tap dancing I wasn't sure I possessed. Where was my staff when I needed them? I glanced at my watch. Just finishing lunch, I would wager.

Trapped in my conundrum, I jumped when doors slid open and I came face-to-face with a woman I didn't expect to see. Not Aziza for sure. Caucasian, hair pulled back, the veiled brim of her hat pulled low, and glam from head-to-toe.

I greeted her with a smile and a nod as she slid back the metal grate. She seemed as surprised to see me as I was her. Ready to dismiss her, one detail caught my eye as I stepped aside, giving her room to move into the space I vacated:

Her purse.

A very rare vintage Hermès Kelly bag, white with bronze trim, and accented with gold fittings. An instant case of purse lust hit my heart. I'd never seen one like it and could only imagine how much such a distinctive, recognizable piece would cost. I wanted to ask her where she got it and what it set her back, but one just didn't do that sort of thing, not here, and especially not if one was the owner of the Club and, as such, straddled the line between staff and peer.

What is she doing here?

4

Donna

I'm facing a woman: a tall, slim, brunette—quite pretty, and around my age.

Surprise flashes across her face. Apparently, she was not expecting to run into anyone.

Welcome to the club, hon.

Damn it! In a few minutes, she'll find Hummingbird's body. I've got to get out of here–*now!*

As she moves past me, we exchange nods. But before doing so, I shift the angle of my head to lower the veil of my brimmed hat.

No need to worry since her gaze has dropped to my handbag. From the way her eyes widen, I guess she recognizes its worth.

After stepping into the elevator, I casually reach for the button that will take me back to Dominic's third-floor room. I stand at a half-turn. If she's watching me, she'll see a bored woman smoothing her gloves into place.

During the interminable ride to Dominic's floor, I'm working out my exit strategy. This mission called for a simple pick-up, so I had no reason to ask Arnie to loop the club's video-cam footage before my arrival. Now I do. I've got to call him immediately.

After I change out of this getup, Dominic will take "Princess Maja" to dinner outside the club. When he returns, he'll be alone.

If the manager, Ahern, asks him any questions, I'm sure Dominic can come up with some tale that positions him, as always, the playboy hero who dumped yet another adoring fangirl.

Suddenly, I remember that the tall brunette was admiring my purse.

It will be a clue to pass forward to the police.

Granted, should they try to trace it, it'll lead to a dead end. Buyer 1515 doesn't exist.

But since the handbag is one of a kind, I can never take it out again in public.

I frown as I look down at my purse. Well, heck, I guess it just wasn't meant to be.

I'll just leave it to Mary and Trisha in my last will and testament. By then the trail should be cold, and heaven knows its value will have gone up even higher.

I count the seconds before this ancient elevator descends to the third floor. When it finally arrives, I stroll out as if I don't have a care in the world. Reaching Dominic's door, I tap twice.

I hear him whistling as he moves toward it. He opens it, but before he can say anything I rush in past him and close the door firmly.

"Hummingbird is dead," I hiss.

Frowning, he exclaims, "You *killed* her?"

"No, you ninny! She was dead when I got there! Not only that, but when I left the Royal Suite someone was getting off the elevator when I was getting on. The woman may be able to recognize me. She admired my purse. She may use it as a clue to pass forward to the police. We've got to call Ryan and the others to let them know."

When I flop down on his ridiculously shaped bed, the damn thing rolls with the wave I've created.

Frowning, Dominic looks at me sideways. "You've created quite a tsunami, Old Girl! You must be heavier than you look."

If looks could kill, instead of rolling his eyes Dominic would be rolling in some unmarked grave.

With a click of my cell, Dominic and I are connected to the

whole team: Jack, Abu, and Arnie, who are hanging in Jack's and my suite at the Ritz; and Ryan and Emma, in Los Angeles.

I'm quick to the point: "I found Hummingbird at the rendezvous—but *she's dead.*"

The connection's dead air is finally broken by Ryan's wary question: "How was she killed?"

"Not by a bullet, or a knife. Her neck wasn't broken either." He can read my miffed tone: *And not by me, thank you very much.* I add, "However, there were a couple of odd, tiny wounds on the back of her neck."

"At the very least, were you able to secure the intel?" Ryan asks.

"Maybe. I took her cell phone and also the amulet around her neck, since you'd mentioned it as an identifying feature. I also took the items she held in her hands: an antique vase and a couple of hotel security cards on a key ring. Maybe she needed it to get into the suite."

"If so, she'd have only needed one of the cards, not both," Jack counters.

"Good point," I reply. "Abu, I'm texting you and Emma a photo of Aziza's tattoo and amulet now. See if you can make heads or tails of it."

"Got it," Abu confirms. "The lettering is Arabic, but these aren't words."

"It may be a code," Emma reasons.

"Emma, get the SIGINT team to work on deciphering it," Ryan commands. "Arnie, see if you can hack the key cards."

"Will do," Arnie assures him.

"Hummingbird was tatted with symbols identical to those on the talisman," I inform them.

"When you recover the body, an MI6 autopsy will determine the exact cause of death and send us better photos of the tattoo," Ryan says. "If she took the time and trouble to tattoo it to her body, it must be important."

"We're recovering…*what?*" Jack, Abu, and I exclaim in unison.

"You heard me," Ryan replies. "*The body.*"

5

Lucky

A set of grand, inlaid, wooden doors at the end, barred my way. The formal entrance to the suite, they opened to the grand foyer and main room of the Royal Suite—if my key worked. The rest of the suite formed a U, wrapping around the main hallway that I currently strode down. Doors on either side opened to service areas within the suite. On my right would be the master wing with bedroom, closet and a bath the size of my apartment. The other housed the kitchen facilities and two guest suites. Accommodations for Princes and Maharajas, Queens, Hollywood A-listers and perhaps a minor luminary who could tote the freight.

Another text dinged.

Remember, all stops to keep Ben happy.

My father, the ultimate control freak.

Still thinking about that friggin' purse, I fumbled with my key, trying to figure out which way it went in the slot and how to hold it so my thumb was properly positioned. The security measures were redundant but necessary. Many of our guests had targets on their backs. Whether it was the Russians trying to punish a defector or kidnappers looking for a human chess piece, or simply an unrequited lover or jilted business partner, the effect was the same—bad news for them and bad press for us, not to mention mounds of paperwork and police crawling all over the place. All of which had a chilling effect on business.

Which somehow brought me around to the woman with the purse. She didn't work for us. And she could only have come from the Royal Suite. No one was in the suite. So how did she get up here? Maybe she had been in the suite and left something? Perhaps. Why did I care? She looked like she belonged here—well, maybe trying a bit too hard, but, in my experience, those intent on doing mischief didn't walk around with a purse worth serious five-figures.

I needed to find Aziza, then meet her uncle, Sheik Ben, dazzle him with my best suck-up, and get on a plane to Paris.

I knocked, but no answer. Aziza must be in another part of the suite. I contorted myself to get the key in the slot. Turns out I didn't need it—the handle turned easily and the door swung inward on silent hinges like the door of a bank vault.

"Hello?" I called. The lights in the room were still dark. The only illumination filtered in through the large French doors, four sets of them floor-to-ceiling, marching across the far wall. "Aziza?" At least the drapes had been pushed back, the folds of velvet held to the side with silk ropes. I shut the door behind me and flicked on the lights. Lamps dotted around the room shed a warm glow. A large crystal chandelier in the circular foyer dripped light as it cascaded from the fourteen-foot ceiling. Underneath it, a huge floral display in a cut crystal vase erupted from the three-legged wooden table beneath it. Sprigs of red and green pussy willows, and curled branches with wide gold ribbon winding through it; the whole thing demanded attention. I paused to give it its due.

Red Dahlia, I thought.

"Aziza?" I called again. Where was she? Surely, she could hear me.

A bar removed from a Scottish castle before the turn of the century several centuries ago curved from the wall to my left. A swinging door to the left of the bar hid the entrance to the food service areas. A dining room table with seating for twelve separated the bar area from the great room. Several hand-knotted silk

Persian carpets softened the wood floor. Overstuffed couches and wing-backed chairs clustered around glass-topped tables creating nice conversation areas. Oil paintings of people no one remembered filled spots on the wall. Bookcases lined the front wall. Books that looked great but probably hadn't been cracked since the turn of the last century filled the shelves. The obligatory rare Chinese pottery had been tastefully arranged among the books. An odd gap caught my eye. A faint circle shadowed the wood shelf. A vase was missing—a very important vase—three-quarters of a million dollars important.

I would've seen the insurance claim on that, but none had hit my desk.

A tingle of fear prickled my skin.

"Aziza?" My voice held an edge now. "Aziza, where are you?"

Light leaked from the crack under the door closing off the hallway to the master suite. I followed it, more careful now. It came from the bedroom. I eased down the hallway, pausing to look in before I charged ahead.

The body of a woman, face down, arms and legs akimbo, her short skirt riding up to show a tattoo on the back of her thigh, so new the skin around the symbol was still pink.

Her long black hair fanned to the side, exposed her neck and a sliver of her face. Two marks, angry and red, marred the flawless olive skin of the back of her neck.

I knelt beside her, pressing two fingers to the hollow above her clavicle. Her skin still warm, but no pulse.

"Fuck." I rocked back on my heels then pushed to my feet. I took in the room as I pulled my phone from my purse.

What the hell should I do now?

Out of my comfort zone, I'd wandered into the deep end and needed someone to give me a hand. But who? I scanned the room, looking for anything out of place.

Nothing.

I backed out of the room, then ran for the door. I had called the Club from the car, so I hit redial. The front desk picked up before it even rang on my end. "This is Ms. O'Toole." I worked calm into my voice, which held steady. "May I have Security please?"

"Yes, Miss."

A female voice answered, announcing I'd actually reached the extension I'd asked for. Without letting her finish announcing her identity, I started shouting...well, muted shouting. More like demands in a you-may-not-ignore-me tone. "I need everyone in this whole place looking for a woman in a cream and gold Chanel suit—short pencil skirt, lovely tapered jacket. Her hair is..."

I paused. Because of her hat, I had no idea what color it is.

"She's wearing a...a matching hat," I stuttered. Then I remembered the purse. "She's carrying a vintage Hermès Kelly bag, bronze and white with gold embellishments. Find her—*now!*"

"Yes, ma'am."

"Don't alarm the guests but find her. It's crucial. Do you understand? Do not let her get away." At the front door, I illuminated the Do Not Disturb light then pulled the door behind me, making sure it locked.

Then I turned. Stifling the urge to run, I strode toward the elevator.

6

Donna

"*Move* Hummingbird's body?" I'm stunned at Ryan's suggestion. "But...*why*?"

"This wasn't just any asset," Ryan explains. "The dead woman —Aziza Halabi—is the daughter of a Saudi Arabian crown prince: Sheik Muhammad bin Al Saud. We're trying to stop an international incident, not start one! MI6's report will soften the blow for the royal family."

"By that, you mean, her espionage role?" Jack asks.

"Yes—and the fact that she was working in the first place—in a private club, of all places."

Emma snorts. "Because women in her country and of her position are practically imprisoned."

"To her credit, Aziza was able to convince the Crown Prince to loosen the tether to some extent," Ryan counters. "She was in England for university. She is—*was*— an International Studies major at Oxford." He sighs. "If what we have is her intel and it's correct, her country will mourn her as a true patriot."

"We'll have to move fast," I reply. "Unfortunately, when I summoned the elevator, a woman was just coming out of it. She seemed worried—and she was surprised to run into me. Since the Royal Suite is the only guest accommodations on the floor, by now she'll have realized I was in there, especially since I left the door as I found it: cracked open. Needless to say, I didn't stick around to see if the woman actually walked into the suite. Even if she did, I found Aziza's body in the master bedroom."

"If this woman didn't immediately see the poor girl, she may have just called out her name, gotten no response, then turned around and left," Dominic suggests.

"This may be why we aren't hearing an ambulance or police sirens," Jack points out.

"Not as of the last few minutes. But, eventually, someone will find her," Ryan replies. "When they do, all hell will break loose. All the more reason to get Donna out—*now.*"

"Arnie, as soon as possible, I'll need you to wipe me from the security feeds throughout the club," I say. "I left Dominic's room around 20:05 and took the vintage elevator to the penthouse level —fifth floor. There were security cams in the elevator and in the halls."

"On it," Arnie murmurs.

"You can't do a simple loop," Ryan reminds him. "Since Donna ran into someone, you'll have to erase Donna but leave the woman."

Arnie sighs. "I'll do my best with the time I have." I hear him clicking away on his computer keyboard.

"I'll give you a hand by looping Dominic's floor," Emma adds.

"Thanks, Em." The relief is obvious in Arnie's voice. "Ah, hell! The mystery woman is leaving the Royal Suite now! Strange. She doesn't seem scared. More like, angry."

Ryan sighs. "She was in there long enough to have found Aziza."

"That's odd. The usual response to a dead body is fear or tears," I exclaim.

"Not if she was in on the murder," Dominic replies.

"And if so, we have to find out who she is, and who she works for," Jack declares.

"As of now, this woman is certainly our prime suspect," I agree. "On the other hand, Aziza's killer may have arrived before her as opposed to after her and most certainly left the suite before Donna arrived for the pickup."

"Good point," Ryan says. "Emma, after you've finished looping Dominic's floor, pull up the security footage for the hallway leading to the Royal Suite. Begin an hour prior to Aziza's arrival and up until Donna's ETA for the pickup."

"Will do, Chief," Emma replies.

"Also, run the mystery woman through facial recognition analysis. We need to know who we're dealing with."

"On it," she assures him.

"Jack and Abu, you'll do the wet work," Ryan adds.

"Getting a dead body out of there won't be easy," Jack mutters.

"From what I can see of the activity taking place in the club, one of its reception areas is preparing for some sort of event," Dominic chimes in. "Maybe that will help."

"Checking the security feed now…" Emma adds. "You're right. A few workmen, dressed in coveralls, are going in and out…In fact, I'm following two guys who are carrying some rolled-up carpets…They're taking them down a side hall. It goes to a service area just beyond the kitchen." She pauses for a few moments. Finally: "They went out a door that leads to a loading dock on the back alley. They've dropped the carpets there."

"That's where we'll start," Abu declares.

"You'll have to get the carpet up to the Royal Suite without being seen," I remind them. "It won't be easy since the elevators are for guests and staff only."

"Crikey! I've got the perfect solution!" Dominic exclaims. "The suite's kitchen happens to have a dumbwaiter."

I give him a sideways gaze. "How would you know that?"

"I discovered it quite by necessity—sadly, during an aborted tryst with the wife of an Argentine diplomat whose skeet shooting skill is renowned the world over." Dominic shrugs. "Considering my proximity to his wife, I saw no need to test his claim to fame."

"What a shame," Jack mumbles.

Ryan sighs loudly—a warning to all to keep on task.

"What about the kitchen staff?" I ask.

"The dumbwaiter is located in a butler's pantry," Dominic adds. "And since the Royal Suite is the only one with a formal dining room, the pantry isn't currently in use until the suite is occupied again."

"Then we'd better hurry, since readying it for the next guest was Aziza's excuse for being up there in the first place," I reply.

"I see the pantry," Emma says. "In fact, it is accessed from the same service hall that leads to the loading dock."

"Perhaps Jack and Abu should raid the catering staff's lockers in order to get upstairs," Dominic suggests.

"Easily done," Emma replies. "From what I'm seeing, the employee dressing room can also be accessed from that corridor. I'm in the room now...For the time being, it's empty. And from what I can see, it contains personnel lockers. There's a door marked 'Uniform Closet.'"

"That makes life easier. Wear your eyes and ears, everyone," Ryan warns.

"Will do," Jack assures him. "Abu and I are over and out." We hear him ring off.

"If the mystery woman was the killer, she may consider *you* a witness," Dominic points out to me.

"Dominic, all the more reason you have to get Donna out of the club immediately," Ryan declares. "But hang around in case Jack and Abu need you to create a diversion. You're also to tail the mystery woman. If necessary, intercept and interrogate."

"With pleasure," Dominic purrs.

"Donna, you'd better move fast—and safe journey." I'm touched by the concern in Ryan's voice.

I RUN TO THE BEDROOM CLOSET IN DOMINIC'S SUITE, PULL OUT THE RED leather dress suit, and toss it on the bed: a heart-shaped monstrosity that undulates under the merest touch.

Ugh!

I can't let my disgust slow me down. Quickly, I unbutton my

jacket and blouse. Finally, I step out of my skirt and toss the discarded Chanel outfit into my suitcase. It deserves better treatment, but I haven't the time. Still, I grumble, "Dominic, really! A waterbed? That's…so…"

"I know, hard to resist, isn't it?" From his joyous tone, he actually means that.

As I slip the dress over my hips, I retort, "This doesn't look like the kind of joint that caters to…to…well, you know—"

Dominic chuckles. "Rumpy-pumpy shenanigans? I've come to learn that if you spend enough money in any club, their world is your pleasure palace."

His voice sounds too close for comfort. I look around to see him leaning against the wall. Frowning, I growl, "May I have some privacy? I've got to get back into your fantasy fuck suit if I'm going to make it out of this supposedly hoity-toity club without drawing attention to myself." *Talk about a misnomer!*

"You'll need someone to help you zip it up," he reminds me.

"At least, turn around until I do." I pull up the dress, then grab my Princess Maja wig in one hand and the outfit's red stiletto heels in the other. Scanning the room for a mirror, I realize Dominic could see me all along because he's staring up at the ceiling—

Which has a mirror over the bed.

He rewards my blush with a wink—

But then curses when the shoe I throw at him hits its mark.

WE DESCEND INTO THE LOBBY AT ARM'S LENGTH, BUT BY THE TIME THE elevator door opens Dominic has once again draped his arm around my waist.

In fact, I now find myself in a lip-lock.

Why, that son of a bitch…

Okay, admittedly, he isn't a half-bad kisser.

Yeah, okay, I'll survive.

For the sake of Babylon London's staff, Dominic and I exchange subtle smiles and lust-filled gazes. Dominic's pat on my ass is a step too far, but breaking his hand in the club's lobby would defeat the prime objective: getting me out of here without incident.

At that moment, I see Jack and Abu on the far side of the lobby, walking out of a room with large double doors. Between them, they've hoisted a carpet onto their shoulders.

Thank goodness they're already here.

"Yo, Jack—Mystery Woman is waiting for the Royal Suite's service elevator, so grab the public one instead," Emma insists.

Instead, they head toward the one public elevator that ascends to the Royal Suite.

It's only after the doorman summons one of London's iconic black cabs that I breathe easy again. Just for show, Dominic gives me a searing kiss before ushering me into it.

"I'm rather enjoying this," he whispers as he nuzzles my neck.

"Don't tell Jack," I warn him.

Dominic glances skyward. "Not to worry. Mum's the word, Ducky." He shrugs. "He's a very lucky man."

That bit of sweetness earns him a stroke on the cheek. Still, to change the subject, I urge him, "I don't know if our mystery woman is still here, but if so, intercept her."

He waves me off, but his ear-to-ear grin is his vow that he plans on doing exactly that.

As a precaution, in a Scandinavian drawl I ask the cab to take me only as far as Selfridges, as if I haven't a care in the world. He drops me off on the Oxford Street side. I walk through the store with the goal of exiting on the Orchard Street side.

As I pass the Hermès concession, it hits me: *I left my handbag in Dominic's room.*

Damn it!

Considering his predilection for cozy company, I'll make him promise to place it deep into a suitcase. I'd hate for one of his many conquests to pilfer it, like some sort of trophy.

If they do, he owes me—okay, make that Acme—it's one hundred and ten thousand Euros!

By now, I'm safely ensconced in a second cab instructed to drop me off a few blocks from the Ritz. We're inching our way through Park Lane's stop-and-go traffic, giving me plenty of time to tune into the real-time machinations of my team.

While Arnie takes on the meticulous task of erasing me from the floor's archival footage, Emma furtively whispers that the elevator's security camera is now on a loop that shows it as empty. The same goes for the cameras on the Royal Suite's hallway, the service hall, the butler's pantry, and the loading dock.

Jack and Abu, now liveried as club waiters with aproned food carts, enter the empty vintage elevator.

And, as Arnie previously did for me, the second they step onto the fifth floor, Emma hacks the code that keeps it from going beyond the fourth floor.

They reach the suite's front door. Since they don't have a properly coded RFID keycard, Jack pulls something from his pocket that works just as well: a little gadget that spoofs the suite's Vingcard Vision lock.

As Abu and Jack enter the suite, I relay in a whisper, "The master bedroom is down the hall to the left."

The moment they enter it, they unroll the carpet beside the dead woman's body. The frowns on their faces confirm that rigor mortis has set in. This means they'll have to be very careful. Gently, they place Aziza onto the carpet and roll it up. Lifting it evenly, they take it into the dining room.

The dumbwaiter is in an alcove. Thank goodness, it is wide enough. While Jack maneuvers the carpet into it, Abu lowers the dumbwaiter slowly until the carpet is vertical within the chute.

They press the button that sends it descending five stories.

Immediately, they are out the suite's front door. Jack locks it behind them.

It takes the vintage elevator two minutes, tops, to descend. Still, each passing second seems like a year.

Luckily, by the time the elevator opens again in the lobby, no one is waiting for it. As previously planned, Jack and Abu walk quickly to the service hall.

Just as they enter the pantry, the dumbwaiter groans to a stop.

"Talk about perfect timing," Emma mutters.

With immense care, Abu and Jack pull the rolled carpet from the dumbwaiter.

"You're clear to go down the service hall to the loading dock," Emma hisses.

They're out the door with the carpet.

Two minutes later, their white, unmarked, paneled van veers away from the dock.

My taxi has just pulled up to my destination—the corner of Piccadilly and Bolton—when I hear Ryan say, "Good work, boys."

Arnie exclaims, "Donna is now a ghost. But, Princess Maja lives on."

"Lucky lady," I mutter.

7

Lucky

*W*ith the vise of panic squeezing my chest, I chose the service elevator. With a dead woman rapidly cooling in the Royal Suite, the refined one servicing this floor was much too slow. Talk about keeping someone on ice.

How many laws was I breaking? Probably enough to be a permanent ward of the state.

I swallowed a nervous giggle—murder always made me twitchy. Running the risk of being accused of it made it impossible to breathe.

The elevator took way longer than usual—I was almost apoplectic by the time it arrived. As soon as I could, I eased sideways through the opening then began pummeling the door-close button. The door didn't shut as fast as I wanted, and left me waiting, alone with my heart pounding in my ears.

I didn't want time to think. Thinking wasn't going to help. The young woman was a Saudi citizen. Her uncle our most important partner and client. Who could help? MI5? The local police? The Queen? The American Embassy?

Of course, no American was involved…except me.

I needed help in the worst way. But I had no idea who to call.

But, at least I knew who to blame. I called my father.

As the elevator spit me out in the hallway behind the lobby, he answered with a cheery, "How's everything?" Thankfully, no one waited or lurked within earshot—January wasn't exactly high season in London.

Fluent in sarcasm, I matched his tone. "Oh, really terrific. Just peachy, actually."

"No need to be smart with me. What's—"

"Lucky?" My mother came on the line. She must've picked up the same time my father had answered. "Is that you? You sound so far away and so not like yourself."

"Mother, I can't talk right now. Can you please get off the line?"

"No, I most certainly cannot." I could almost see her puffing up with indignation. "That is no way to talk to your mother." Just as quickly, her tone shifted to breathless with a hint of clueless. "I've been thinking..."

Never a good thing, but I didn't think it would help if I pointed that out. Standing by myself, in a foreign country, with a dead body on my hands, jail time in my future and an incipient diplomatic incident, I was not in a position to cast the first stone. Once my mother had the bit in her teeth, she was going to run no matter how hard I pulled against her, so I let her.

Besides, at this point, the only outcome I saw had me in the Tower of London watching through a slit in the rock wall while they built my gallows, so what was the hurry?

My father, suffering from the Curse of the Y-chromosome, still hadn't learned that lesson. "Mona, please. Let Lucky and I talk. It's business."

"Albert, I refuse to be left out any longer." She added frost to the indignation. Truly impressive.

"Father, it's okay. Let her be." I shifted the phone to the other ear. "What is it, Mother?"

"Ms. O'Toole?" A tap on my shoulder.

More frost. Nigel, his face a mask of disdain, demanded my attention. I held up a finger. "Wait your turn."

"I will not! I'm your mother!" Mona's voice cut like a wire garrote.

I turned my back on Nigel. "Not you, mother. Sorry. Go ahead."

After a moment of silent gloat, my mother waded in, her voice conspiratorial. "Well, you know how we have these twins?"

An odd start. If I hadn't already lost the feeling in my hands and both feet due to my panic-restricted blood flow, I would've started pacing to burn off the anger welling. "Yes, of course."

Another tap on my shoulder, this one more insistent.

I whirled on Nigel. "Damn. What is it?"

"I'm getting to it." My mother went back to huffy.

"Not you, mother." I put my thumb over what I thought was my phone's microphone. "Quickly," I said to Nigel.

In a microsecond his look told me what he thought of my rudeness. I needed to take lessons—that look was championship stuff. Eye for an eye and all of that, I wanted to tell him but that would take time and air I didn't have.

"The sheik is arriving. We will put him in the Royal Suite as planned. I'm assuming it's adequately prepared? I can't seem to reach Aziza. You've sent her on a wild goose chase?"

I ignored the insult as my vision started to swim. "Fine." I uncovered the microphone then his words hit. I whirled on him. "What? You can't do that!" Stars floated in front of me. I'd been holding my breath. It rushed out of me in a whoosh. Blood flooded from my head.

Nigel reared back.

"But I haven't told you yet what I'm planning." My mother complained in my ear.

"No whining!" I sagged onto the nearest chair, then bent at the waist, stuffing my head between my knees.

"I assure you I am not whining." Nigel's tone was clipped.

"Not you." In the few nanoseconds of shocked silence, I took a deep breath. My father had been strangely quiet. Now I heard a soft chuckle. "Thanks so much, father." My vision clearing a bit, I sat up but didn't trust my feet. "Mother, give me a moment. Nigel, do not put the sheik in the Royal Suite. Ready other accommodations."

"There are no other." It was his civilized way of saying *You should know that.*

"Lucky, I want to tell you about their names!" My mother gave a verbal stomp of the foot.

"Mother! For God's sake! Shut up!"

A sharp intake of air hissed in my ear—a warning salvo. Damn the torpedoes. "Hold the sheik at the front desk. I'll escort him myself."

Nigel gave me a nod and a tight smile and turned on his heel.

"Mother, you have the stage, but make it fast. Like, ten words or less, fast."

"You said shut up."

"And I'm going to hang up if you can't understand my situation is dire on this end. Spit it out. Ten seconds."

"Lucky!"

"Eight."

"You know the twins don't have names yet?" She was taking a verbal stroll, calling my bluff.

"Of course. Six."

"Oh, for God's sake, Mona!" My father spluttered, out of patience.

"Albert, I'm talking!"

And I was witnessing the theater of the absurd they call family.

It's like somehow the Powers That Be get everything arranged perfectly, the compatible personalities clumped together in familial units, then, just before babies are born and marriages made…or vice versa…somebody evil shuffles the deck just to see what happens.

My family is what happens. A future homicide in the making. The question always was which one of us would break first.

Force that she is, my mother would never be put off by such a trifling thing as her husband's fury. "And you know how they're girls?"

"Four seconds."

"Stop it, Lucky! You sound just like your father," She raised her voice as if he couldn't hear. "But a whole lot nicer."

"Things are a bit dicey on this end, and it's getting late here, Mother. Two seconds to make your point." I rose and started toward the reception desk, ready to disconnect. I could blame my father later. Right now I needed to keep Sheik Ben from stumbling over the body of his dead niece.

"I've decided on names!" Mona announced as if alerting everyone to the Second Coming.

"Really?" my father and I said in unison. Her pronouncement stopped me mid-stride.

Of course, she wouldn't have consulted the father of her children—that wasn't Mother's modus operandi. I don't know why I was surprised. Maybe because no matter what, the woman never, ever learned anything.

My phone beeped a message. Someone else wanted my attention. Terrific.

I held the phone in front of my face and squinted at it. Jean-Charles.

We have arrived.

Great. Now he copped an attitude. A lot of that going around—I must be putting something out into the Universe I wasn't aware of. Hell, all I wanted to do was keep my job and stay out of jail—normally not a problem. However, today was far from normal which relegated Jean-Charles to a low priority.

Life was imploding before my eyes.

Wednesday night. I still had forty-eight hours to make the party in Paris. If I didn't, I had a feeling my Prince would not come searching with a glass slipper.

"What names are you considering?" my father asked while I half-listened, distracted by all the plates I had spinning.

Mona drew in an audible breath and I braced for impact. "Storm and Rayne. That would be Rayne spelled with a 'Y.'"

A hooker in her youth, by the time I was born my mother had risen to be the madam of an eponymous brothel in Pahrump, the closest town of any size in a county where prostitution was legal. Technically, in Clark County where Vegas resides, girls couldn't legally advertise they were employed in the world's oldest profession. With sixteen thousand hookers in Vegas, I thought reality had erased that technicality, but nobody asked me. And each year the Vice Squad rounded up the same nine hookers, booked them, then let them go in a grand show of competence, diligence and compassion—at least that's what they wanted us to think.

"Weren't they X-Men?" I stammered.

"Were they? Even better." My mother sounded triumphant.

"Really tough hanging such odd monikers on pretty little girls. Makes them stand out, when all they'll want to do at some point is fit in."

"But standing out is what makes them special."

"They'll get there. You don't need to force the issue. Trust me on this one."

"But odd names are all the rage. I mean North and Apple? Seriously?"

"But you said you think standing out, going against the majority is what makes you special. Why don't you keep thinking? You'll come up with the perfect names."

A moment of silence during which I had an out-of-body experience. Was this really happening?

"If you think so." She didn't sound happy about it but at least she didn't argue.

I heard a click. "Is she gone?"

"Frankly, ever since the twins were born, she's been gone." My father sounded tired and exasperated. "What's the big goddammit on your end?"

With time in short supply, I cut short our conversation and pocketed my phone.

I strode into the lobby just in time to witness Nigel holding the elevator door open for Sheik Ben. "Sheik Ben," I said, struggling to keep the squeak out of my voice. Nigel gave me a wide-eyed look of terror in response to my glare. Controlling a client as difficult as the sheik was an impossibility. The best even someone with my clout could hope for would be to herd him in an acceptable direction. Being female put me at a disadvantage, though. But my father couldn't send the son he didn't have.

I bolted into the elevator, waving Nigel away. His look of relief told me our accounts were settled—we were back to boss and employee, no hurt feelings. He slid back the metal grate, trapping me with Sheik Ben. I smoothed my dress before straightening my spine, willing some bone into it.

Maybe ten years my senior Sheik Ben looked younger, despite the glower. Apparently, wealth beyond the dreams of avarice could keep the hands of time from advancing. How I would love to test that theory. Another life, maybe. I'd be lucky to get out of today alive. "Sheik Ben, so good to see you." I gave a fake smile and a tiny bow.

"Lucky, cut the crap." His clipped British accent made anger sound palatable. Oxford had suffered through four years of Ben's education. He'd come away with a killer accent and manners—when he felt like using them. "We both know you don't want to be here, and neither do I."

I leaned against the wall, minimizing my height advantage. His hand tailored suit in a light Italian wool did its best to add taper to his stocky body. A shock of black hair sprouted through the open collar of his white button-down. He'd shaved on his way to the hotel—no five-o'clock shadow and a dot of blood had dried to a dark brown on his chin. When he smiled, he would be considered Hollywood handsome. Without it, like today, he looked capable of casual cruelty. Not a good look on anyone.

"I'd rather be in Paris, for sure. But I've been asked to stand in for my father who, as you know, can't travel due to health issues."

"Health issues." He gave a snort. "Thought I told you to cut the crap."

My give-a-damn snapped. "Look, you throw your money around, keep us all dancing like puppets with you pulling the strings. For one, I've had enough. I'm here because my father asked me. Personally, I find the fact you males are so…" Warning bells sounded in the depths of my empty head and somehow, I paid attention, catching myself before I dove head-first off the cliff. I pulled in air, quieting my panic…sort of. "I apologize. Not my place."

"Don't pander to me. You suck at it. I like the fire much better."
He gave me a flash of that smile and I saw a hint of what everybody was talking about. "Are you going to depress a button and
have this miserable piece of machinery lift us to the fifth floor
or not?"

"No."

A hint of surprise fractured his composure. "No? Why then are
we here? Somehow I don't think I'm your type for elevator sex."

It was a miracle I didn't laugh in his face. Elevator sex! My
creep meter pegged. He should be grateful I didn't kill clients, at
least not often. And he should be grateful he lived where he did.
No way would he survive in any western country in this #metoo
world. Of course, he was a product of his culture. I wondered what
our excuse was.

"I'm sure I'd be flattered at your attentions," I said. We both
knew that was a lie. "Your women don't work, so, well, that leaves
me out." Yeah, I had to get in a bit of a jab. Frankly I felt like an
elbow to his nose might knock some sense into him, but I had
more crow than I could swallow on my plate already. "However,
there is an issue with the suite." To tell him or not? Flying blind, I
figured falling on my petard would look better in the long run.

He waved a hand. "If it's not ready, have them work around
me. I'm tired and I need a drink and a shower. My brother…" He
cast a look my direction giving me a glimpse before he shut
it down.

Great, we were bonding over family issues.

"It's not that. It's Aziza."

"She is in the suite then, waiting for me? That's terrific. You
have saved me great trouble."

Taking a moment, I inserted my card and pushed the button. I
didn't speak until we arrived. Somehow, this time marching down
the long hall brought visions of walking to my death. A bit melo-
dramatic, but I hadn't eaten in twenty-four hours and my brain
was starved of glucose. A new excuse and a rare one. As my
mother said, I never missed a drink or a meal.

"Sheik Ben." With a hand on his arm, I stopped him. He turned toward me. When I looked at the doors to the suite, the do not disturb light burned like a red eye next to the door. No one had been in. She'd still be there. "Aziza is dead. I'm very sorry."

"What?" His voice dropped to a lethal tone. "How?"

"I don't know. I found her and had just come back downstairs to call the police when you arrived." I telescoped it a bit. A good half-hour had passed, but I didn't think it mattered.

"I must see her." He charged toward the door, then stopped and whirled. In my haste to follow, I almost ran him down, stopping inches from him and ending up with my chin to his nose. He grabbed my arm and dug in his fingers. "I hold you accountable. This is your fault. We have worked together a long time. You've never let me down before. Your office made arrangements for my stay. You're responsible."

Although his grip hurt like hell and was offensive in the extreme, I refused to give him the satisfaction of responding to either. To me, his logic chain had more than a few weak links. I'd get to the bottom of what had happened and why, then I'd have my pound of flesh.

One thing he got right: the murder happened on my watch.

He continued his beeline for the suite.

Hot on his heels, I knew it would be futile to try to slow him down, much less stop him. "I have the key."

He grabbed the handle and cranked. The door opened.

I was sure I'd locked it.

I followed him through the great room.

The vase was still missing.

"Sheik Ben. Wait!"

He continued his charge down the hall to the master suite. He disappeared inside with me a second behind. I skidded to a stop beside him in the center of the room.

The body was gone.

8

Donna

*B*y the time Jack gets back from delivering Aziza's corpse to MI6, I'm no longer Princess Maja. The princess' wig, scarf, and dress suit are tied up in a bag that will soon find its way into the Thames.

It's great to be me again.

From Jack's long, lingering kiss, I gather he thinks so too.

Suddenly, he sniffs the air. "Are you wearing perfume?"

"Um…" Oh, heck. He's caught a whiff of Dominic's musky signature scent: Floris Number 89. Not at all surprising, considering that Dominic stuck to me like glue during our fleeting public moments as faux paramours.

"Wait…" Some unpleasant memory etches faint lines on Jack's brow. "That's Dominic's stench."

"You win the prize." I roll my eyes. "He reeks of it, and I didn't have time for a bath since he…we…"

"'Since we,' what?" His eyes narrow and his smile shifts into a smirk.

"You're going to make me say it, aren't you? Okay, then…yes, he kissed me—in the lobby, as part of our ruse."

Jack's eyes narrow. "Did you enjoy it?"

I shudder. "We're talking about Dominic, remember?"

61

"Yes, I know who he is, starting with 'Winner of the Under-cover Lover Award' five years in a row." Jack crosses his arms at his waist. "And we all know why he's held the title for so long."

"Only because you retired from the contest!"

My sharp glare doesn't stop him from muttering, "Lucky you."

"Jack Craig, if you're implying that Dominic and I went 'rumpy-pumpy' on that heart-shaped waterbed of his, you're as nutty as he is randy!"

"His suite has a waterbed—and it's *heart-shaped?*" Jack's double take is worthy of a Loony Tunes cartoon. "How did it feel?"

I'm shaking with anger. "How would I know? I was too busy changing disguises between rendezvousing with a corpse, dodging her possible killer, and being petted like a prize pooch by Acme's horniest honeytrap!"

Jack bites his lip. I can't tell if he's pissed at the situation or is trying to keep from laughing.

Neither is acceptable. On the one hand, he's a fool to think a man-whore like Dominic would appeal to me. And on the other, it is *so* not cool to make fun of me—his beloved, his main squeeze, the one who makes his heart go pitter-patter when I first come into view—

As opposed to being another of Dominic's afterthoughts.

Before I can make this clear to him in no uncertain terms, our cell phones hum in tandem, Instinctively, we reach for them. It's Ryan:

All hands on deck.

Jack is saved by the buzz announcing a team teleconference, and he knows it.

To prove it, there's a tap on our door.

I open it. Arnie and Abu stand there. Arnie holds three sizable brown paper sacks. "Fish and chips," he announces. "I got plenty for everyone."

"So, here's what's happened with Mystery Woman during the past half-hour," Emma begins.

Babylon London security footage appears on Arnie's computer screen. In it, two men get into the elevator.

"I recognize one of them," Ryan says. "That is Sheik Mohammed Ben Halabi. He's Aziza's uncle."

Oh...*Hell.*

"The other is the club's manager," Dominic informs him. "Nigel...Thingamabob."

"Ahern," I remind him. Suddenly, I exclaim excitedly, "Oh, my God! Mystery Woman joined them by the elevator!"

"So, that's the bird I'm to intercept?" Dominic murmurs. "Well, well! She's quite tasty."

But of course she'd appeal to him: Tall, dark, and beautiful, she's just his type.

Then again, every woman north of eighteen and south of sixty would fit that description.

She'll soon notice him too.

Hey, better him than me.

"Ha! She told the other man to take a hike so that she can go up to the suite with the sheik," Jack notes.

"Too bad the club's security doesn't have audio," Ryan mutters.

"No kidding," I murmur. "Still, you can see the tension between her and the sheik."

"From the looks of things, he's giving her an earful," Ryan agrees.

"But she's holding her own," Dominic says. Intrigued, he adds, "Look at how she leans against the wall as if she's toying with him."

In your dreams.

"The elevator stopped at the penthouse floor," Abu points out.

"If she found Aziza's body, why would she have taken him to see it when she hasn't even notified the police yet?" Emma wonders out loud.

"The only logical reason is that she doesn't want to cause an international incident," Ryan reasons.

"We may not be able to hear what's happening, but her actions speak volumes," Jack counters. "In the first place, she shooed away the club's manager before he could see what had happened up there. Also, she already knows the sheik. If she told him about the body, he isn't acting as if he's upset about his niece's death. For that matter, neither is she. And remember: other than Donna, Abu, and me, Mystery Woman was the last person to go in and out of the suite."

We all think about this for a moment. Finally, I say, "Jack's right. She's our prime suspect."

"Emma, any luck with Interpol about Mystery Woman?" Ryan asks.

"Not yet," Emma admits.

"At least we've got one bit of decent news," Ryan continues. "I've heard from our contact at MI6. We should have the autopsy results in a few hours. In the meantime, Emma and the SigInt team are reviewing the photos of the talisman and the tattoo to determine if either or both are part of a cipher."

"Arnie, have you been able to hack the key cards?" I ask.

Choking on a chip, Arnie mumbles, "I'm back on it…as soon as I finish my cod."

Ryan sighs then declares, "In the meantime, Donna, you and Jack should scrub Aziza's apartment in Oxford. She may have left a clue as to whether you actually retrieved the intel, and what it pertains to."

"We'll leave now." Jack looks at his watch. "It should take us about two hours to get there."

"I'll text over the address. It's off campus. Word of warning: Aziza has a roommate—another student. Her name is Roxanna Marmaduke. Apparently, it's been a convenient living arrangement, but the girls weren't close. From Roxanna's Facebook and Instagram pages, she looks to be quite the party animal."

"If so, and since this is the weekend, she may be out on the town. That would make it easier for us to let ourselves in, and to get out quickly," I reply.

"That would be fortunate," Ryan agrees. "But if she's home,

perhaps Jack should divert her while you go in for reconnaissance."

"Sure, I can do that," Jack assures him nonchalantly.

Ah, here we go—payback for Dominic's little peck.

"I'll bet you can," I mutter.

Jack's smirk indicates he's heard me.

"I've texted you Roxanna's social media links so you can ID her. Break a leg, folks." Ryan rings off.

The text hits my phone a nanosecond before it reaches Jack's.

Nonchalantly, I open it and find myself staring at the woman in question. The arm holding the camera is extended in such a way that the shot is angled from high above her face, giving viewers a bird's eye of her more than ample breasts, squeezed tightly into the hot pink lace push-up bra peeking out from the tight blouse tied at her waist. As with most selfies, she purses her lips, hollowing out her already sky-high cheeks. Her auburn hair falls straight and long below her shoulders.

When my eyes shift in his direction, Jack tries to hide his grin by heading toward the closet. "What you're wearing is okay to play cat burglar, but I'd better change."

He takes a pair of skinny gray jeans from one hanger and a black, fitted blazer from another. I drop onto the bed and watch as he strips off his shirt for a fresh one—a crew neck tee shirt that hugs his massive chest.

I whistle appreciatively. "I'm sure Roxanna will be duly impressed."

He shrugs as he steps out of his loafers. "It's a dirty job, but someone has to do it. Too bad Dominic isn't tagging along. It sounds right up his alley."

"He'll have his hands full with Mystery Woman."

"Better him than me," Jack says as he pulls on his jeans and zips up.

"Why do you say that?" I ask.

Tucking his shirt into his pants, he replies, "Because, unlike me, he enjoys playing the raven. I take your viewpoint: it's an unpleasant but sometimes necessary part of our jobs."

Jack is extending an olive branch.

My way of taking it is to roll off the bed, reach for his jacket, and hold it out so that he can slip his arms into it. Afterward, I smooth it over his shoulders.

Honestly, this is wasted action since his response is to take me in his arms to pull me back onto the bed with him.

I don't fight it. Instead, I lean into his embrace.

And I plunge into his kiss.

But when he starts to shrug off his jacket, I sigh, then whisper, "We can't, Jack. Not now. Work before play, right?"

He groans but pauses. Finally, he nods. "Okay, then. But when we get back—"

I interrupt him with a kiss that seals my promise:

It will be worth the wait.

JACK AND I DRIVE SLOWLY BY THE TWO-STORY RED BRICK TUDOR townhouse shared by Aziza and Roxanna before parking a few blocks away.

Their home is on Walton Cres, one of Oxford's many narrow streets that snake around the city's colleges. Except for an occasional pop of color on a front door, the townhouses are indistinguishable. In Aziza's case, the door is sky blue and solid wood with a peephole and a glass transom overhead.

After getting out of our car, we walk back toward the house. When we reach it, we pause and lean in toward each other, as if engaged in a conversation. In reality, we're assessing our covert entry options.

Each townhouse shares a common wall with another. Narrow alleys separate four townhouses from the others on the street, forming a block. A side door leads from each house into the closest alley.

A waist-high brick wall gives each home twenty or so feet of breathing room from the sidewalk. There's a bit of a front yard, but the tall, thick box hedge that surrounds Aziza's yard keeps prying eyes at bay. Still, separately, we peer deep into it. One interior light is on: downstairs, illuminating the large, front bay window.

To enter the narrow walk to the front stoop, one must first open the ornate iron gate. The stoop's light is on as well.

Jack glances down at the screen of his cell phone. "Roxanna is at a nearby pub, with a couple of girlfriends." He mutes a video posted just a moment ago on her Instagram page. It shows her mugging with two other gal pals. When some guy leaps into view, Roxanna shoves him away, annoyed. The other girls, laughing raucously, are egging him on as he chugs his beer.

"Good," I declare as I snap on a pair of nitrile gloves from the canvas Tesco bag slung over my shoulder that marks me as just another housewife walking home from the grocery store. "Keep monitoring Roxanna's actions and play lookout while I go in. This should take twenty minutes, tops."

Jack nods. "Put your cell on buzz. If she leaves the pub, I'll text you."

I do as he asks.

We kiss before Jack crosses the street. Casually, he leans against a lamppost, as if waiting for a friend.

As I saunter to the alley beside Roxanna's house, he deflects a curious glance of a passerby by quickly turning his head and looks down at his cell phone, as if a call has just come in.

THE BACKDOOR LOCK IS EASY TO PICK.

The bright, narrow beam of my flashlight reveals a messy kitchen. Dirty dishes are in the sink. A small table holds the remains of a half-eaten breakfast: a plate sprinkled with crumbs, a coffee mug ringed with lipstick, and open mail.

The bills are addressed to Roxanna. The few envelopes addressed to Aziza are left sealed. One is a bank statement. Another thicker envelope identifies Oxford University as the sender.

A third envelope, the size of a greeting card, has her name

written in box letters. There is no return address. I slip all the mail in the Tesco sack. Aziza has no use for it, but maybe Acme will.

The light in the living room keeps me out of there. No need for someone to spot me through the window. Still, I take a quick glance. Mismatched settees flank a fireplace. Over it, someone has hung a poster of happy celebrity couples: Ryan Gosling and his wife, Eva Mendez, at the Oscars; another red-carpet photo of Justin Timberlake and his wife, Jessica Biel; and yet another of Prince Harry, taken during that celebrated first post-wedding kiss with the American actress, Meghan Markle.

The poster's headline, pocked with frowny faces, declares:

ANOTHER ONE BITES THE DUST!

MY PATH TO THE UPSTAIRS ROOMS IS RIDDLED WITH OBSTACLES. A basket of laundry blocks the foot of the stairwell leading to the bedrooms above. Where the stairs take a turn, a pyramid of books is stacked high enough that one nudge with a heel could send them tumbling. A black lace bra dangles from the banister. Seeing it, I can only pray that all my harping about tidiness will deafen my eldest daughter, Mary, to the clarion call of messy roomies by the time she leaves for college next fall.

The door closest to the landing is wide open, revealing a bedroom. The walls are painted cherry red. A mattress sits on a platform so low that it might as well be on the floor. You'd have to swim through a sea of clothes and accessories—fishnet stockings, booties, thigh-high boots, and six-inch heels—to get to it.

A black-and-white mural-sized poster of the nineteen-fifties pin-up girl, Bettie Page, hangs over the bed. The iconic model is in a leopard bikini. Her breasts are barely contained by its halter-top. With hands raised above her head and entangled in her black tresses, she lunges to one side, straining the string holding the loin-cloth over the front of her bikini bottom.

A penis-shaped vibrator large enough to satisfy King Kong's

lady friend sticks out from beneath a pillow. It's labeled: SLICK WILLY

Talk about pleasant dreams.

Photos in frames of all sizes cover the top of the bureau. In them, Roxanna takes center stage. Sometimes she's in the middle of a gaggle of giggling girlfriends. In others, she is entwined with some guy in a VIP booth at some lounge. In most cases, she and the men are glassy-eyed. Whereas one of her hands holds her cell phone's camera aloft, the other is consistently poised in the international signal for FUCK YOU. The men mimic her gesture while keeping the other hand below Roxanna's waist.

I'm beginning to think that Roxanna is what the Brits would call a slag.

The next door, also open, is a bathroom. The vanity counter on the left side of the sink is strewn with makeup, hairbrushes, neon blue and purple spray-on hair color canisters, and a flat iron.

The other side of the sink's vanity is empty except for a single hairbrush. There are a few dark strands in it. My guess: they belong to Aziza. I pull them from the brush and place them in a Ziploc bag that I've taken from the break-in kit in the Tesco bag.

I open the medicine cabinet above the sink. A plastic packet of birth control pills has Roxanna's name on it. A jar of KY Intense Woman's Arousal Gel sits next to it, as does a 144-count box of condoms: Trojan Ultra-Ribbed Ecstasy.

You've got to give Roxanna credit: she leaves nothing to chance.

She also has a prescription for Erythromycin. So, she has Chlamydia? Yikes.

I see no birth control pills for Aziza, but I may find them in her bedroom.

I move down the hall to the final door. It's closed, but it isn't locked.

Entering it, I feel as if I'm in a different apartment altogether. The room faces the front of the house. Modern furnishings counterbalance its traditional elements—tall double-hung paned windows, deep ceiling and floor molding, and beige and white trompe l'oeil wallpaper. The bed's four coiled posts, lacquered in ebony, reach almost to the ceiling. The bed is covered in a white embroidered comforter and a mountain of pillows and sits high above the intricate Persian rug that covers the wide-plank bleached floor.

The bedside tables, dresser, and a desk are also ebony. The surfaces are devoid of items, except for an elegant red leather-tooled Quran that sits on one of the bed stands.

I put it in my pouch. One of the bed stand's drawers is filled with rolled scarves. The other has rolled socks. The shelf below holds Aziza's schoolbooks: Computer Science. Physics. Trigonometry. The other bed stand's shelf has back issues of Wired, PC World, Open Source for You, and Digit.

Aziza was one serious lady.

I check the drawers for false bottoms or a note taped behind them but find nothing. The same goes for behind and under the bed stands. I open the books and flip them over. Nothing falls out.

I look under and around the bed. Again, I find nothing.

Hurriedly, I put everything back and head over to the desk, which is centered against the middle window. It is simple in design: just three drawers that parallel the desk's pristine surface. Also lacquered black, its coiled legs match the pattern of the bed's posts. The drawers are locked but easy to break with the right pick.

Pens and empty lined notebooks are in the left drawer. The right one contains a slim photo album. I thumb through it. Like Aziza, all the women in the photos wear hijabs—the Muslim headdress. Aziza looks a few years younger than the dead woman I found today. In all the pictures, she is smiling or laughing. Several photos have her and some of the other women with men who wear white keffiyehs. The drawer also holds a checkbook. I put it, along with the photo album, in my sack.

A laptop computer is in the center drawer. Bingo! I put it in the Tesco bag and lock all the drawers again.

I move to the dresser. One by one, I take out the drawers. Aziza's clothes are folded neatly. Again, no false bottoms, and nothing taped to the drawers' exterior sides.

I've just checked Aziza's closet for hidden compartments when I hear laughter, and then a door shutting.

Damn it–Roxanna must be home!

Slinging the Tesco sack over my shoulder, I tiptoe out of Aziza's room and to the staircase. When I reach the landing, I figure out why Jack didn't text me: his chuckle is easy to recognize.

So is his voice as he says, "You say, you have a roommate? Did you meet her at university?"

"Not exactly. We were introduced by…well, a mutual friend. She's the shy type. Bookish, you know? He thought she needed someone who could look after her."

"Is he her boyfriend?"

Roxanna snickers. "Hardly!"

"So, she and you are close?"

"If you're asking if she's 'friendly,' like me, the answer is no," Roxanna declares.

She must be proving this because all of a sudden I don't hear a peep out of them.

Grrrr…

"Is your roommate upstairs now?" Jack must be standing close to the stairwell because his voice is suddenly louder. I guess he figures I haven't heard them yet. Ha! Even their silences speak volumes.

"No. She's working tonight," Roxanna replies. "In fact, she's rarely home these days." In a babyish voice, she adds, "I'm here all by my little lonesome. But if you're into threesomes, I can call a friend."

"Not necessary," Jack assures her. "I'm into you."

Considering the next few quiet minutes, I imagine she's rewarding him for that little white lie.

"Let me show you my etchings. They're upstairs." Roxanna's sensual simper promises to deliver much more than any Etch-a-Sketch can provide.

"I'll just bet they are." Jack's husky taunt elicits another giggle from her.

"What? You don't believe me?"

"Lead the way," he dares her.

"First things first," she purrs.

Whatever she's showing him now is demonstrated silently.

Finally, Roxanna exclaims, "Well now…that will do just fine."

I hear footsteps on the staircase.

Darn it, I'm now too far away to leap back into Aziza's room. And since I don't have time to pick the lock again, I duck into the bathroom.

If Roxanna and Jack aren't stomping up the stairs, they are slamming into walls like two rhinos in heat. They must have stopped at the threshold of her bedroom door because I hear a few moans before Roxanna growls, "In there, big boy! I'll be right back."

She's walking my way. I barely have time to hop into the bathtub and duck behind the shower curtain.

I peek out in time to see Roxanna open the medicine cabinet and pull out the KY arousal gel. She also opens the condom box and pulls out a couple of condom packets. Pausing, she stares down at them and says, "Sod it!"

Realizing she's having second thoughts about Jack, I almost sigh out loud.

My relief is short-lived when she waltzes out the door with the whole box.

Why, that little slut!

Serenaded by a cacophony of heaving petting, I slip out the bathroom, down the stairs, and out the kitchen door.

When I'm a block from Roxanna's house, I call Jack's phone. After he picks up, I declare loudly, "Darling, why haven't you called home? The children refuse to go to bed without hearing you sing them their bedtime song!"

Jack takes the hint. Sighing, he mutters, "I'll be right home, dear."

He's at the car in less than three minutes.

I hold up the Tesco bag. "Mission accomplished." As I hop in the driver's seat, he gives me a thumbs-up and tosses me the car fob.

I wait until we're on the M40 before saying, "I hope she kept her knickers on. Otherwise, you may have to see a doctor."

Jack laughs. "Not to worry. I took that as a given. Besides, I don't think I could have lived up to her expectations."

"Why do you say that?" I ask innocently.

He holds up Slick Willy.

I'm laughing so hard that I almost drive off the road. "Why did you take that?"

"I didn't, I swear! When I insisted I had to go home to my wife, she threw it at me." He shrugs. "I thought it might make a good gag gift."

"Gag is right," I declare. "Well, if it's any consolation, you've always lived up to my expectations."

In appreciation, Jack kisses the back of my hand. This simple gesture sends a surge of desire through me.

We make it back to the Ritz in record time.

Somewhere between Northolt and Greenford, Slick Willy was tossed out the window. It's for the best. I'm sure it'll find a home and make some lucky lady very happy.

9

Lucky

"What kind of cruel joke is this?" His head lowered, the sheik looked at me under the shelf of dark brows like a bear eying dinner. "You had me worried sick. What would I tell my brother? Aziza was a sick child. My brother was quite attached."

Tongue-tied with shock, I could only stand there, mouth open, staring at the floor.

The body was gone. The vase was still missing. The door was unlocked yet I had locked it. Where was the connection? Someone was playing games with me. Someone who wouldn't live long after I found them.

The mystery lady I'd met at the elevator. She had to be the key.

I looked up and ran right into the sheik's glare. "Shouldn't you be a bit more broken up?" I stammered, riding a wave of the absurd. None of this could really be happening, could it? "She was your niece after all."

"And a pain in the ass and an embarrassment to my family."

"And you were sent to fetch her." Now I understood more fully why he was pissed—nothing more demeaning than being his older brother's toady. I wondered what Sheik Ben had done to curry his brother's disfavor. Who knew? The whole Arab thing was inscrutable to someone with Vegas sensibilities, not that I didn't try. But, underneath all of it, men were men. And men, I understood. Okay, rephrase that, men I could anticipate. "All you're worried about is what you'd tell her father?"

"Of course not." He shook off my accusation. "What game are you playing?"

"I assure you, I am not playing any game." I gave him my best corporate stare. "Seriously? I run a multi-national business empire. Most days relatively effectively. On any given day, more money than you can fathom passes through our properties." The minute I said it, I knew that wasn't true. He and his family had a firm grip on the world's oil spigot. I rushed on. "I assure you, playing a horrible game with our most valued partner would not be within my capabilities." I walked around the area where I'd seen Aziza. "Her body was here, stomach down. I could see the new tattoo on the back of her right thigh."

"She would never get a tattoo. It is forbidden!"

"Perhaps Aziza didn't care to share." My thoughts raced. I needed to get him out of this room. A murder had occurred here— she'd been dead, I was sure of it. Even though not an official crime scene, it would be—when I found the body. I needed to preserve the evidence, such as it might be, as much as I could. "I need a drink."

The sheik followed me back into the great room, but neither of us headed toward the bar. Beads of sweat popped on my skin. One traced a winding trail down the side of my face. Pretending to push my hair back, I swiped the moisture away. "Is it hot in here?" I stepped to the nearest French door and opened it. Unlike in the states, here no one cared if anyone wanted to leap to their death— it opened easily. I felt the sheik's eyes boring holes in my back. Where the hell had the body gone? The cool, damp night air helped. Keeping my back to the sheik but watching his reflection in the glass, I drank the air like wine in huge restorative gulps. "You must admit, your niece wasn't forthcoming with you or the rest of her family. She kept her job here under wraps. The girl was going off the grid, and you were sent to fetch her home, which would probably end up like that poor girl snatched off the yacht never to be heard from again." Oops, a bit too far. The temperature in the room rose. Pissing people off, an odd skill for a customer service rep, but we all have our crosses to bear.

"Do you really wish to insult me?" His voice had gone lethal.

"No." I turned back to face him, then leaned on the door frame, my hands behind me to keep them from shaking. I'd found bodies before, but I'd never lost one. "Her skin was still warm, but I couldn't detect any pulse."

He held his arms wide and circled slowly. "Then, where is she?" Anger radiated off of him.

"I don't know, but I will find her. Maybe you can help me. When was your last contact with your niece?"

He moved to stare out the window next to me. "We are not close. She speaks mostly with her mother, from what I am told. My brother thought it best that I arrive without fanfare."

"So, no one told her you were coming?"

"Not that I'm aware of. And I told your office to be circumspect about who they were making the room arrangements for." He gave me a slitty side-eye. "Perhaps they weren't discreet."

No way the leak came from my office, but it would be futile and reek of desperation to argue that point now. I needed a solid footing of facts. "Well, someone wasn't discreet. Aziza was up here readying your room, or so I was told."

"That, my dear Lucky, is on you."

There was something in what he'd told me earlier... "You said before Aziza wasn't answering her phone. Yet now you tell me you haven't tried contacting her. Which is it?"

"My brother said she was not answering when her mother called. He was most put out."

A ring of the buzzer interrupted my train of thought. The door swung open admitting the butler who nodded.

"Gerald," The sheik said, his voice icy. A look passed between he and the butler. It wasn't a good look. Something was there. Anger, maybe?

Gerald's expression flattened as he held the door for a phalanx of bellmen, each one rolling in a piece of new Louis Vuitton luggage.

I launched myself from my perch. "No, no, no! You can't stay here." I rushed toward my staff members who, in grand British fashion, forged ahead despite my not-so-thinly veiled order. I turned on the sheik. "Stop them." I felt compelled to protect my future crime scene—Aziza deserved that.

One of the bellmen glanced his way. He waved him on. "I've booked this room. I intend to stay here. As for you, stay out of my way. And you should seriously consider professional help."

A not so subtle cue that it was time to take my leave.

THE SHEIK HAD A POINT. MY PSYCHE HAD BEEN PULLING APART AT THE seams for some time now. The Lucky O'Toole Self-Betterment Program, an abandoned effort, had failed miserably. My downward slide was now complete—I was not only finding dead bodies, now everyone thought I was imagining them.

But I wasn't. I saw what I saw. And it was up to me to prove it.

As I waited for the elevator, I scanned the hallway for the security cameras, noting their placement. Two had a direct shot at the elevator.

Security was on the second floor behind the casino.

The elevator opened into a different world. My kind of world. Here I could see hints of the Babylon back home. Long streams of colored fabric waved along twenty-four-foot ceilings lending an air of intimacy. Dark purple paint adorned the walls. Gold wall sconces with flames under glass, as if from burning bundled reeds, cast enough light to see, but not a great deal more. A comforting environment. Casinos that had inquisition-style lighting made me nervous and desperate to escape—not the feeling a casino owner wanted to engender in their players, at least by my way of thinking. The carpet, thick and lush to muffle sound, provided an air of elegance with its beautiful colors and patterns. Gaming tables tucked under tented fabric in colorful hues occupied the front of the room. Poker to my right and other table games to my left, baccarat being the most popular along with craps. A high-roller room, invisible from here, catered to the Asian predilection for high stakes Baccarat hid in the far corner of the casino.

Play was light. Frank Sinatra crooned above the soft sounds of the early-birds settling in to wager the hours away. The night was still young. Most would probably be dining in our five-star restaurant on the roof. This being a private club, the restaurant didn't have a name—something I thought a gross oversight. Especially given the fact we opened a few reservations to the public. A large doorway to my right, halfway down the wall, opened into the bar, which did have a name, The Library, but everyone referred to it as the War Room given the many high-dollar business deals hashed out there. The Library was home to the requisite grand wooden bar pilfered from some Scottish castle in days gone by. Secretly I thought the Scots had a factory for those bars hidden somewhere. These days everyone seemed to have an antique Scottish bar. How many of them could there really be?

Shielded from prying eyes by dark, one-way glass, Security hung over the back of the casino on a short mezzanine level. My keycard gained me entry. I paused for a moment to let my eyes adjust to the darkness. Everything here mimicked Security back home but on a much smaller scale. Several figures huddled in front of a wall of video monitors to my right. The first twelve showed ever changing feeds from the cameras dotted around the property. The rest of them comprising the bulk of the monitors showed constant feeds of each gaming table from overhead. From that vantage point both the dealer and the player's hands were always in view.

An office was on my left, the lights dark. And the whole of the casino stretched in front of me through the floor-to-ceiling window that comprised the far wall. The view pulled me—a human moth looking for light. I loved watching commerce in action.

A presence eased in at my elbow. "Rather spectacular, isn't it?" The soft voice belonged to Bree Corbyn, our Security Head.

Short, a bit lumpy, with a ruddy face and a riot of blonde curls,

Bree would be one of that last people I'd want to meet in a dark alley, but the first one I'd want on my side. There was a rumor her hands were registered as lethal weapons and were insured by Lloyd's. I hadn't personally checked the validity of the whispers. I didn't need to—at the heart of every bit of gossip was a kernel of truth.

She sipped from a delicate tea cup, the steam visible as it curled.

"I think I was a voyeur in a former life," I said as I refocused on the view. My stomach rumbled.

"A former life? As far as I can tell, this is legal voyeurism." In the light from the casino I could see her lips curl into a smile.

"Stopping short of taking it to a personal level."

"Of course. Although you Yanks are dreaming up more ways to invade privacy than anybody I've seen."

"Those are the politicians—a hand in your wallet, a camera in your bedroom."

"What a world." We both paused in a moment of mourning for the world as it had been.

"I need your help. First thing, cancel Aziza's master keycard."

"Is she being let go?"

I didn't have a good answer.

Bree could tell she'd put me on the spot. "Not to worry. Consider it done. And the second thing? I'm assuming this involves the woman you had everyone scouring the club for?"

I squeezed her arm in gratitude. "I'm assuming you didn't find her?"

"You would've been the first alerted." She paused as if choosing her words. "The odd thing is, we found no trace on any of the feeds of the woman you described."

First a missing body, now a missing suspect. Games. I hated games. "What about the two cameras in the hall leading to the Royal Suite? I was there. The elevator doors opened and there she was, surprising me. She seemed a bit taken aback as well, as if she wasn't expecting anyone to come up in the elevator."

Bree shook her head and took another sip of her tea. "She wasn't there. You were, but no one else."

"But I saw her." I absorbed all of what she said. This whole thing seemed like an M. Night Shyamalan movie. Did I see dead people, too? Or was I going crazy? I seemed okay to me. But, if I was crazy, and I thought I was okay, that would mean I was crazy, right? I abandoned that line of reasoning before my head exploded, but my heart fell. "You don't believe me either."

"Actually, I do." She lifted her cup toward her office. "Let me show you."

I followed her to her office. She didn't click on the lights.

"Take a load off."

With piles of paper occupying the two rather spindly chairs, I propped a butt cheek on the corner of her desk while she cued up a video clip. Once she had it set, she motioned me closer. I lurked over her shoulder like a vulture.

"The first clip is the feed from the two cameras watching the elevator on the Royal Suite floor." She punched a few buttons, then clicked through a drop-down menu.

"Can you take it back far enough to see if a young woman on our staff...Aziza, you know her?"

"I do."

"She was supposed to ready the Royal Suite. I'd like to see if anyone went up to the suite with her."

"Your mystery lady in Chanel?"

"Perhaps. Or anyone else." She shot me a side-eye. "Just curious."

"I'll take it back thirty minutes then run it forward much faster than real-time. We'll be able to see anybody who entered the suite."

"That should be enough time." We both watched the feed and time sped by on the time stamp. "There!"

Bree slowed the tape as I pointed. We watched Aziza enter the suite alone. I noted the time. Twenty minutes before I showed up. "Okay, now go forward twenty minutes or to when I arrived. I appeared on the screen as I stepped off the elevator, paused for a moment, then I proceeded down the hall.

I bolted upright as if someone hit me in the ass with a Taser set on stun. I pointed at the screen. "She was right there! I know I didn't create her out of thin air—she carried a bag I never would've imagined."

Bree swiveled around and gave me a flat stare. "A purse?"

"Vintage Hermès." I shrugged. "It's a thing."

"Not a Hermès gal?"

"Totally, just overpriced for my sensibilities." I pointed to the screen. "Why are we talking about this? What made the woman disappear?"

Bree turned back around. "She didn't disappear. Watch this." She overlaid two different cuts, one showing me pausing and stepping slightly aside, then the other of me right after that. She ran them out a few seconds.

"What? It just shows me pausing to let her in the elevator then charging down the hall. The only thing missing…is her."

"Let me run it frame by frame."

I squinted in concentration focusing on the screen and looking for I-didn't-know-what. She ran it to the end. "Still nothing."

She backed it up. "Here." She pointed to a section. "Look there. What do you see?"

"Run it again." After the second time, I had it. "My movements don't flow completely. It's like I stood still but before the camera rolled again, I moved slightly."

I stepped back as Bree swiveled around completely. "Somebody tapped into our computers and manipulated the feed. Really sophisticated, but I think they were in a bit of a hurry."

"Sophisticated?"

"Like government spooks. I should know."

"Government? Legit or not?"

She shrugged. "Who knows these days?"

I couldn't imagine what country's toes we'd stepped on, but the chess game of world politics was not my venue. "So they were in a hurry? Hence the slight hitch."

"Right. Normally, your eye wouldn't even see it in real time if you weren't looking for it. But they knew you'd be looking and they left it anyway. That's why I think they did this on the fly."

"To cover their tracks."

"Did you look for the woman on any of the other feeds from around the property?" I asked even though I knew she would have.

"The woman is nowhere. It's as if she was never here."

"But you could track her through the club by finding the spots on the feeds where the images have been manipulated, right?"

Bree blew out a puff of air as she sipped what had to be now tepid tea…with milk. My stomach curdled at the thought. "In theory, sure, but we would have to know where to look. Without any hints as to her route out of the club, it'd be needles in very large haystacks."

"I'd really like to know if she talked to anybody."

"I'll get somebody on it, but—"

"It'll take time, I know. As many sets of eyeballs as you can spare." I thought for a minute. The woman had to get in yes, and they, whoever they are, had to get Aziza's body out. Two separate problems. "And could you check the exterior feeds as well? Maybe focus on the back first, the loading dock and all that?" The woman probably walked in the front door. That one I could tackle myself.

"What am I looking for?"

I shrugged and looked a bit sheepish. "Anything unusual."

"Trite." At least she smiled. "More time."

"I know. It's really important."

She looked at me for a tick longer than necessary. "I see that. You got it."

"Somehow, that woman got in here and up to the Royal Suite, which even God couldn't do without the appropriate credentials. Somebody had to let her up there." I thought about telling Bree about Aziza and my dilemma, but since that cat was not out of the bag with anyone at the club, and, since I had no body and hence no crime, *and* since the disappearing body would only cement my looney-tune status among the staff, I kept that whole thing to myself. "I'd really like to know how and, while you're at it, why would be nice."

"Piece of cake." A bit of sarcasm to seal the deal.

"Could the same folks who hacked into the video feeds also have breached our firewall into the rest of the system?"

"I would've told you nobody could've done what I know they've already done. Our security is state-of-the-art. Very, very few would have the capabilities."

"So, in theory, they could've triggered the elevator and disabled a room lock?"

"Elevator, yes. Room lock, no. That system is sequestered in-house—no internet, no outside access."

Through the glass wall of her office, I stared at the video monitors. "Who are these people?" And why did they want Aziza?

10

Donna

"So, what do we want to discuss first—the good news, or the bad?" Ryan asks.

Arnie and Abu have joined Jack and me in our suite for a conference call we've initiated with Ryan and Emma at Acme headquarters. Dominic is A.W.O.L. For his sake, I hope it's for a very good reason—that being, Mystery Woman.

"Let's start with some good news," I suggest.

"Great idea," Ryan exclaims. "Do you want to go first?"

Hearing Ryan's hopeful tone, Jack frowns. "Our mission was a mixed bag," he admits.

"I've got a little of both too," Arnie admits.

"Likewise," Emma weighs in.

"Shall we draw straws?" I suggest. "That way, we give Ryan something to smile about before breaking his heart again."

"Yeah…thanks for that, Donna," Ryan replies sarcastically. "I'll draw for you. Emma first, Arnie next, and the Craigs go last. I'll interject where I see fit."

No arguments there.

"I'll be happy to share my good news." Emma's buoyancy gives me hope. "We now know the name of our mystery lady."

"Through Dominic's reconnaissance?" Abu asks.

Emma guffaws. "Hardly! And Interpol had nothing on her. However, TSA was a treasure trove. Because she travels all the time, its facial recognition system immediately identified her. Her name is Lucky O'Toole. She's the scion to the Rothstein family of Chicago—you know, the one that owns casinos all over the world, including the Babylon in Sin City *and* the London club, which Dominic frequents with such pleasure."

"And where Aziza worked," Jack replies.

"Until she was murdered today," I add. "Speaking of Dominic, why isn't he on the call?"

"We last heard from him two hours ago," Ryan barks gruffly. "He was on his way to the club's casino. Who knows what kind of mischief he's gotten himself into since then."

I try not to laugh as I ask, "Don't we have eyes and ears on him?"

"Apparently, he didn't think it necessary to clue us in on how he was going to accomplish his mission," Ryan retorts.

Jack laughs. "In hindsight, maybe that's a good thing."

"I can tap into the club's security cameras," Arnie offers.

Ryan sighs at the thought. "So that we're not distracted by his shenanigans, do it after this call."

Arnie's eyes open wide at the possibilities. Finally, he chokes out, "Right, Chief."

"Now, for my not-so-great news," Emma says. "Starting with two hours prior to Aziza's arrival in the Royal Suite and up until the point where Donna left Dominic's room and ascended to the fifth floor, no one other than Aziza went in and out of it."

"Are you sure?" I ask, stunned. "Not even the O'Toole woman?"

"Positive. A few hours before Aziza got there, two elderly housekeepers went in and out together. But that's it."

Jack frowns. "So, despite her suspicious actions, this Lucky person may not have killed Aziza."

"Still, the fact that she went to the suite and didn't report what she saw still makes her a Person of Interest," Ryan points out. "Since we're on the subject of Aziza, I've got something to report.

Her autopsy results have come in from MI6." He pauses before adding, "Officially, she died of a heart attack."

His declaration is met with stunned silence.

I stammer, "But...she was so young!"

"You're right," Ryan agrees. "She was taken before her time. Someone made sure of that. The marks you found on the back of her neck indicate she was hit with a stun gun. The shock to her heart killed her."

"Stun guns don't usually kill—unless the victim had a heart condition," I reason.

"It may not have been diagnosed," Emma says. "Maybe her perpetrator only wanted to disable her in order to swipe the intel and get out before she could pass it forward."

"Or perhaps the killer knew of her condition and used the stun gun to make it look like a heart attack," Jack argues.

"If her condition had been diagnosed, it would be in her health record," I point out. "I would imagine her college would have a copy. It might also be in her personnel record."

"If it is in her personnel record, Lucky O'Toole would have had access to it," Jack replies.

"Arnie, hack the club's database to see if it has this information. If so, it certainly keeps Ms. O'Toole in line as our prime suspect," Ryan commands.

"No problem, Boss," Arnie replies. "I planted a trojan backdoor in the Babylon's database. I'll lurk around now and see what I can pull up." We hear him tapping away.

"By the way, folks: the inscription on the amulet is identical to Aziza's tattoo, but not entirely so," Ryan adds. "There is one extra character. SigInt is attempting to decipher the full description. Which brings us to Aziza's key cards. Arnie, you're up to bat."

Arnie sighs. "Okay, so, my great news is that I hacked both of Aziza's key cards."

"So far, so good," Ryan replies hopefully. "Go on."

"The first one is a master key for all the rooms in the club. Nothing sketchy there, since it's something she would carry because she's the manager's Girl Friday."

"Aziza must have used it to get into the Royal Suite, and then left it open for me," I reply.

"And the killer," Jack adds.

"Unless the killer had his or her own key," Emma suggests.

"And if the killer is this Lucky lady who owns the joint, she may have had one anyway—or would have known where to lay her hands on one," Abu reasons.

"The second card was encoded with a simple cipher. I had no problem breaking it," Arnie continues. "Now, for the bad news: the intel Aziza put on the card are video recordings of some Saudi businessmen handing over cash and munitions to the very terrorists the Saudi royal family claims are being supported by Qatar."

"I've verified that what Aziza claims is matched by the Arabic being spoken on the videos," Abu adds.

Jack lets loose with a low whistle. "If it's true that some Saudi bad actors are trying to undermine UAE citizens' allegiances to the Saudi royal family, well, that's a pretty big get!"

"Yes, that's what it looks like," Arnie replies.

"The Saudi royal family has done everything it can to bring Qatar to its knees," Ryan adds. "The FBI has already validated Al Jazeera's contention that the UAE hacked the Qatar News Organization. It has also restricted Qatar's airspace, and it's coerced the international banking community to cut ties with Qatar. Now the UAE is demanding that the U.S. and U.N. sanction Qatar as well."

"So, here's my bad news." Arnie takes a deep breath. "Aziza's message stops short of naming the men in the video."

"Is it because she doesn't know who they are?" I ask.

"No," Arnie responds. "Not only does she claim that she can identify the bad actors, she also knows *how* they are funneling the money to the terrorists. She wrote that she'd hand over a cipher key to read the rest of the intel secured on the card, but only after attaining CIA's written assurance that it would protect her and a few others who have risked their lives to let the truth come to light —no matter who the real culprits turn out to be."

"I guess now is a good time to tell you our news," I add. "When I searched Aziza's place, I grabbed her computer along with a couple of other items; a photo album, her mail, checkbook, and her Quran. One of those items may hold a key to the missing intel."

"Or it may lead us to those she wanted to protect. If we find them, they may also have copies of the intel she wanted to pass forward," Jack points out.

"Well, that's a start," Ryan replies.

"Can we meet with Aziza's handler?" Jack asks. "Maybe he can shed some light on who she was talking about."

"I'll see if I can set up a meeting," Ryan promises.

"Okay, yeah, here's a bit of great news. Slide it into my column, thank you very much!" Arnie exclaims.

"Tell us first and then I'll give credit if credit is due," Ryan retorts.

"I'm inside the Babylon's personnel files. Aziza's dossier does indicate a heart condition."

"So, it is possible that Lucky knew about it," I reason.

"Speaking of which, I wonder how Dominic is doing with her now?" Emma asks.

"He'd better be pulling out all the stops," Ryan grumbles.

Jack chuckles. "I'm sure he's doing all he can to pull out *something.*"

"Bad choice of words," I say as I smack his arm.

Ryan groans. "It's been too long a day for lousy puns, even at Dominic's expense. Get some sleep, people. You deserve it."

11

Lucky

*I*f only the train of life would pull into the next station and let me off.

I could catch a later one…when I started breathing again.

With no body, no clues, a ticked off fiancé, a crazy mother, and a father slipping in all aspects of his life, I wandered the casino, trying not to think about any of it. Normally my happy place, the casino didn't work its magic tonight. Of course, this wasn't Vegas where magic was everywhere. This was buttoned up and la-dee-da London. Today, its normal charm eluded me.

But, if I couldn't *be* home, I could pull an ET and phone home.

First, privacy. The front desk directed me to my room. While they'd honored my desire to have a no muss-no fuss kind of room, knowing my love of a good view, they'd given me one at the end of the hall overlooking the street and the small park across the way. I too had a wall of French doors that opened to a tiny balcony large enough for a café table with two chairs. Normally I would throw open the doors no matter the weather. Tonight, I resisted. Only one floor, the fourth, separated my room from Sheik Ben's and I'd opened a side window in his suite. If I planned to talk about him, I didn't want an eavesdropper.

My suitcase had been put away, my things tucked out of sight. I loved that personal butler touch. I wished we could provide it for everyone at the Babylon, but, with over three thousand rooms in our Vegas flagship, that level of service penciled-out only for the Kasbah, our extra-primo, invitation-only, hidden enclave.

I fluffed the pillows on the bed, kicked off my shoes, then arranged myself so I could drink in the view of lights and the city.

Miss P answered after two rings. "Problem solved?"

I'd forgotten she hadn't been looped in. At a loss as to where to start, I took my mother's frequent advice and started at the beginning—the *only* advice I'd ever take from my mother. Miss P listened without comment until I wound down.

"Wow." She actually seemed a bit ruffled which was so unlike her. As someone who'd been raised on a farm in Iowa, followed the Grateful Dead sleeping with Jerry Garcia along the way (although she never actually had confirmed that) and then married for the first time at fifty to a hunkalicious Aussie fifteen years her junior, she needed a good shove to be rocked off center.

"Not helpful and not inspiring confidence."

"Give me a moment."

While she gathered herself, I perused the room service menu. With my blood sugar at a low ebb and my stomach so empty it had stopped complaining and simply ached, this was probably not a good time for options. Like going to the grocery store hungry, I'd probably end up with all of Aisle Seven, which translated into everything on the menu.

"What do you need on this end?" Ah, Miss P had returned, her tone back to helpful.

"Sheik Ben told me he called our office to have someone make his arrangements here."

"That's correct. I took the call."

"Anything unusual besides him putting that on us?" Sheik Ben had standing orders at the club as did every member. It would've been far easier for him to call London rather than route everything through my office.

"I thought that odd and mentioned it to your father, when he called to check that I had everything under control. He mentioned in passing that the sheik was in New York. I interpreted that as a reason he called us."

Other than he had a sat phone in his plane, but pointless to mention that now. "Okay. Anything else?"

"The sheik seemed put out he had to relay his normal requests."

"And they were?"

Papers rustled in the background. Miss P wrote everything on spiral-bound pads. "Krug Clos du Mesnil, only the 2000 would do, Beluga, his personal silk sheets, yellow roses, and Gerald, his favorite butler, who must be available 24/7 for the sheik's entire stay."

Funny the sheik had requested him. They hadn't looked happy to see each other. "I met the butler. Is he one of our full-time staff?"

"Yes, but only joined us last year."

"And you're sure you ordered yellow flowers?"

"Yes, yellow roses, Teasing Georgia yellow roses, to be exact."

"I'll take your word for it. Who did you talk with? Do you remember?"

More rustling. "Nigel Ahern. He told me he'd have Julie take care of it."

No mention of Aziza. "That's it? He didn't tell you to be discreet?"

"He would never have to. That's a given." Her voice puffed up with a bit of huffy.

"I know that. You know that. He knows that. But he mentioned that specifically, that he had reiterated discretion, so I thought I'd ask."

"He didn't."

I'd take Miss P's word over anyone else's. Besides, with the Royal Suite being readied with Sheik Ben's normal requests, everyone would have known he was coming. "Interesting."

"You're sure the young woman was dead?" Her voice dropped to a whisper.

I'd asked myself the same question: could I have been mistaken? Had Aziza merely been unconscious, then awakened and walked out of the suite? "I'm sure." My certainty made my heart heavy. Closing my eyes, I leaned my head back on the pillows and pictured the suite, the body, and when I'd found her. I could feel her cooling skin with only a hint of warmth left, the missing pulse under my fingers when I pressed them to her neck. Yes, she'd been dead.

Both Miss P and I remained silent for a few seconds.

"How do you think they got the poor young woman's body out?"

"I have wracked my brain. There's only one elevator to that floor. Security is tight with cameras everywhere. Yes, they could've looped the tape, but…" I trailed off.

"You didn't clue security in about the missing girl." Miss P knew me far too well—both a blessing and a curse.

"Without a body, I got nuthin'."

"And they'd start dismissing you as a nut job."

"A bit indelicate, but yes. I figure that if somebody just carried a body through the public spaces, someone would say something, even here where pulses are practically non-existent."

"Agreed."

"That leaves the back of the house. I've asked Bree, the security head, to look at those tapes. I don't know what else to do. I'd love to go prowl around the Royal Suite, but I can't do that until the sheik goes out."

"Even then."

"I'll be careful." I tapped my chin with a forefinger as I contemplated the world outside my window. The mist had grown thicker, encircling the lights in a halo of white. "I do need you to do one more thing."

WHEN THE CALL CAME IN, I'D MADE IT THROUGH HALF OF THE PASTA I'd ordered but had yet to muster any energy to get out of my clothes and into a warm bath, which proved to be a good thing.

"Ms. O'Toole, this is Julie at the front desk. We have a situation in the casino. Mr. Ahern has gone home for the evening. He suggested you might like to handle it."

I couldn't think of anything nice to say, so, miraculously, I didn't. Nigel wouldn't be done out of his pound of flesh, I guessed. Frankly, I was too amped to sleep, so 'a situation' was just what the doctor ordered. "What's going on?"

"We have a…gentleman…winning big at one of the baccarat tables."

"From your hesitation I take it he's not a gentleman?"

"I shouldn't say, Miss."

"Got it." Nothing I hated more than a guest in my establishment making the staff uncomfortable. "Is the dealer crying foul?"

"Well, we usually stop short of making any accusations where the members are concerned, but the dealer would like some assistance, yes. The man in question is beating the odds by a large margin."

And killing the house. "He's a member, then?"

"Yes." I could almost hear the wrinkle to her nose in distaste.

"I assume security is rolled in on this?"

"Yes, ma'am. They have been watching, but nothing so far."

"Have you been able to identify any accomplices to the man in question?"

"Bathrooms are empty. The other players are known and not doing anything that would raise suspicion."

A lone wolf. "On my way." I tested my feet, still steady, then headed for the door. A pause in front of the mirror confirmed I didn't look any better than I had yesterday, probably didn't smell any better either, but I would have to do. I pressed the housekeeping button on my way out—cold food congealing in my room when I returned would not be appealing. A text pinged my phone as I strode toward the elevator. Jean-Charles again. I hadn't answered his first text. And since I still didn't have anything to tell him that wouldn't piss him off, I ignored this one as well.

Delaying our come-to-Jesus-moment would only make it worse. But, right now, I was maxed out and just didn't have the fight in me.

Identifying the table in question proved easier than I'd thought. The other gamblers had abandoned nearby tables and now stood in a ring three people deep, each person jockeying for a view. With a few whispered *pleases* and *excuse mes*, I wormed my way through until I wedged myself next to the dealer, keeping him between me and the guy with the hot hand who was seated to the dealer's left five seats down. "Hey, Adam," I whispered, my mouth close to the dealer's ear. "Looks like you're the center of attention tonight."

A thin, dark-skinned, earnest-eyed young man with a penchant for numbers and a calm, efficient manner at the table, Adam Kalb had been with us for several years, practically since the day we'd opened the club. I'd hired him myself and I hadn't been disappointed.

He smiled but didn't turn as he centered his attention on the game. "Yes, ma'am. This particular gentleman does run hot and cold, but he's super-heated tonight."

Hence the reason he'd pushed the button to gain some special scrutiny from Security and management. "Anything overt that hit your radar?"

His mouth turned down at the corners. "Not that I could see."

A cheer went up as the man won yet again.

"I think I'll dig a little deeper, see what kind of snakes I can find."

This time Adam flicked a side-glance my way. Dark, soulful eyes betrayed his concern. "Be careful, Miss Lucky."

His warning struck me as a bit over-the-top. The guy was a card sharp mining for dollars, well, pounds, at my establishment. Not the best way to be invited back. Everyone in the casino was an invitee and, as such, they could have their invitations revoked on a whim. The card counters were shown the door. The cheats were prosecuted. The key was figuring out which one we had tonight. I backed out of my tiny human parking place and repositioned myself halfway down the table on the dealer's right.

A man sat opposite me, chips piled in front of him, his blue eyes aglow with the thrill of the chase. His blonde hair was cut short—the gel was unnecessary, but an interesting insight. Tonight, he wore a white dinner jacket, a hand-tied red bow tie, and a tilt to his lantern jaw. Did men get to wear white after Labor Day? I couldn't remember, but he did look out of season if not out of place. A James Bond wannabe. London clubs were full of them. But he did have the look that everything in life was a wager, a weighing of the odds. Intriguing, but way overdone.

He glanced up quickly, then away, then back again almost as quickly, this time for a longer look. I met his gaze and gave a welcoming half-smile. He took the bait, motioning me around the table.

I eased into the seat next to him which another gentleman, tapped out and ready to repair to the bar, had vacated. "I'm Lucky."

He pressed a gentle kiss to the back of my hand. Warm. Sensual. Guess he blew right by the ring on my left ring finger. "No, it is I who counts myself lucky." He managed to say that with a straight face. Clearly his skills exceeded mine, which triggered a warning bell.

"My name is Fleming. Dominic Fleming." He even used the Bond. James Bond inflection.

I narrowed my eyes slightly, hoping to bring him into focus. The whole shtick was designed to disarm me with charm, I could see that. Despite it having the opposite effect, I figured playing along for a bit wouldn't hurt. "You are having a good evening, so far?"

"It just improved greatly."

I painted on a smile and prayed someone would turn him off… or break his nose. "Tell me, how is it you have such luck tonight?" Cheating, most likely. He had cards hidden somewhere—the trick would be finding them.

"If you'll let me buy you a drink, I'll tell you." He motioned to the dealer to cash him out as if I'd already agreed.

The guy was getting on my last nerve. I waited while the dealer counted the chips then handed Dominic his receipt. He held the back of my chair, then pulled it out as I rose allowing me to exit from the table easily. Maybe he was no gentleman, but he was certainly going through the motions.

He headed toward the lobby.

"The bar is the other way."

"I'd rather run naked through Hyde Park than drink the swill they stock here." He gave me a smile that only partially hid a leer. "I have proper refreshments in my room."

So, when exactly did I lose the upper hand here? I followed him onto one of the newer elevators. He pushed three.

My floor—a curious bit of synchronicity. He stopped halfway down the hall. "Here we are."

With a view of the brick wall of the adjacent building, his room wasn't nearly as posh as mine. Add in the heart-shaped bed with a mirror over it and I'd swear we were back in Sin City. "I didn't know..." I decided silence was safer, so I bit down hard on the foot I'd already stuck in my mouth. He was clearly a man with lots of money and no taste. "Mr. Fleming, what do you do exactly?"

He gave me the once over. "Win."

I rolled my eyes.

Either he missed it, or he was blinded by some personal Double-0 Section fantasy. "You look like a bubbles kind of lady."

"Bottled bubbles, yes."

"I assume Krug is sufficient." He bent to reach into the fridge, giving me a nice ass shot. Acceptable.

I watched him carefully to make sure he didn't offload any cards he might have had up his sleeve.

When he handed me my flute of bright bubbles, I jumped in before he could work his angle. "So, tell me."

He looked bemused. "What?"

"How you were able to take so much off the house tonight."

He held his glass to the light. "They say the best winemakers capture light in a bottle when they craft Champagne."

"I prefer to think happiness. I live in a world filled with light."

A slight purse of the lips preceded an almost imperceptible nod followed by a taste. "Nice." He raised his glass. "To happiness."

I raised mine then tested my bubbles, letting them linger on my tongue. Little explosions of happiness. "So, how'd you do it?" No way was he distracting me with all the genteel manners, the suave accent, and the tight ass. Okay, maybe a little, but he tried way too hard to be taken seriously.

"Take money off *your* house?"

So, he knew who I was. Idle fancy or something more? "Yes, *my* house."

"You think I cheated." As he took another sip, his expression remained impassive—not even a hint of offense clouded his baby blues. "How?"

"Well, no identified accomplices, so changing out cards, I should think."

He opened his arms wide. "Then they should be somewhere on my person. You're welcome to look for them."

A game. I could see it from the glint in his eyes. Regardless, I had to call his bluff. "Take off your jacket."

The corner of his mouth ticked up as he did as I asked, shifting his flute from one hand to the other. On the crook of a finger he extended the jacket.

I checked the pockets and the lining. No cards. I laid the jacket on a wing-backed chair by the window. No way was I going near that bed.

"What next?"

I stepped in close to him, which made him shiver as he leaned in. The warmth of his skin radiated through the thin cotton of his shirt as I ran my hands over his torso. Six-pack? Check. Nice pecs. Check. Lats that flared just enough. Yep, those, too. Muscles roped down each arm. Unlike his personality, his body was drool-worthy...and not hiding any cards. I leaned back.

He raised an eyebrow—there was challenge in the invitation.

Circling him with both arms, I dipped two fingers inside his waistband, and ran them along the inside. Still no cards. Reaching the front, I dipped further.

A sharp intake of air, followed by a warm chuckle.

I looked down to hide my smile. He was enjoying this distraction even more than I'd hoped. Squatting, I ran my hands down his legs then lifted each cuff, checking his socks. "You're clean." Out of the corner of my eye, I caught the glint of something gold shoved under the bed. While I made a fuss of straightening his pants legs and making sure the cuffs were crisp and placed, I took a harder look.

The purse!

The white and cream Hermès Kelly bag! I wasn't dreaming. The lady I'd seen at the elevator wasn't a figment. She was real.

And she'd been here!

"I'm blessed with a gift for card play." Fleming's declaration brought me back.

I couldn't let him know I'd seen the purse. I forced myself to calm and plastered on a smile as I let him help me to my feet. "And not for foreplay, I'm afraid." I had to get out of here. I turned on my heel and made for the door.

He darted around me. For a moment I thought he'd try to block my exit. Instead, he held the door open. "Until next time."

He hadn't spilled a drop of the Champagne.

I could feel him watching me, so I turned toward the elevators —I for sure didn't want him to get a bead on which room was mine.

Knowing I shouldn't, I glanced back as I waited for the elevator.

He raised his glass and gave me a wink.

What game was he playing? And what had he and the woman wanted with Aziza?

Forty hours. That's all I had left to figure this out, solve the murder and save life as I knew it.

As the elevator slowed, I braced myself for energy and excitement, an intoxicating mix. When the doors opened...nothing. Oh yeah, London. Julie still manned the front desk. "Pay Mr. Fleming his winnings, but please encourage him not to play too often."

"Yes, ma'am."

"Just call me Lucky. Ma'am makes me feel old."

She stood there blinking rapidly. I got it. To a twenty-year-old I was Methuselah.

"What do you know about Mr. Fleming?"

Julie's face flushed—the pink of anger that drew her mouth into a thin line. "He's quite the flirt, and rather indiscriminate. We get a lot of complaints about…" Her face flushed crimson.

Remembering the heart-shaped bed with the mirror above it, I shuddered. "I bet. He keeps a lot of money in play?"

She nodded. Keep enough money working for the house and management would turn a blind eye, even indulge a member's proclivities. But, I had my limits. "Any idea how he makes it?"

"Imports, or so he says."

Carrying the whole Bond thing to the absurd. "Right." We shared a smile—Bond, a common thread through generations of women. "Who'd he come in with?"

Julie glanced around, then leaned across the counter, her voice hushed. "Princess Maja of Sweden. She's rather fond of red leather."

My mystery lady favored Chanel and Hermès.

My stomach growled. That half-bowl of pasta had evaporated. "If anybody needs me, I'll be in the kitchen conning someone into cooking me something decent." Jean-Charles would know just what to fix. Teddy would know how to make me laugh. And I wasn't sure I wanted either of them. Teddy couldn't be trusted— he'd broken my heart once already. And Jean-Charles had a full life, one I'd have to fit into rather than the other way around. So far, he hadn't struck me as a meet-in-the-middle kind of guy. Come to think of it, I wasn't sure I had any compromise in me either.

Life, it always exacted a price for a gift.

———————

AT THE FAR END OF THE CASINO, UNDER THE OVERHANG OF THE

Security mezzanine, I pushed through a set of swinging double doors and walked right into the middle of an argument.

Nigel Ahern was nose-to-nose with a man of Middle Eastern descent, if I had to guess. Both were red with anger. Nigel had set me up to deal with Dominic—he hadn't gone home. But I'd deal with him later.

"Where is my rug?" Nigel said—clipped word darts.

"Exactly, where is *my* rug? You called me to pick up three, but there are only two."

"There were three here earlier today." Nigel's implication was clear—the man had stolen it.

A head taller than both of them, I inserted my rather large body between them. "Gentlemen." I wormed my hand next to my chest, then extended it as best I could toward the man I didn't know. "I'm Lucky O'Toole, owner of this establishment."

He looked at me through tiny slits for eyes. "You're the boss?"

"Yes."

He turned away from Nigel, a look of haughty triumph on his face. "Then you are who I will do business with." He wiped his hand on dirty trousers. "I am Mr. Dehkordi. People just call me Dek." He pressed a hand to his chest. "Like my father before me, and his father before him, I am the best Persian rug man in all the land. I come every month to take the rugs to clean them, sometimes more often if necessary. Earlier, I received a call to pick up three rugs tonight and return them tomorrow. This is very difficult. The rugs are delicate works of art. But I will do this because you are such a long and good customer. When I get here, there are only two."

"There were three." Nigel injected his venom into the conversation.

I looked at the rugs—two tubes of carpet rolled for pick up. Then I looked around the rest of the kitchen area, then peeked around the corner to the butler's pantry. "What's that?" I pointed to a metal door maybe four feet square, the handle on the bottom.

"What?" Nigel was having trouble following my shift.

"That." I pointed again.

"The dumbwaiter."

Not something we had in Vegas. "Where does it go?"

"The Royal Suite."

A dumbwaiter. A missing rug.

I knew how the killer had gotten into the Royal Suite and how she'd gotten Aziza's body out.

12

Donna

"*W*hy won't Dominic pick up?" I grouse to Jack.

It's almost nine o'clock in the morning. In the past few hours the rest of the team has gotten numerous texts from Ryan, increasingly alarmed that Dominic has yet to call in.

I'm dialing our British operative's cell phone for the fifth time. This time, however, I'm not hanging up until I get him on the line.

To face me, Jack rolls over on the bed to give me his full attention. "Your guess is as good—or as bad—as mine."

"By 'good,' do you mean that he may still be in bed with the O'Toole woman?"

Jack laughs. "You'd have to ask *her* if it was 'good.' It'll give you gals something to dish about."

I stick my finger in my mouth and feign a gag reflex, then retort, "I have many questions for Lucky, but Dominic's so-called prowess is not one of them—"

"A pity, Old Girl—since it's all too obvious you'd welcome a bit of spice in your drab little housewifely life." Through the phone, Dominic's voice is cool and clipped.

It's also loud enough that Jack can hear him too. While my face flushes, Jack purses his lips to keep from laughing aloud.

I shush him before putting the phone on speaker. "It's about time you picked up," I chide Dominic. "Ryan is practically apoplectic with worry!"

"He need not be," Dominic retorts sulkily. "I was just catching up on some...*sleep.* Everything is under control." He sounds a bit put out.

Jack and I exchange worried glances. "How was your encounter with Ms. O'Toole?" Jack asks.

"My winnings at the baccarat table caught her attention, and she accepted my invitation to join me for a drink in my room," he responds airily.

"Talk about ideal circumstances," I reply.

"So, did Lucky reveal anything to you?" Jack asks. "And by that, I don't mean the obvious."

"What Jack is asking is did you get anything out of her?" I ask.

Jack smirks as he adds, "As opposed to putting anything *into* her."

"Crikey, Craigs! Get your minds out of the gutter!" Dominic, usually the punster, actually sounds disgusted. "If you must know, nothing was, as Jack so vulgarly puts it, 'revealed' by her...or for that matter 'put into' her." His sigh drips with disappointment. "Instead, she gave me quite a dressing down."

"Not in the usual way, I take it?" Jack does nothing to hide his glee.

"I only wish!" Dominic sounds practically wistful. "Admittedly, I was manhandled a bit by Ms. O'Toole. Unfortunately, it was only a pat-down to assure I hadn't cheated at the baccarat table."

"Did you?" I ask.

"My darling Mrs. Craig, I keep secrets, or I discover them. But I never *reveal* them."

I'm sure it's Dominic's pomposity that has Jack rolling his eyes. "What happened next?

"Oddly enough...*nothing.*" The word sticks in Dominic's throat. "From the look on her very beautiful face, she certainly appreciated what she felt—*literally,* if not emotionally. But the moment the pat down was completed, she...well, she just *took her leave!*"

"Oh..." Jack and I murmur in unison.

"Pardon?" Dominic's tone warns us against pitying him.

I opt for silence.

Not Jack. He practically crows, "Wow! So, you really *were* just sleeping all this time!"

My frown warns him not to rub it in.

"Not *alone*," Dominic sniffs. "Just...not with Lucky." He must realize how disappointed he sounds because he quickly adds, "The subsequent conquest was worth it, if only to gather important intel on the target."

Not to mention how it might have assuaged his bruised ego.

I smirk, "By conquest, do you mean Lavinia, or Prunella?"

"Sorry. I didn't mean to mislead you. I meant to say *'conquests,'* as in both lovely ladies." The pride in his voice is broken with truculence as he adds: "Unlike Ms. O'Toole, I saw no need to crush anyone's feelings."

I shake my head at his audacity. "How very kind of you. I'm sure they were both very appreciative."

"Thank you for that, dear Donna." As always, Dominic somehow missed the sarcasm in my statement. "Indeed, their displays of gratitude were quite uplifting...Ah! Take note, Jack, as *that* was a jolly pun."

"Duly noted." Jack shakes his head. "So, what exactly did your playmates divulge about Ms. O'Toole?"

"They consider her *buttoned-up*. A *perfectionist*. Puts business before *pleasure*." Dominic's voice, low and languid, sounds as if he's giving the play-by-play of a sex tape. I know him too well. He's titillated by the thought of breaking her icy demeanor.

"And rumor has it that she is engaged—*to a Frenchman*." Dominic's sigh was almost orgasmic.

Ah, the ultimate challenge! Cuckolding a son from the Land of Love.

Jack bows his head in disgust. When he's able to collect himself, he mutters, "We'll let you go, Dominic. I'm sure you're anxious to report back to Ryan. God knows he's chomping at the bit to hear from you."

"Oh...yes. About that, Old Chum. You wouldn't mind covering for me, would you? Perhaps tell him that I'm working diligently to achieve...well, for a lack of a better word, shall we call it 'infiltration?'" He laughs weakly. "Another indelicate pun, but apt."

I've never heard Dominic so disheartened. I pipe up, "Jack would be glad to contact Ryan on your behalf."

Jack slaps his forehead in disgust. I grimace as he grouses, "I'll do it, but *you owe me.*"

He says it to Dominic but he points to me too.

To nudge Dominic out of his malaise, I murmur, "In any event, you're still on Lucky's radar—right?"

There's a long silence before Dominic vows, "Not to worry. After tonight, she'll be obsessed with me."

He clicks off.

Jack tosses the phone away. "Have you ever noticed that I'm 'Old Chum' only when he wants something from me?"

"What have you got to complain about? No matter how many times I've pulled his fat out of the fire, I'm always 'Old Girl'— emphasis on the old," I retort. "Hey, that last thing he said before hanging up—it sounded...I don't know. Ominous, I guess. What do you think he meant by it?"

"Frankly, I couldn't care less. Dominic needs to cut the lovesick schoolboy routine and get Lucky to tell him why she felt the need to check on Aziza as you were leaving; and if she came across the dead woman's body. And if so, why wasn't it a shock to her?"

"If he's smitten with her, he may not want to be the one to ask hard questions."

Jack frowns "Why not?"

"She may be his...you know, his Valentina." After this slips out I bite my tongue.

Jack flinches at the name of his now deceased wife. "Or your Carl," he replies evenly.

"Fair enough," I murmur.

Valentina stole Acme intelligence from Jack, and then faked her own death—but not before turning the intel over to her lover: my ex-husband Carl, who also disappeared, presumed dead.

Jack is right. Love is complicated.

Up until now Dominic has always used sex as his super power. Here's hoping Lucky O'Toole isn't his Kryptonite.

"DOMINIC ASKED YOU TO CALL ME ON HIS BEHALF?" RYAN IS shouting so loud that Jack must lower the volume on his cell phone. "Why the hell would he do that?"

"He's still...under cover." How Jack is able to say that without snickering is beyond me. To keep from giggling I purse my lips.

Ryan's silence is more ominous than his snarl. Finally, he says, "I see. Well, relay a message to him. If I don't hear from him in the next twenty-four hours, he can stay in his homeland at the risk of MI6 rescinding his Acme-granted Interpol clearance based on the incident that got him tossed out of the agency in the first place."

Yikes.

"For what?" Jack wonders.

"That's classified," Ryan retorts.

"Aw, come on. Give us a hint," I ask.

Silence.

I'm not above begging. "Pretty please?"

"Prince Harry. Vegas," Ryan retorts. "Need I say more?"

Jack's eyes open wide. Like me, the incident is easy to remember considering the avalanche of news coverage it garnered.

"I'll make sure Dominic calls you with an update," Jack promises.

Ryan grunts his thanks. "By the way, I've asked Abu to tail the O'Toole woman whenever she leaves the hotel. If she's working with others, we need to know it."

"Smart move," I reply. As much as he'd love to, Dominic can't have eyes on the O'Toole woman at all times. And if she spotted him, she'd surely find it suspicious based on the interaction they've already had—or, apparently haven't had.

"As for your meeting with Aziza's handler, it's to take place at 12:00 today," Ryan adds. "You and Donna are to meet him on the southeast bench facing the Joy of Life fountain in Hyde Park. He'll be on the lookout for a canoodling couple."

"That's easy enough," I reply.

"His code name is Vulture," Ryan continues. "He'll have a pair of binoculars with him, and he'll use it in a sentence after you give him the passphrase, 'What a splendid place for bird watching.'"

"Got it," Jack says.

"Thanks, Craigs. Now, let's wrap this thing up." He rings off.

I frown. "No one is more anxious to do that than me. I've already gotten a ranting phone call from Penelope Bing, grousing about Aunt Phyllis' choice for the prom's theme: 'Game of Thrones'"

"That sounds innocent enough," Jack replies.

"It would be—if she hadn't ordered a pyrotechnics show and a roomful of medieval weaponry."

"Frankly, I think it'll be a big hit with the students," Jack counters. "Penelope is just jealous because she didn't think of it first."

"You're probably right. Now that Peter is about to remarry, Penelope is afraid of losing Cheever's affections to his new step-mom. Even Jeff has admitted that Peter's fiancée is quite a hottie." I sigh. "I guess Penelope is worried that Aunt Phyllis is stealing her thunder."

"If she's so worried about it, why doesn't she take over as prom coordinator?"

I slap my mouth in mock shock. "But that might mean breaking a nail! And besides, if the prom is a flop, who would she blame then?"

Jack tweaks my nose. "As always, you—even from fifty-five hundred nautical miles away."

My cell buzzes with another text. As I read it, I groan.

"What is it now?" Jack asks.

"Penelope again. My God, it's the middle of the night there! Doesn't that woman ever sleep?"

"Not when she's got a victim in her sights," Jack reminds me. "In this case, Aunt Phyllis—and you. What does she write now?"

"For some cockeyed reason, Aunt Phyllis thought that hiring a

Goth band made up of little people would be the ideal entertainment at the dance!"

Jack shrugs. "At the very least, it fits the theme, what with the popularity of Peter Dinklage's character—Tyrion Lannister."

I finagle with my cell phone settings. "They can duke it out. I'm muting their texts until we land in Los Angeles. In the meantime, we'd better get ready to meet 'Vulture.'"

"Not before we call Dominic and read him the riot act," Jack reminds me. He hits the digits of the man in question.

"Yes?" Dominic mutters.

"Call Ryan."

"Dear Chap, isn't that what you were supposed to do for me?"

"'Dear Chap' did as requested and took it on the chin for you," Jack retorts. "Ryan sends you a message in return. If you don't call within twenty-four hours, then you can quote-unquote, 'stay in his homeland at the risk of MI6 rescinding his Acme-granted Interpol clearance.' He said you'd know what that means."

Silence.

Finally, Dominic sighs. "I'll call now."

I hate to hit him when he's down, but it's time I remind him that he's got something near and dear to my heart: "Dominic, can we meet up in a couple of hours? How about Berkeley Square Gardens at, say, thirteen hundred. Bring the Hermès handbag. Mama misses her new baby."

With all the traffic going in and out of his room, he'd better return it before one of his liaisons finds it too tempting to resist.

"But...but what if Lucky leaves the club in the meantime?" Dominic sputters. "Ryan will have my head if I miss another chance to interrogate her!"

"Ryan knows you've got her covered inside the Babylon. He's asked Abu to tail her should she roam from the club," Jack informs him.

"*Abu?*" Dominic's voice cracks. "So, that's it! Ryan is losing confidence in me!"

The look on Jack's face reflects mine. Obviously, Dominic's response has him just as worried.

"Not at all," I say in the same soothing tone I used with the kids when they were teething toddlers. "It's just that you're on Lucky's radar, whereas Abu won't be noticed. Listen, Dominic, the park is only a few blocks from the club."

"Your damn purse can wait!" he retorts. "Ms. O'Toole is the first priority."

I flinch at his fear. Covering the phone's mic, I hiss, "I've never seen him like this! He's losing it over that woman!"

"Not on my watch," Jack vows. "We've got to get him out of the club, if only to talk some sense into him," He takes the phone. "Dominic, you agreed you owed me one. Well, this is the one. No arguments! You'll meet us in Berkeley Square Gardens at 13:00. It'll take all of ten minutes, tops, which still gives you plenty of time to get back and into your goddam bespoke tuxedo in order to impress Ms. O'Toole at the casino table."

"Blimey..." Dominic's anguish is palpable. Finally: "Well then, so be it."

The phone line goes dead.

"I've never seen him so lovesick," Jack mutters.

"Men are always taken with the woman who plays the hardest to get," I point out.

"No—in this case, I'd say he's got it—*and bad*," Jack counters.

If so, it's with the worst person possible: Our target, Lucky O'Toole.

We've got to make him realize what's at stake.

JACK AND I STROLL ARM IN ARM INTO HYDE PARK. WE'RE DRESSED casually—jeans and heavy jackets, woolen caps tugged low, and scarves around our necks. We also wear sunglasses—wishful thinking that the sun will win its game of peek-a-boo with a frigid, thickening fog.

We're not shy with our public displays of affection. The fact that it's part of our cover makes it all the sweeter. Sure beats all the times we must pretend we don't know each other.

We are twenty minutes early. The park bench that is the rendezvous point with Aziza's handler is currently Ground Zero for a gaggle of giggling schoolgirls, no more than seven or eight years old, who are taking their recess. Other students dip their hands into the fountain's basin in order to sprinkle chilly drops of water on each other and then run away, squealing with delight.

Ten minutes later their teachers round them up and walk them out of the park, leaving us to sit on a far side of the designated wooden bench.

I lean my head on Jack's shoulder.

"That's not exactly 'canoodling,'" he reminds me.

"You're right. And since we're to give off all the right signals…" I swing my legs into his lap and stroke his cheek.

He puts his arms around me and pulls me closer.

When our lips meet, it's all too easy to lose myself in our kiss. As my eyelids close, drowsy with delight, the sounds around us seem to intensify. The chirping birds flying overhead are symphonic. The bits and pieces of conversations of others as they walk by rise and fall with a self-deprecating British lilt. It's a welcomed reprieve from the humble bragging you're sure to hear in my neighborhood of L.A. movers-and-shakers and yummy mommies.

My eyes finally open when the crunch of gentle footsteps on gravel stops short.

The man, short and slight, wears a heavy wool reefer and bowler hat pushed so low that it covers his eyebrows and grazes his dark glasses. He sports a fake goatee and mustache: Well, at least the goatee is pasted on. A faint auburn smudge is a telltale sign that his mustache has been dyed to match his chin fringe.

And yes, he wears binoculars around his neck.

Jack nods genially. "What a splendid place for bird watching."

"Indeed," the man declares. "In fact, from here I've even spotted a vulture or two…" As his voice trails off, his eyes grow large.

Jack follows his stare—

To me. More specifically, to my right ring finger.

When the man takes off his sunglasses to get a better look, I find myself staring at Nigel Ahern.

I'm shocked enough to leap off Jack's lap.

I land on gravel.

"*You?*" Nigel and I hiss in unison.

"Sit down—both of you," Jack warns us in a low snarl.

With as much dignity as I can muster, I rise and take my place beside Jack on the bench.

Slowly, Nigel lowers himself beside me.

I collect myself enough to murmur, "I'm certainly surprised to see you in this capacity, Mr. Ahern."

"You surprise me as well, 'Princess Maja.'" He does a piss poor job hiding his smirk. "Although, I suppose, I should have suspected the princess would eventually come into play in this mission."

"I don't know how. She didn't exist until the moment I stepped foot into your club."

"As a mute, no less." He glances skyward, as if the answer to all riddles could be found in the fog draping our heads. "Mr. Fleming's ploys should be less transparent."

I shake with anger. "He gave me away?"

"Not at all," Nigel assures me. "If you must know, when I bowed over your hand, I noticed you'd chipped a nail." He points to my right ring finger.

"You're quite observant." I shrug, silently cursing the oversight. Note to Self: *always* carry your last polish shade with you, along with a bit of polish remover, especially if you're going to beat someone to a bloody pulp.

"My keen eye has saved me on numerous occasions." He bobs his head proudly. "As for Mr. Fleming, as an MI6 case officer, I am quite aware of his bona fides as an international *bon vivant*. Whereas his exploits—or, more correctly, his *sexploits*—provide great cover for his missions, they've also made him legendary in our tight-knit covert community. Who hasn't snuck a peek at his Interpol dossier, if only for a few moments of titillating diversion, courtesy of the perennial winner of the Undercover Lover

Award?"

"I, for one," Jack mutters. He glances in my direction.

My blush is my tell. If he's looking for company, he ain't getting it from me.

Noting my discomfort, Nigel adds, "Rest assured Mr. Fleming's cover is safe with me. I must admit, though, I've admired his technique—from afar, that is. As for his relationship with Princess Maja, I assumed she was a target as opposed to one of us. Dominic usually works alone, for obvious reasons."

No better time for me to change the subject. "We are sorry about the loss of your asset, Aziza."

Nigel's eyes cloud with tears. "She was a true patriot—not just to her country and region, but to the Organization."

"Did Aziza reveal to you the contents of the intel, or at least give you a clue?" I ask.

He lowers his head. "No. But because her goal was to foster peace in the Middle East, her intel was always useful in that regard. This time, however, she warned me that it was explosive in its nature and insisted that it was to be passed up the line by her and only her. She said it was her way to protect me...in case anything should happen to her. She knew she was in danger."

"What did you think when she disappeared last night?" Jack asked.

"I did my best not to panic—especially when a maid informed me that something was amiss in the room."

"What did she mean by that?" I ask.

"Aziza left a clue for me, in the Royal suite," Nigel explains. "The flowers were all wrong."

Jack frowns. "I don't understand."

"The sheik usually requests yellow roses. The housekeepers are keen to his demands, and I know they'd followed through with the right order. But the flowers had been replaced with red dahlias."

"And you think this had something to do with Aziza's disappearance?"

Nigel nods. "I'm sure of it. We'd worked it out as a signal that she'd be in danger." Nigel shakes his head angrily. "I must admit, it shook me to my core! I'm sure the club's owner felt my demeanor was off-kilter."

"You mean Lucky O'Toole," I say.

His eyes widen, surprised I'd know her name. "Yes. Albeit, Ms. O'Toole's actions were no less strange. She appeared yesterday with just a few hours' warning. She specifically asked for Aziza. When she heard she was in the Royal Suite assuring that the next guest's requests had been met, Ms. O'Toole went up immediately as opposed to leaving word for Aziza to join her in the manager's office. When it became obvious to me that Aziza had somehow disappeared into thin air, I asked Ms. O'Toole if she knew where she might have gone. Ms. O'Toole's answer was both coy and ambiguous."

"A strange reaction indeed," I murmur. "I assume you already know that after I reported finding Aziza, MI6 asked that we retrieve her body immediately for analysis—in fact, prior to the next guest's arrival."

"Thank you for doing so." The grief in Nigel's tone undercuts his politeness. "As you already know, Sheik Mohammed Ben Halabi is—was—Aziza's uncle. But he was not aware that she worked at the club. Purposely, she was rarely scheduled during his stays. Had he found out about it, he would have insisted we fire her and MI6 would have lost a very valuable asset."

"If that was the case, why was Aziza working yesterday?" Jack asks.

"The sheik's arrival came with little notice," Nigel replies.

"Just like Ms. O'Toole's," I murmur.

Nigel nods. "In fact, she insisted on showing the sheik up to the suite without me."

Hearing this, Jack nudges me.

"Has anyone noticed Aziza's absence today?" I ask.

Nigel thinks for a moment. "Thus far one of our receptionists, Julie, expressed wonder at Aziza's absence. The ladies were more acquaintances than friends, but they shared a mutual respect. Also, one of the croupiers: Adam Kalb. Apparently, she borrowed something from him and he had wondered if she'd left it in the office."

Jack nods at this information. "How about Ms. O'Toole? Considering her rush to meet with Aziza yesterday, I would think she'd have been openly speculating about her employee's whereabouts this morning."

Nigel frowns at the mention of Lucky. "She mentioned nothing last night. And I didn't run into Ms. O'Toole this morning, but it is inevitable." He looks at his watch. "In fact, I'm due back at the club now."

"What do you know about Ms. O'Toole, and for that matter the Rothstein family in general?" Jack asks.

"They are brash. They are on top of all the club's revenue sources, seemingly to the farthing." Nigel shrugs. "May I just say they are Americans, and all that implies?"

"You may," Jack retorts wryly. "Have you noticed anything that may lead you to believe that they may be laundering money?"

Nigel thinks for a moment. Finally, he shakes his head. "Again, they keep a tight rein on revenue and expenses, but the operations and accounting staffs are tip-top, and well vetted. As such, any peculiarities would seem out of sorts to them, and they would mention it."

"We're almost certain Ms. O'Toole saw the body," I reveal.

Nigel's back stiffens. "If so, she would have surely mentioned it to me!"

"That's what we thought, too, especially if it upset her—either personally, or in regard to its effect on the club's guests," I reply. "But she hasn't said a word. Strange, isn't it?"

"Mr. Ahern, when you next speak to Ms. O'Toole, perhaps you could ask her if Aziza came through with the help she needed. Report back to us as to her demeanor and her response."

Nigel's eyes grow large. "You believe she is responsible for Aziza's death?"

"She is the prime suspect. Should she do or say anything out of the ordinary, please let Acme know as soon as possible." Jack declares. "Based on the intel Aziza risked her life for, time is of the essence."

Nigel nods imperceptibly. "But of course." He lowers his gaze to his watch. "I must be heading back to the club now. A pleasure to meet you both formally." His pleasantry aside, his lower lip trembles. Nigel is shaken by the thought that whatever Aziza stumbled onto, Lucky O'Toole and her family are somehow involved.

Their casinos may provide them cover, but it may also be their downfall.

BY THE TIME JACK AND I ARRIVE AT BERKELEY SQUARE, A DENSE FOG has forced the sun to give up all hope of blessing London with its brightness. Sparkling snowflakes, rapidly crystalizing in the frigid air, dance drunkenly around us.

Jack nods toward a bench located between two entries of the oval, gated park. It faces south: the side closest to Babylon London. "I'll wait here. Why don't you grab a seat on the opposite side of the square?"

"Why?" I ask.

"Considering the Rothstein family's aversion to financial losses, Dominic's interaction with Lucky O'Toole certainly puts him on her radar—but, unfortunately, not in the amorous way we'd hoped. On the off chance that he took an SDR, he'd be coming from another direction."

Normally, an undercover agent rendezvousing with the rest of his team would follow standard procedure and take a predetermined surveillance detection route, which would allow him to duck and dodge anyone trailing him. Unfortunately, Dominic is behaving more like a lovesick schoolboy.

"Sadly, my guess is that you'll see him before I do." Bowing my head against a sudden flurry of flakes, I head off across a diagonal park lane.

TO MY RELIEF, WITHIN MINUTES I SPOT DOMINIC. HE CARRIES A

Harrods shopping bag. It's the one from my Princess Maja shopping spree, but now it must hold my Hermès purse, thank goodness.

He's walking down Bruton Street, on the park's northeast side. But when he's a block away, he stops short before seeing me. Apparently, something or someone has caught his eye.

Getting up, I wave my hat at him in order to get his attention, but by then he is walking in the opposite direction.

Where the hell does he think he's going?

I call his name. When he hears it, reluctantly he turns toward me.

I rush in his direction.

Jack must have seen me get up and wave because now he's a few strides behind me as I cross the street.

When I reach Dominic, I ask, "What's wrong? Did you get turned around?"

He frowns. "Don't be silly! I know this city like the back of my hand. It's just that…Well, I thought I saw…someone."

Jack, now even with us, rolls his eyes. "Let me guess—Lucky O'Toole."

But just in case he's not mistaken, I look beyond him. The street is empty, and no wonder. Snow is falling even harder now. This is a street frequented by posh shoppers. Why stare at a bauble or blouse from a freezing sidewalk when you could be welcomed by shop girls bearing warm smiles and a glass of bubbly?

Jack puts his hand on Dominic's shoulder. "You've got it bad, man."

"But, I'm sure it was…Just…Never mind." Dominic's indignation melts into shame.

I point to a pub further up the block: the Coach & Horses. "I need to warm up," I say. "And from the looks of things, you need a drink."

He nods.

The pub, back in the direction of his ghost, will give Dominic a second chance to see that she was merely a figment of his imagination.

She's also become an obsession. We need to have a serious talk.

THE PUB IS QUIET. WHILE DOMINIC AND I TAKE A BACK BOOTH, JACK goes up to the bar and orders a round of our usual libations: a martini for Dominic and a glass of a decent red wine for me. Jack takes a scotch, neat.

I'm dying to divulge the name of Aziza's handler to Dominic, but because I know Jack will want to see the look on Dominic's face too, I hold my tongue while he pays the barmaid. She motions that she'll bring over the drinks as soon as they're poured.

After Jack slips into the booth next to me, he turns to Dominic. "So, did you straighten things out with Ryan?"

"Our fearless leader and I are of like mind that one way or another, Ms. O'Toole must be coerced into telling us all she knows." Dominic grimaces. "Our opinions diverge on the methodology."

"I see," Jack replies. "You think you can scratch her belly and she'll purr out the answers we need."

The bar maid has walked over with our drinks in time to catch this tantalizing tidbit. Intrigued, she studies Dominic.

For the first time since I've known him, Dominic misses his chance to dazzle a woman with his patented Yes-I-Want-You gaze coupled with his And-You'll-Enjoy-Every-Moment-of-It grin. Instead, he stares longingly at the olive in his martini glass.

I wince at the thought that he envisions Lucky O'Toole's head as its pimento.

The disappointed barmaid shrugs and walks off.

It's now my turn to get him to see reason. "Here's something that may change your mind, Dominic. We met with Aziza's handler. Want to take a guess as to who it is?"

"Surprise me." Removing the olive, he puts his glass to his lips.

"Nigel Ahern."

My timing couldn't be worse. Dominic is so surprised that he spews his drink all over Jack.

To my husband's credit, he stays quiet and keeps calm. His only show of exasperation is to wipe his face with Dominic's cashmere scarf.

"Not to worry. I'll get it dry-cleaned," Dominic assures him. "And I insist on buying the next round."

"How magnanimous." The irony in Jack's voice is lost on our lovelorn colleague. "Dominic, as you can imagine, Nigel is upset to have lost Aziza, both as a friend and an asset. He also added that Ms. O'Toole arrived virtually unannounced, immediately asked to see Aziza alone, and in fact was in such a hurry to see her that she followed her up to the Royal Suite as opposed to waiting for her to return from it."

"I see," Dominic's voice is barely a whisper.

"Then you must also see the need to get over yourself," Jack adds. "There are other ways to skin a cat. It's time to play hardball."

"But Old Boy, I still don't feel it's necessary. She just needs a little...well, massaging." At the thought, a shadow of a smile rises on his lips.

"I am not 'old,' and I'm not your 'boy,'" Jack growls through gritted teeth. "I'm your mission leader. And in that capacity, I'm commanding you to–"

In the hope of silencing Jack, I take his palm and squeeze it. "Dominic, darling, what Jack is trying to say is that your approach may need some finessing."

Dominic's eyes narrow. "What are you implying?"

"Only that the woman is obviously more frigid than you anticipated—and it has nothing to do with you. If she had anything to do with Aziza's murder, she's in panic mode."

Relief floods his face. I've swatted away his worst fear. His ego has been assuaged.

I reach across the table and take Dominic's hand in mine. "And I understand that you want to clear her."

Hesitantly, he nods.

"If she were acting innocent, this would be so much easier," I continue. "Unfortunately, she isn't."

"So…what should I do?" Dominic asks.

Jack snorts. "Quit thinking with your dick, for starters. If you want to clear her, she needs to come up with answers."

"Metaphorically speaking, I've found that flies are much easier to catch with honey than with vinegar."

"Use any method you want. However, if you can't 'massage' Ms. O'Toole into giving us her side of the story, you're to wrap her up and bring her home…metaphorically speaking."

Jack slides a small clear packet toward Dominic. It contains a white powder: the tranquilizer Rohypnol.

Dominic looks as if he's been given a death warrant. Slowly, he slips it into his pocket, gets up, and walks out the door.

13

Lucky

*S*leep had been fitful. I was awake when my phone vibrated on my nightstand. I squinted at the caller ID as my stomach growled. Still hungry—a metaphor for my life at the moment: no matter what I put in, I remained unsatisfied.

I rolled onto my back. "Hey. Pretty late there."

"Just eleven or so," Miss P said. "Things are barely getting rolling."

Time differences eluded me. As did most of my life at the moment. "I assume you have something for me? Either that or you've taken to missing me more than usual."

"I'm bereft without you."

I marveled at her deadpan delivery. "And I'm running away from home, both fantasies of mine. Whatcha got?"

"That purse you asked me to research? You were right—it's one of a kind and it has some interesting recent history." The comforting shuffle of her papers echoed across the distance. "It came up for auction recently, a private sale at Christeby's but quite widely publicized."

"Who was selling her baubles?"

"Normally, I can find out that stuff on the QT, but this time someone had a tight lid on it."

"Interesting. I should think the purse would bring at least fifty grand." My interest in our mystery lady increased.

"That's where it gets interesting. You're pretty close to the estimated selling price. It actually went for almost three times that."

I pushed myself up in bed. The blinds were open. The rain had stopped—not that it was sunny by any stretch, merely a lighter gloom. "Any idea why?"

"Somebody wanted that bag badly."

During our years together, Miss P had picked up my penchant for stating the obvious. "I wonder why?" As I thought, a tiny dart of sun pierced the gloom. It didn't last long. "Is Sharon Walker still at Christeby's London office?"

"Yes."

"Will you arrange an appointment for a civilized hour, say around eleven?" That would give me time to take full advantage of the restorative properties of my spectacular bathtub followed by a leisurely breakfast. Running on fumes, I'd be no good to anybody if I didn't pull myself together.

"I'll make the request and have her confirm with you directly."

"Perfect. That should give me time to find my smile."

"And perhaps some manners. Jean-Charles called here to confirm you arrived safely." Concern rather than accusation filled her voice.

"He gave me an ultimatum. You know how much I like threats, even thinly veiled and delivered in a French accent. We are at loggerheads over whose career comes first."

"It doesn't have to be an I-win-you-lose sort of thing. Each circumstance is unique. Compromise and communication are the keys to making any relationship work, especially one as complicated as yours."

"Yes, well, ultimatums usually don't indicate a willingness to meet in the middle."

Miss P didn't have an answer for that.

"Besides, the whole thing may be moot as I doubt I'll meet it any way."

"You still can make the party. Let someone else handle things there."

"So, I have to give in." It wasn't a question.

"It all depends on what you want."

"And how much I'm willing to sacrifice of myself to get it." Which we both knew was pretty much zero. I wanted the magic, the joy of being with someone who let me be me and loved me for it. If I got that, they'd get everything I had in return. "I'll let you know what I find out from Sharon. Thanks."

"Call him, Lucky."

I ended the call.

TODAY THE BREAKFAST BUFFET LINED THE BACK WALL OF THE LIBRARY, a small room wallpapered in shelves of floor-to-ceiling books. A tiered tray held various exotic fruits to begin. Then came platters of pastries to tempt me, followed by steam tables, which I opened one at a time. I returned to the beginning of the line choosing two croissants—this close to France they had to be crisp with flakes holding as much butter as possible—followed by one toad-in-the-hole and a scoop of beans, a curious English tradition that for some reason I liked. I found a small table by the front window. As soon as I took my seat, a white-coated waiter materialized. "Tea, miss?"

An English tradition I hadn't learned to appreciate—tea still reminded me of dirty dishwater. "American coffee, please."

"Yes, miss." Somehow, he managed to convey his disappointment in my lack of refinement and make me feel good about it.

Bree caught me polishing off my second croissant. I dabbed at the flakes I could feel on my chin as I motioned her to the chair opposite.

"Can't stay, thanks." Bree looked bright in her blue pea coat and wild blonde curls. The cold had slapped her cheeks pink. "Saw you on my way to my office and thought I'd tell you in person what I planned to phone you about. I checked the loading dock tapes personally. Only thing amiss was a white van. Three men, faces always away from the cameras."

"Let me guess, they loaded one rolled up Persian carpet that probably was heavier than it looked into the back of their truck."

Her eyes widened. "Precisely."

"Anything unique about the van that might help in tracking it down?"

"No. Clean, unblemished, no stickers, no plates. I'm sorry."

"No worries. Glad to have a theory confirmed." I warmed my cup with fresh coffee from a silver pot snug in its quilted warmer. "Oh, there is one more thing." I told her about Dominic and the woman he came in with.

"And you need a photo?"

Bree read me almost as well as Miss P. "Yes, please. And I'd like to know what purse she carried."

Bree's eyebrows shot toward her hairline, but she nodded and didn't give word to the unspoken question I saw in her eyes. "Anything I need to know or can help with?"

I felt bad about freezing her out, but truth was I still couldn't prove a crime had been committed. "When I know a bit more, I'll need your help."

A smile, then a crisp nod and I was alone.

While working on my second pot of coffee and the last section of the *Financial Times* which I'd savored in the forgotten luxury of time, my phone chirped. I'd changed the notification tone to something more civilized, so I didn't jump out of my skin. A text from Sharon confirming an eleven o'clock meeting. I had forty-five minutes. Christeby's was also in Mayfair, a few blocks away on New Bond Street. Given the lighter gloom outside with only a hint of flurries riding on a biting breeze, I decided to walk.

Bree caught me as I headed toward the front entrance. "Here," she held out a photo.

The woman in red.

"I couldn't find any personal detail—the lady wore sunglasses and a headscarf. The only thing showing were blond bangs. And her bag was red leather, Michael Kors. It matched her luggage."

I folded the photo and put it in my pocket. "Thanks." I cinched my Burberry tight and grabbed an umbrella from the bellman who huddled in his thick red wool coat, rubbing his hands against the cold. The walk took me across Piccadilly, a street I loved. The urge to detour through Piccadilly Circus to enjoy the shops and their offerings, from first edition books to leaded miniature soldiers—a bit of purely British retail magic—proved almost irresistible. But I found the resolve somewhere and forged on.

Christeby's occupied a building much like the one that housed the Babylon London Club, on a similar block. These buildings had been here long before we showed up and would still be here long after I was nothing but a faded notation in a yellowed birth register in Nye County, Nevada. Something about that made me feel good as I trudged up the steps thinking about all who had done the same before me.

Sharon had left a credential for me. No sooner than I'd been ushered through security, then I found myself sitting in front of her after a quick hug. Her office walls were home to various prints and paintings, most vaguely recognizable and all a testament to her taste.

Stylish, with an ash-blonde bob and heavy large purple eyeglass frames that owled her brown eyes, she gave me a warm smile. "Lucky, it's been too long. May I offer you some tea?" At my look she laughed, a sound like wind chimes in a soft breeze. "I forgot. Coffee then?"

"No thanks. I've had enough to keep me alert into next week." Through the years, Sharon and her firm had made millions off my family's penchant for art, both buying and selling. I was hoping that would be enough to get some info on who bought that Hermès bag. "I'm here about a Hermès Kelly bag you sold last week."

She leaned back and crossed her legs. "Crème and gold?"

"Went for a lot more than anticipated." She had to remember—her fee was based on the take.

"Yes, there was a lot of interest in that bag. The Russians. The Americans. The Koreans. Everybody jumped in."

"Any idea why?"

"What's your interest?"

"On the QT?" I wondered how much I could trust her.

"Understood."

"A lady, a person of interest in a major crime, carried that purse as she left the scene." I fudged as much as I could. News of a murder at the club would race through London despite the promised discretion.

"I see. You want to know who bought that bag." Her posture tensed.

"No. It would cost you your job to share that info with me—I'd never put you on the spot like that. But, any help you can give me would be most appreciated. She was heavily disguised, and I couldn't get a good look at her—not even enough to be able to pick her out of a line-up."

She relaxed, and I could see my approach had the desired effect —she wanted to help. "I can't look up any contact information, but I can give you a description not only of her but of who she was with." She settled back to tell her story.

I listened, imagining the scene, the fevered bidding, multiple countries joining the fray, all checking with someone remotely before raising their bids.

Government. The word popped into my head as if sent directly up the vagus nerve from my gut.

That old gut instinct. Could it be right?

Bree had said the video looping at the club was very sophisti-cated—government-agency-sophisticated.

I fiddled with my Birkin—silently thanking the Big Boss for providing me with the right calling card. If you want to talk with the ducks, you have to look like a duck…or something like that. "So, the mystery lady was brunette, shoulder-length hair, not short, not tall, nice figure?"

"Rather ordinary. Pretty, not ravishing." A woman's take on another woman. "She did the bidding."

"Interesting." Her description was perfect for someone who wanted to fit in, go unnoticed, unrecognized. Not much but at least it gave me something to go on. "And the gentleman with her?"

"There were two, one beside her and another patrolling the room, watching the action."

"That's allowed?"

"No one complained. Everything is done out in the open at an auction."

"Tell me about the man with our mystery bidder."

"He was more memorable. Talk, dark, wicked smile...you know." She trailed off holding onto a note of dreamy. "Green eyes, dark curls and one of those things in his chin." She made an up-down motion on her chin with her index finger.

"A cleft?"

"Yes, that's it."

"And the other gentleman? Blond, blue eyes, dapper with an air of over-inflated ego?"

A frown pinched the skin between her perfectly arched brows. "And a bit touchy."

Dominic Fleming.

"I'm sorry I couldn't be more help."

I stood and extended my hand. "You've been a great help, thank you."

While she hadn't told me how to find her, she'd told me what to look for.

IT HAD STARTED TO SNOW LIGHTLY. THE FOG HAD FROSTED THE FEW trees lining the street, freezing to the bare branches. That, coupled with the foreign architecture and the odd sirens bleating in the distance, transported me—right into a snow globe. I turned up my collar and ducked my head against the pelting of the soft flakes. Never one to travel the same bit of real estate if I could avoid it, I chose a different route back to the club. I'd spent an hour or so perusing the galleries at Christeby's and was enjoying the lingering. The stores on Bruton would be equally diverting. I always loved the Stella McCartney windows. And the street ended in a nice park, Berkeley Square Gardens. Plant life wasn't plentiful in Vegas, so I deviated to walk through it whenever possible.

Several blocks of life flowing past pretty windows filled with beautiful things I would never pay retail for, and pretty people enjoying the post-holiday flurries and the blood stopped pounding in my ears.

The park loomed ahead, making me choose either right or left to follow the road around. I don't know what made me look, but I took a glance into the gardens. A figure, trim in a perfectly tailored overcoat, his fedora pulled low, the brim obscuring half his face. Something about him sparked a memory—six pack abs, a nice flare to his lats, warm skin, the heat of his lips pressed to the back of my hand, his arrogance... evident even now in his choice to follow me and not even try to hide.

He hadn't glanced my way, but I had the sense he knew I was there. My anger seeped in through the cold...and a prickle of fear. He'd been with the mystery woman—she'd been in his room. Aziza had died. I needed to know what game they were playing. Right now, it struck me as best to not let him know I was onto him.

I stood for a moment as if caught in the net of indecision. Which way should I go? I pretended to be focused on the poster hanging from the lamppost, announcing the next auction at Christeby's—Andy Warhol. I'd like that. Out of the corner of my eye, I saw Dominic turn to move in my direction. I glanced at my wrist as if looking at a watch—a completely superfluous bit of extravagance in Vegas where time didn't matter. Tapping my chin, I pretended to be weighing options, then I took a left, heading toward Piccadilly. At the first alley, I ducked in.

Out of Dominic's sight, I flattened myself against the building, counted to three, then risked a peek. Dominic strode in my direction. Perhaps I should let him catch me. His story alone would be worth the irritation at being followed. Or I could simply break his nose. I was leaning toward the second option, when a voice called out, drawing Dominic up short.

A woman, holding her coat closed, rushed toward him. Brown

hair, medium height. Her small beanie provided little cover against the cold. I could see her face clearly. Could she be our mystery woman?

I couldn't take them both. Besides, I thought it best to not let them know I was onto them. Thinking they still operated in the clear, maybe they'd make a mistake.

I pulled out my phone. Holding it around the corner, but using the building to shield myself, I started snapping photos. After checking I'd gotten some good full-face shots of the mystery woman, and several acceptable ones of Mr. Fleming, I dropped the phone in my coat pocket and stepped out from the alley. Keeping close to the building, I headed toward the club.

Foot traffic was light, so I didn't need to dodge as I ate up concrete with long strides—one of the advantages to being six feet tall. My focus elsewhere as I churned on what I knew, what I didn't, and who I wanted to kill first, I was surprised when my shoulder connected rather solidly with a gentleman walking the opposite way.

I staggered slightly.

He grabbed my shoulders to steady me. "I'm terribly sorry." He let go, letting his hands trail lightly down my arms until sure I had regained equilibrium.

I glanced into dark eyes. "No worries. My fault as well."

Without a backward glance, I hurried on.

NIGEL STOOD AT THE FRONT DESK, HIS BACK TO ME, WHEN I RODE IN on a broomstick of pissed off and gotcha. "Mr. Ahern, a moment of your time."

He jumped at my voice probably thinking the hint of pissed off was for him. He needn't have worried—I had bigger fish. I reached into my pocket for my phone. Odd—the pocket was empty. Pretty sure I put it there, I checked the other pocket to be sure. Empty as well. "What the hell?"

"Is something amiss?" Nigel asked in a bored voice.

I wanted to start yelling, "You mean besides Aziza being murdered, Dominic Fleming playing a dangerous game right under my nose with some female chameleon, a sheik who is salivating to shish-kebob me, a *very* irritating mother, and, to top it off, a future former fiancé who was probably the catch of a lifetime? You mean, other than that?" Instead, I took a deep breath and said simply, "My phone. I can't find my phone."

"Should I ping it?"

Pinging *him* held some appeal. Pinging my phone, not so much. It must be on my person. I thought back. I had it by the gardens— I'd taken the photos I wanted to show Nigel. Then I put it in my pocket...

The man who'd bumped into me!

He'd lifted it!

Damn. "Nigel, have the nearest Apple store send over a new phone."

"An eight or a ten?"

At my glare, he wilted. "Yes, Ms. O'Toole. Is that all?"

"No, I want to know if you've seen someone in the club. I had her photo in my phone. She's an acquaintance of Mr. Fleming's." I described the mystery woman as Sharon had described her to me. The woman I'd seen in the gardens.

"And where did you see her?"

"I saw them together in Berkeley Gardens. And she's been to Mr. Fleming's room."

"You know that how?"

"I saw her purse in his room." Why was I letting the pinhead grill me? "Answer the question, please."

Nigel looked at me a smidge too long making me desperate to wipe the manners he hid behind right off his smug little rat face. But, today I decided to be a grown up.

She'd been in my club. Someone would know her or at least have seen her.

I needed a name.

Nigel stepped back, distancing himself from me. "No, I've not seen her."

"Really?" My heart sank. "But she carried a one-of-a-kind Hermès bag when I saw her. Later I saw the same bag tucked under Mr. Fleming's bed."

"But I must ask, why are you following Mr. Fleming? He might object."

My eyes went slitty. "And what are you implying?"

He retreated even further. "You saw her with Mr. Fleming, you said so yourself."

"Yes," my tone turned venomous. "There are three possible conclusions and you have leaped to the wrong one. I suspect the lady he came in with had something to do with the disappearance of Sheik Ben's niece."

"Aziza is missing?" He seemed surprised, but not overmuch. "Why have I not been alerted? And you think Mr. Fleming had something to do with Aziza?"

I'd said too much. I took a step, closing the distance. "What is it between you and Mr. Fleming? And what do you know that you're not telling me?"

He leaned back slightly but held his ground. "I...I...I don't know what you mean."

The front desk and bell staff was all ears. This was not the place to dress-down their boss. "Interesting accommodations have been made for him. We'll discuss his special treatment later. Have you seen the woman or not?"

"No, I've not seen her."

"She hasn't been in the company of Mr. Fleming?"

Nigel crossed his hands in front of himself, protecting his privates. A reflex, I had no doubt, but a telling one.

Was he lying?

"No, Mr. Fleming came in with a Swedish princess. The princess bears no resemblance to the lady you describe."

"Unless the lady I saw is hiding skin-tight red leather under her over coat."

"They are not the same. I would not be untruthful."

Now I was sure he would be.

14

Donna

*W*e've only been back at the Ritz a few minutes when we hear a knock on our door.

Jack looks through the peephole. "It's Abu and Arnie."

When he opens it, Arnie peeks in first. On the other hand, Abu saunters in as if he owns the joint. Catching my eye, he pulls something out of his pocket—a cell phone. "Smile! You're on Candid Camera," he says, as he tosses it to me.

I catch it one-handed.

"It belongs to Lucky O'Toole," Abu explains. "Arnie has already unlocked it."

With Jack looking over my shoulder, I tap the photo app. Low and behold the most recent pictures are of Dominic and me, standing together on Bruton Street.

"So, she wasn't just a figment of his imagination!" Jack declares. "This confirms our suspicions that Dominic is on her radar—and not in a good way."

I frown. "And now I am too, thanks to our lovelorn colleague's failure to catch her tailing him. Arnie, what else did you grab from this device?"

"Everything—contacts, emails, texts. Just scanning it, nothing jumped out in regard to Aziza. However, Lucky's father was quite insistent that she make this sudden trip to Babylon Club London. I've forwarded it to Acme ComInt for more in-depth analysis. Oh, and I erased the photos of Dominic and you from her cloud storage. But if you want to keep these as a souvenir—"

"Not necessary." I roll my eyes.

Arnie leans in, as if he's got a secret to share. "I also perused her upcoming travel itinerary. She's due in Paris in less than forty-eight hours. Her fiancé isn't too happy that she rushed here to take care of some emergency instead of leaving Vegas with him for the City of Lights. The dude wasn't above a couple of passive-aggressive digs."

I snicker. "Maybe we should mention that to Dominic. From the way he reacted about the Frenchman's existence, it may give him the confidence to get what we need out of her."

"After the ultimatum we gave him, he should already have enough incentive," Jack retorts. "But just in case he doesn't, the fact that she tailed him should put him on high alert." He punches in Dominic's telephone number. After three minutes, Jack mutters, "Why the hell doesn't he pick up?"

Arnie pipes up, "He's probably in the middle of the ritual he does before a covert ops."

I raise a brow. "Pardon?" I asked in my best British accent.

"I heard him discussing it on the 'Spooklandia' podcast," Arnie admits. "Dominic does this twelve-point mind-over-matter regime that he swears makes him irresistible to women." Smugly, he adds, "I have to admit, I tried it and it certainly made a few ladies smile."

Jack, confounded, shakes his head. "You're joking, right?"

Arnie blushes. "Well...okay just one *lady*. Emma."

"Was she smiling or laughing?" I ask.

Perplexed, Arnie frowns. "Well...now that you mention it..."

A text pops on my phone. It's from Ryan and it reads:

VULTURE. NOW. GPug. JL. N

Jack has received it too. "Well, we know by Nigel's code name that Ryan is telling us that Nigel needs to meet again. It must be an emergency."

"Since we met in Green Park, obviously he wants to do so again," I reason.

"But what do you think 'ug' stands for?" Jack asks.

"Underground station," Abu deduces.

"The fact that he asks to meet at the underground stop closest to us must mean that he doesn't want us anywhere near the club," I reason.

"Makes sense," Jack replies. "He wants to keep you as far away as possible. And the underground is crowded enough that we'll be hiding in plain sight."

Arnie pulls up the station's internal map. "Three trains go into the station. 'One is the Jubilee Line."

"That's the 'JL.'" I reason. "Does it go north to south?"

Arnie nods.

"So, we've now got our 'N,'" Jack declares.

He and I grab our coats again and we're gone.

NIGEL STANDS BY HIMSELF AT THE FAR END OF THE NORTHBOUND platform of Green Park Station's Jubilee line. By leaning against the tiled wall, this already slight man is in the shadows, which obscures him even more. Once again he's got on the dark reefer coat and the bowler snug to his head. He must have been in such a rush to get here that he's not wearing the paste-on goatee.

Jack takes a subway map from a small wall kiosk. Arm in arm we walk past Nigel, chatting as if we're oblivious to his existence. When we get a few feet beyond him, we stop and open the map, as if perusing it, Jack keeps his back to Nigel, who stares out onto the track. Because I turn to face Jack, I can glance over at Nigel.

"Thank you for getting here so promptly," Nigel hisses. "I'd just returned from our rendezvous when Ms. O'Toole stormed back into the lobby."

Without turning around, I mutter, "Let me guess. While she was out, she somehow misplaced her cell phone."

He pauses for so long that at first I think he's disappeared. Finally, he whispers, "How did you know?"

"One of our operatives lifted it," Jack murmurs, "After she took a picture of Mrs. Craig with Mr. Fleming."

Nigel winces. "Yes, she mentioned seeing the two together. She described you as you are now, not as 'Princess Maja.' And she also insists that Mrs. Craig was his guest at the club, despite me insisting that he showed up with an entirely different woman."

"How could she think that?" Jack asks. "All traces of Mrs. Craig have been scrubbed from your surveillance footage. It's just a supposition on her part that the two women are one and the same."

"I made it quite clear to her that, to my knowledge, Mrs. Craig has never set foot in the club." His back stiffens. "She inferred that I was lying to her. She was…well, quite insistent in fact!"

"*Shhh*," I warn him. At this hour apparently a train arrives every three minutes, and the next one is due in two. I scan the platform. Apparently hoping to choose a less crowded car, others have drifted our way: a woman with a sleeping toddler in a stroller; French-speaking tourists laden with shopping bags; and a gray-haired businessman reading a folded copy of *The Times*. The collar of his cashmere coat still sits high on his neck.

To contain his agitation, Nigel purses his lips.

"Have you any idea how she made the connection between Dominic and me?" I ask.

"She mentioned seeing a very expensive handbag in your possession when you visited the club. She said she saw the same bag in Mr. Fleming's room."

Jack groans. "That damn purse isn't made of leather. It's pure albatross!"

"Yeah? Well too bad. It's a keeper," I growl.

Still shaken, Nigel glances around. "The woman is insufferable —especially when she's on the warpath, as she is now! As much as I fear blowing my cover, because of poor Aziza's fate, I now fear for my life—as should Mr. Fleming. I have yet to see him in order to warn him, and, frankly, I don't dare do so within the club. Because of his club winnings, she has a legitimate excuse to watch him like a hawk"— his voice trembles as he adds—"just as she's now watching me."

I'm concerned that Nigel isn't just worried about his cover being blown. He's pop-eyed with fear.

"We'll get word to Dominic immediately," I assure him.

Jack looks skyward. My guess is he's wondering if Dominic is still going through his love 'em and leave 'em ritual.

The train arrives with an increasingly ominous hum before stopping suddenly with a deafening whoosh. The departing passengers surge around us, giving us the cover needed to get away. Jack and I follow the tight crowd toward the staircase while Nigel goes off in the opposite direction, toward an elevator.

We are halfway up the staircase when Jack turns. "We forgot to mention to Nigel: should it be necessary for us to exfiltrate Lucky, somehow he'll have to cover her absence with the Rothstein Organization. We should head back and mention it to him."

I nod. "He was on his way to the elevator. You meet him there. I'll walk back down now, in case he circled back to follow us up these stairs."

We part with a kiss.

BY THE TIME I GET BACK TO THE NORTHBOUND PLATFORM, ALL passengers have dispersed. I hurry down its far side, where I last saw Nigel. But I stop short when I notice that an OUT OF ORDER sign has been strung across the small hall leading to the elevator. In my silence, another's footsteps can be heard, but then suddenly stop. I see a figure, but it's too far away to make out whether it's him.

"Nigel?" I call out.

The figure takes off in a quick trot—away from me.

Instinctively, I run toward him. But as I pass the hallway I glance back toward the elevator. What I see stops me in my tracks: a leg, extended on the ground, keeps the door from closing.

I run to the prone figure:

Nigel.

Although his body is still convulsing, his eyes have already rolled back into his head and his pulse is gone. Blood trickles from his left nostril.

The bloodstain, on the left side of his open coat, reveals the location of his fatal wound. I lift his coat. A thin slit in his white shirt, now darkened with blood, tells the story: Nigel was stabbed right below the heart.

There is a camera in the hall and the elevator. Security will have seen who did this to him. Someone may be on the way now.

Still, I'll be damned if I let the killer slip through my fingers.

No one passed me going left toward the stairs, and it ends in another fifty yards to the right. No one is there, but out of the corner of my eye, I see a door closing. A faint click confirms it wasn't my imagination.

I run toward it.

The sign on the door reads EMERGENCY EXIT. I open it and discover a stairwell leading upstairs. Besides the dim lights dotting each step, an overhead light glows above. I make out a man running up the stairs: it's the businessman with the newspaper.

Hearing my footsteps behind him, he stops and turns around. Having followed and murdered Nigel, this man must recognize me too.

Smiling, he pulls the knife out from the folded paper. He knows better than to leave any loose ends.

Gripping the knife high, he runs down the stairs toward me. Between his weapon, his size, and the fact that he's angled above me, he has every advantage.

He'll soon discover he's also got two major liabilities.

He's startled when I pull a pin light from my pocket and flash it in his eyes. This stops him cold, giving me the few seconds I need to punch his nutsack.

As he doubles over, I slam the wrist holding the knife against the wall. The weapon clatters down the stairs.

By now, he's recovered enough to head-butt me, and I go tumbling after the knife.

He's angry, but he's not stupid. Choosing to get the hell out as opposed to finishing me off, he stumbles up the stairwell and out the door at the top, still gasping from my punch.

I get up and scramble after him. When I open the door, I find myself on a side street: Mayfair Place.

The man is long gone.

My first call is to Jack. "I'll be there in a minute," he assures me.

My next call is to Dominic.

"AH, MRS. CRAIG!" DOMINIC'S VOICE IS AS SMOOTH AS VELVET. "I have wonderful news for you."

"You'd better. Someone just tried to kill me and, as you can imagine, I'm a bit peeved about it."

"Well you'll be happy to know that it couldn't have been the deliciously divine Ms. O'Toole."

"Perhaps not personally—unless she made a miraculous recovery from a sex change operation in the past hour—"

"Not Lucky. She is"—he sighs rapturously—"all woman. And all mine! In fact, her way of apologizing for wrongly accusing me of cheating was to send up the club's most expensive bottle of Bordeaux."

"What did she say in the note?" I ask.

"Something quite sensual: 'A bottle for sharing. See you at three o'clock.'" His chuckle is as giddy as a schoolgirl's.

"Did she sign the note?"

"Did she...Honestly, no." By Dominic's tone, he's back on the defensive.

Well, boohoo. I almost got killed, so I couldn't care less. Cruelly, I ask, "Are you sure it wasn't gifted by one of your two fuckcierges?"

"*Chateau Margaux*? Doubtful! Even if Prunella and Lavinia combined their salaries for two years, they could never afford it," he retorts haughtily. "In fact, the poor dears are so tight for tuppence that they actually demanded a loan from me! They suggested the photos they took of us *in flagrante delicto* act as collateral. Inwardly, I scoffed at their terms: interest-free, and with payback terms longer than any sane lender would consider—"

I groan at his cluelessness. "Like, say, *never*?"

"Well...one might see it that way."

"Yes, but that 'one' would have to have a brain. Dominic, those women were shaking you down!"

"Beg pardon?"

"They were blackmailing you."

"Oh...Well, perhaps," He sounds miffed. "In any event, it's a moot point. When I showed them that my camera set-up was far superior to theirs, they became exceedingly testy. They even had the audacity to say they'd report me to management! But when I pointed out that my relationship with Ms. O'Toole was probably on more solid ground than that of a mere employee, they saw the futility in playing *that* card..." Dominic's voice trails off. In time, he mutters, "You may be right."

Like, *duh.*

"As for the sender of the wine, you've made my case for me," he adds gruffly. "It had to be Lucky,"

"Who may have a hit squad at her disposal. Dominic, Nigel was just killed!"

"*What?*..." Shock tosses his bravado off a cliff. Clinging to the last vestige of his romantic fantasy, he retorts, "Why would you think that would have anything to do with Lucky?"

"Because she saw you and me together, on Bruton Street."

"But...How do you know?" He asked, deflated.

"As we told you, Abu is tailing her—and apparently, *she* was tailing *you.* After he saw her taking photos of us, Abu picked her pocket."

"The fact that she took our photo only indicates her jealous nature," he retorts airily. "Not that she's a killer."

"No, you dolt! *It indicates that she knows we work together*. The reason Nigel met with us was to tell us that Lucky saw my purse in your room! She told him so, in a fit of anger. She even described me to him. When he tried to convince her that Princess Maja looked nothing like me, she practically bit off his head."

My revelation draws a groan out of him.

I warn him: "Nigel was knifed in the subway. You're on her turf —*her club*. Just imagine what she'll do to you."

My heart pounds as I recall Nigel: legs sprawled apart, eyes rolled behind their lids, and the bright red stain on his coat.

"You're right. I've fallen in love with the target. My stupidity has cost two patriots their lives." Shame has muted Dominic's voice to a whisper.

Suddenly, I feel sorry for him. "Look," I whisper back, "Just stick to the mission."

"I will," he vows. Softly, he adds, "Do you think the wine is poisoned?"

"Gee, I don't know. But I wouldn't put it past her." Suddenly, I add, "But if it isn't, you need to spike it with the roofie powder before she shows up. We'll be a block or two away in a van. Leave word with the front desk that you're expecting a couple of friends, and that we're to be allowed up to your suite."

"Got it. Syringe through the cork. I'll open it in front of her so that she doesn't suspect." Dominic sighs. "In any event, she'll be the only one who drinks it."

That says a lot about the woman you think you love.

I don't dare say it aloud.

15

Lucky

*N*obody had seen her.

Our mystery woman was a ghost. A ghost who stashed very pricey handbags under beds, but a ghost just the same. I knew I wasn't crazy, but I wasn't getting very far either, and time was slipping like sand. A disguise would explain things. No doubt my mystery woman and the red leather-loving princess were one and the same, not that that would do me any good now. If the mystery woman graced my turf again it wouldn't be as any iteration of herself she'd shown before.

Dominic Fleming was the only common denominator.

I had rebuffed him rather harshly. Perhaps it was time to make up.

He hadn't returned to the club yet, but no doubt he'd turn up eventually. Thankfully, Julie once again held steadfast behind the reception desk. "Will you ping me when Mr. Fleming returns, please?"

"Yes, Miss, of course."

The miss was a nice touch—I'd asked, she'd listened. There was a promotion in her near future. I could see she wanted to say more, but she restrained herself. Yes, a very nice promotion.

While using precious time I didn't have, waiting for the opportunity to seduce someone I wouldn't invite into my home given any other choice, I decided to make a few turns around the casino. The first pass confirmed what I already knew: play was light, and everything was well in hand. Nothing like a well-oiled operation to make me feel redundant. The second pass proved more interesting.

Two men confronted each other in the doorway to the War Room. Backlit by light from the windows beyond, they appeared only as silhouettes. One I'd swear was Sheik Ben. The other, I wasn't sure, but he wore the morning coat and unctuous air of one of my staff. As I inched my way closer, working to not draw attention to myself, I could see from the postures of the two men, the conversation was heated. The sheik repeatedly pressed home his point with a forefinger jab to the other man's chest. My staff member, his hands clasped behind him, his chest puffed, took the obvious berating with equanimity, nary twitching a muscle.

I'd almost made it to eavesdropping distance when both men noticed me. With a lift of his chin, the sheik dismissed the other man. He turned toward me, his eyes lowered.

Gerald.

I nodded as he passed, then joined the sheik. His face a blotchy red, a tick working in his cheek, he tried to hide his seething with a tight smile. "Ms. O'Toole."

Formality. I guess I too had fallen out of grace—a tumble I'd taken many times before. "Sheik Ben." I glanced at the back of his retreating butler. "I take it you've found Gerald and his service wanting. Is there anything I can put to right?" Jeez, I'd been in-country for less than twenty-four hours and I already was losing the easy swing of American English.

"That won't be necessary." His smile flicked again, then fled. "I've not been able to reach my niece. She didn't show up for her shift today."

I didn't feel the need to reiterate the whole she's-dead thing. Once you hear that, it sticks—even if one didn't want to believe it. "I'm turning over every rock. Is everything as you desired in your room?"

"Of course. You keep looking for my niece. I hold you personally responsible." He raised his hand to give me a poke in the chest as he had Gerald, then he thought better of it, letting his hand drop. Wise man.

Normally a stickler for his demands being met precisely, he hadn't mentioned the flowers. After watching him stalk off toward the elevators, I returned to the front desk.

"Mr. Fleming just went up to his room…alone," Julie whispered conspiratorially as I approached.

"Impeccable timing then, thank you." I'd be hearing from him soon enough, I'd wager. My note and the wine should at least warrant a proper thank you. I tried to appear all-business, but I was rather alarmed that she would think I would lower myself to chase the likes of Dominic Fleming. A new low. "I have a question for you. Sheik Ben normally is a real stickler, isn't he?"

"Yes, miss. Silk sheets, his Champagne, yellow flowers, and Gerald. We all know the drill."

And had been stung by the whip when falling short, I gathered from her grimace. "Yet the flowers in his suite are red."

She winced. "I'll get that changed right away." Fluster and fear niggled at her composure. "I have no idea how that happened."

"No need. He hasn't complained. Guess he is trying to introduce a new era of kindness and understanding."

She looked like she didn't believe it.

I didn't either. Miss P had said yellow. Someone had intercepted the order and changed it.

I needed to know who.

This one I could do on my own.

"Julie, just checking, but you did send a bottle of our very best Bordeaux to Mr. Fleming's room?

"Yes, miss. With only your note. No signature." She looked a bit bilious. My stock was falling like it was 1929.

I made my way to the alcove just off the lobby. It used to hold a telegraph then a telephone, now it stood as testament to the cost of change. I closed the bi-fold door and pulled out my phone. Now all I had to do was remember my password into the employee network, then another into the accounting ledger. After so many tries that I only had one left before being sent to the digital hoosegow, I made it past go without being sent to jail. A quick search and I found the flower requisition.

Yesterday.

And I'd been right, Red Dahlias. I gave a low whistle. They must be out of season…waaay out of season. I looked for the signature.

Aziza.

She wasn't even trying to cover her tracks. Something had her spooked, and with good reason. But why change the flowers? And why did she replace them with expensive flowers?

I logged off. One more question without an answer.

Time to get a few from the Fleming peacock. I didn't doubt I could get what I wanted. The larger question was *would* I, before he dove across the line and flipped my last switch.

Time to find out.

I stood up. *Sit up. Stand up. Throw up.* A quote from one of my fave films, *Victor/Victoria* and more than apropos. For the first time ever, I felt a kinship with Julie Andrews in all her petite perfection. I tried to take strength from that.

With patience at a low ebb, I would need it.

"I WONDERED WHO MIGHT SHOW UP. I NEVER EXPECTED IT WOULD BE you." Dominic had changed into lounging pajamas. On most men the look would be fey. On him? Not so much. The broad shoulders, the just-right bit of smooth skin and chest hair visible where he'd left the top button unbuttoned. Handsome for sure, but the fact he knew it, even wore it like a birthright, lessened its effect.

On unsteady knees, I used the doorway to hold my bulk as I tried to look all casual and seductive. I think I probably ended up looking like I had to pee.

Clearly, he was a man of indiscriminate taste—he stepped to the side and invited me in. My bottle of Bordeaux sat on the small table next to the small window with the terrible view. Julie had taken me at my word—Chateau Margaux, sufficiently aged to set me back four figures. Two glasses, both empty, stood next to it. He'd suspected, but he hadn't been sure.

To be honest, doubt pummeled me at the moment as well. I twirled the ring on my left ring finger—a nervous habit. A tentable ring, as my mother called it—so large it could be seen ten tables away. My chef didn't scrimp—on anything. He was a man of his word. And one of very discriminating tastes. I'd made my promise and I intended to honor it.

Now, how to get what I wanted without having to sacrifice my principles or break Mr. Fleming's perfect Roman nose?

I shrugged myself off the doorjamb. "I behaved badly. I'd like to make it up to you."

His cheeks were still flushed from the cold, his fingers cool when they brushed the small of my back as he ushered me inside. A chill shivered through me.

You shouldn't be here.

A young woman had died. And I'd appointed myself Inspector Clouseau. Not that this was new or anything, but just once you'd think I'd learn to accept a seat on the sidelines. As I looked for my own little bit of Switzerland in which to stand—not too close to the bed, and not looking like I was ready to jump out the window—I studiously avoided the sex-in-the-Poconos set-up. "I thought you might let the wine breathe a bit."

"An oversight, but as I didn't know when you might arrive…" Seductions usually weren't lunchtime quickies. "Besides, I thought you might like to do the honors. An impressive and educated choice, I might add."

It was rather thoughtful of him, allowing me to see he hadn't doctored the wine. Although, Dominic Fleming, as overstated as he was, didn't seem the type to have to pull a Bill Cosby, but I appreciated his consideration all the same. I did the honors. "Wine?"

He took the glass I offered. He did the gentlemanly thing,

waiting for me to join him. I poured myself a healthy dose before he set his glass on the table.

Maybe he didn't need a quick shot of liquid courage, but I sure did.

Despite my best efforts to hide it, my hands shook. I'd played out this cat-and-mouse game a hundred times…no, more than that. Sin City invited boorish behavior. Yet, tonight I felt somehow in over my head.

Dominic Fleming was a foolish parody of the man he wanted to be. *Nothing to worry about.* I smiled as I eyed him over the lip of my glass, then took a sip. Sex in a bottle, someone had said when reviewing this particular vintage. Reluctantly, I agreed. One taste and lesser women would shed clothing for more. Probably not the right wine to have sent. Leave it to me to screw up a feigned seduction.

My attention turned back to the man in front of me, oozing virility and confidence. A warning bell echoed somewhere in the dark recesses of my gut which tension tied in knots.

Was he a fool, or merely playing one? A sliver of fear cut through me as my gut gave me the answer I feared. In over my head in a foreign country with no one to ride to the rescue and in a compromising situation. Would that be going out on top or on the bottom?

Neither would be satisfying.

"How do you propose making amends for your boorish behavior," he pressed a hand to his chest, his most delicious chest, "and most hurtful rebuff?"

"Well," I sidled in close and played with the collar of his pajamas. "What could I do to possibly make you feel better?" Jesus, I sounded like a complete idiot. How did women do this without throwing up?

Now I pretty much knew who was the fool in this duo.

Without warning, he grabbed my wrist and jerked me toward the bed behind him. My wine went flying, hitting like blood spatter as the burgundy liquid stitched the wall. "*Shit!*"

He landed on top of me, pinning me beneath him, his hands

encircling my wrists, a knee in my stomach.

Most of my breath left me in a whoosh. "Okay, you like it rough," I wheezed, using my last bit of breath. "I'm down with that." *I was so not down with that!* I sucked in a lungful of air. "But that was a waste of superb vino."

"A small price to pay to taste your delectables."

He *so* did not say that, did he?

He'd called my bluff and raised it. *"Enough!"* I got a knee underneath him, then pushed upwards as hard as I could. At the same time, I lifted my head. Our foreheads met with a meaty thunk. I was prepared; he was not. His grasp on my wrists loosened with surprise. I yanked my hands free. Pushing him all the way off me, I rolled off the other side of the bed. I staggered as I centered myself over my feet. The blow had left me woozy.

Dominic didn't appear at all affected, other than maybe being a bit put out. He rubbed the red splotch on his forehead as he eyed me across the bed. "You and I have slightly different definitions of making nice."

"You gave me every indication you like it rough." My world spun. I blinked rapidly trying to bring the room into focus. Stars flitted by.

"Why are you here? And what game are you playing?" Dominic inched closer, moving around the end of the bed.

"Stay there!" I staggered once to the side. My hand found the window sash.

He stopped.

"What game am *I* playing? *Me?*" The room spun around me as if I was Dorothy being carried to Oz.

I glanced at his glass of wine, still untouched.

I had taken a couple of long pulls on mine before it had been sacrificed to foreplay.

"What did you do?" My vision telescoped until a pinprick of light was all I saw. Then the light went out.

The world faded. Noises retreated.

He caught me as I fell.

Then nothing.

16

Donna

"*T*he deed is done," Dominic is heaving so loudly on speakerphone that I worry he may be having a heart attack. "I feel terrible about it!"

It's almost a quarter after three. Abu has procured a limo and driven us to an alley beside the Babylon Club London. Jack and I are in the back seat with Arnie, who is still hacked into the club's security system. Since Dominic has already told the concierge desk to allow us to go up to his room, we probably won't need to scrub footage. Still, planning for unforeseen circumstances is covert ops standard operating procedure.

The goal is to walk Lucky right out the front door under her own power. By allowing her staff to see her leave of her own free will, they'll accept her absence no matter how long she's gone. If she refuses to tell us the truth about her role in Aziza's death, she may be gone from here—and everywhere—permanently. The CIA doesn't take kindly to one of its operatives being exterminated, let alone two.

"I take it that means Lucky is out cold?"

"Yes. But…I'm keeping her warm," Dominic assures us.

Jack covers the phone's mic with his palm. "What the hell do you think that means?" he hisses to me.

I drop my head, disgusted. "My guess is that he's got her laid out on his bed, surrounded by rose petals and burning scented candles."

Arnie's mouth drops open. "Like Sleeping Beauty?"

"More like a fool in love," I mutter.

"No, more like the narcissistic knucklehead he is, especially to the one woman who's turned down his come-ons," Jack declares.

"Hey, I turned him down, too!" I point out.

"Barely," Jack grumbles.

From his sly smile, I realize he's teasing me.

Arnie is staring at his computer screen. "Well, whattaya know—Dominic has a video camera linked to his phone…and right now he's changing out of his pajamas." Arnie's eyes open wide. "Did they…well, you know—do the dirty deed?"

"If so, and he wore those pajamas, that might have been enough torture for the poor girl," Jack declares.

He deserves—and receives—a pinch for that.

Then I open the car door and pull him through it.

For our disguises, Jack's hair is temporarily streaked blond and rises above his head, like blades of grass on an unruly lawn. He wears round tortoise shell glasses. A bright, red cashmere scarf gives his bespoke tuxedo a jaunty nonchalance.

The curly auburn locks of my wig practically reach my waist. My silver sequined dress covers so little skin that it might better be described as a well-placed Band-Aid. Despite the chill, my silver fox stole hangs off one shoulder; a large, gaudy Mylar handbag over the other.

By the time the bellman opens the front door, Jack has lowered a hand, resting it on the center of my bum, like some cheeky chappy steering his tarty party girl into their first stop of many during this night on the town.

As we waltz in, I look at the front desk, and suddenly it hits me: Nigel isn't there to cast a disdainful yet knowing eye on us.

He did an admirable job of hiding his fervent patriotism beneath a milquetoast demeanor.

As if reading my mind, Jack draws me into a kiss but first whispers, "Don't worry, Lucky will pay for it."

BY THE TIME WE REACH THE CONCIERGE DESK, I'VE PULLED MYSELF OUT of Jack's lip lock and purr, "Breathless Mahoney and Sir John Finsbury to see Mr. Fleming."

I'm sure that Prunella and Lavinia's scowls have nothing to do with my spot on Scottish accent and everything to do with Dominic's rebuttal of their blackmail scheme. Watching Lucky waltz out of here on Dominic's arm will undoubtedly add to their angst.

"Yes, Mr. Fleming is expecting you," Lavinia sniffs. She nods to Prunella, who saunters out from behind the desk to ring for the elevator. When it arrives, she inserts her security card then mumbles, "Third floor, room three double O seven."

"No surprise there," Jack murmurs as the doors close.

As the lift rises, we hide our faces from the camera the most natural way possible: by feigning uncontrollable lust.

The second Jack backs me up against the back wall, his hands and lips wander over me. To make our touchy-feely game easier for him, my left leg snakes over his hip. When I draw him in so close, he murmurs, "I want to be able to walk out of here on two legs, not three."

Okay, full disclosure here: we ain't faking nothin'.

The elevator announces our floor with a chime that seems to have been stolen from Big Ben.

Come to think of it that might be a cute nickname for Jack's third leg. After our mission is accomplished, I'll ask him what he thinks of this idea. It'll give us something fun to remember this mission by, other than death, deceit, and a torture session that may be necessary but won't be easy on any of us—

Least of all, Lucky.

I AM HAPPY TO REPORT THAT MS. O'TOOLE IS NOT THE SUBJECT OF A Sleeping Beauty diorama. Still, I find it disconcerting to find her on Dominic's lap, propped up like a rag doll.

Tenderly, he strokes her cheek. She mumbles something, but I can't make it out. "Fuck off," maybe?

To Dominic, even that indistinguishable utterance is a term of endearment. Still, he is concerned enough that a tiny wrinkle is creasing his Botoxed brow. "During the interrogation, Craigs, I only ask that you don't break her pert little nose!"

"Gee, okay. Any other requests?" I open my bag as if rummaging for a notepad. Instead, I pull out a couple of clear, snap-on two-hand restraints along with a black wool crepe cape that we'll fling over Lucky to shield the fact that her march through the lobby is being coerced.

My question puts a grateful smile on Dominic's lips. "Since you asked: please spare her eyes. They are the most lovely shade of blue!" He lifts one of her eyelids to make his point.

Jack gives a grudging nod. "I'll see what I can do. Hey, Dom, listen: I have no problem going in with a good cop-bad cop stance —you, being the good cop, of course. But, should things get a little rough—waterboarding, electric shock, I have to cut off a finger joint or two—can I count on you to hold it together? No crying, no tearful pleas to stop? You know, nothing that may make Ryan ask us to put you out of your misery too…" Jack's voice trails off.

Still, he waits patiently for an answer.

I take it as a good sign that Dominic's back stiffens with indig-nation. "You're planning a full black-site interrogation? My God, man! By rough, I thought you meant a little slap and tickle— which, quite frankly, I could have easily handled here without you."

Oh, brother. "I think you have your answer," I inform Jack.

Before Jack slaps Dominic silly, I move between them. "Stand her up," I tell Dominic.

He does as I ask, but Lucky almost tips over.

Thankfully, Jack catches her.

I snap one side of a two-hand restraint on Lucky's left wrist. I then position Dominic on her right and take his left arm and put it around her waist before snapping the second part of her restraint on his left hand.

"Now, put your hand over hers."

As Dominic does this, Lucky's cuffed arm bends naturally, giving the impression of intimate closeness. "Now, walk her around the room a few times."

At first, her movements are slow and sloppy, like a marionette with a few snipped strings. Soon, though, her sluggishness is barely noticeable.

Staring at them in wonder, Jack asks, "How did you come up with this idea?"

"When I go to Trisha's ballet classes, I watch the choreography," I explain. "Of course, the students aren't doped and slurring their words."

Just as Lucky is doing now, unfortunately.

"What can we do about that?" Jack asks.

"We converse with her," I reply. "Jack, you walk on Lucky's left side. Be alert in case she slips or trips. Dominic, you and Jack should talk to each other, as if she's all there and you're having an intense conversation with her. I'll laugh and chime in periodically."

I take the cape and tie it around Lucky. It covers the restraints, no problem.

"Are we ready?" I ask.

Dominic nods hesitantly.

And we're off.

"You guys look great," Arnie murmurs through our earbuds. He's watching us through the club's feed.

The elevator chimes when it reaches the ground floor. Dominic and Jack, steering Lucky between them, begin a heated discussion of a recent Premier League football game between Tottenham Hotspur and Newcastle United. Walking beside Jack, I giggle and lean in as if sharing asides with Lucky, whose tongue is too thick to form words with vowels.

We've almost made it to the front door when one of the receptionists comes rushing over: the sweet one, Julie. "Ms. O'Toole? Ms. O'Toole! I'm sorry to disturb you, but Mr. Ahern seems to have disappeared—"

At that second, Dominic suddenly stops short, and Lucky's head swings right: giving Dominic the perfect opportunity to kiss her.

It is a long kiss.

Too long.

My God, if he doesn't let her come up for air, he may kill her before we get the answers we need...

I turn to Julie, who seems to have turned to stone. From the look on her face, she's more than shocked; she's horrified.

To break the spell, I tap her on the shoulder. "Are you inquiring about the club's manager, dear?...Yes?...As it turns out, Ms. O'Toole received a phone call just as we left Mr. Fleming's room. It seems that Mr. Ahern was called away on a family emergency."

"Oh..." Julie frowns, seemingly perplexed by this new bit of information.

As Dominic and Jack sweep Lucky out the door, I add, "She tried to reach someone else in the front office—someone by the name of Julie, I think?"

"That would be me."

"Ah, brilliant! She wanted to ask you to take over Mr. Ahern's duties this evening while she entertains Mr. Fleming." I nod in their direction. "Don't they make an adorable couple? Granted, it all happened so very fast!" Nudging her, I add, "It may look as if he's swept her off her feet, but in truth, she made the first move— with a bottle of Chateaux Margaux! Smart, wasn't it?" I wink knowingly. "Well, ta-ta for now!"

"WHERE IS THE BLACK SITE?" I ASK.

Lucky has passed out in the back of the limousine. Dominic cradles her head in his lap. In that dubious position, it dawns on me that, at least for now, Lucky isn't living up to her name.

Dominic shrugs at my question. "Barchester Manor. It's across from Regent's Park, on Outer Circle."

"Posh area," I murmur.

"It should be. I paid enough for it," Dominic murmurs.

I raise a brow.

"Acme rents it from me, but I'm allowed to use it when I'm in town."

"Is it secluded?" Jack asks.

"It's on four acres." Dominic glares at Jack. "No one should hear her screams if that's what you're asking."

It is, but Dominic already knows this.

It's only a fifteen-minute ride.

A brick wall surrounds the home and its massive gardens. Dominic gives Abu the security code that swings open the wrought iron gate. A four-story brick Gothic-era mansion crowns the circular quarter-mile gravel driveway.

The estate's exterior boasts three arched entry doors. A turret sits on its left like a crown shoved to one side of a monarch's head. Above the gabled attic, there are enough chimneys to employ an army of sweeps.

"Give us the tour," Jack suggests to Dominic. "Arnie, come in with us. Abu, watch Sleeping Beauty for a few minutes, okay?"

Abu nods as he repositions the rearview mirror on Lucky.

The interior is just as impressive: each of the main floor's rooms —foyer, living room, dining room, library—is traditionally styled with oversized Queen Anne furnishings and portraits of regal ancestors. And yet, no modern amenity is spared.

"This is more like a grand hotel than a black site," Jack notes.

Dominic nods towards an alcove tucked off the central hall. "You've yet to see the dungeon."

The alcove holds an elevator. When Dominic pushes the button, it opens immediately. *"Entrez vous."*

WE DESCEND INTO A BASEMENT. OKAY, TO BE HONEST, IT'S MORE LIKE some dominatrix's fantasy lair.

One of its black lacquer walls is covered with a torturer's treasure trove of paddles, whips, and chains. Backlit shelves cover another wall. One is filled with dummy heads wearing an assortment of ball gags and submission masks. Another shelf displays dildos of various shapes and sizes standing at attention.

In a corner of the room, a standing closet holds various costumes as well as colorful leather or rubber catsuits, crotchless pants, and barely-there restraints.

Spanking benches, hard chairs, and various torture contraptions are filtered throughout the room. There are also a couple of cages. One hangs from the ceiling.

Incredulous, Jack swings it gently. "Do you mean to tell me that Ryan approved this—*this porn star's playpen* as our official London black site?"

"Well...no, not exactly," Dominic shrugs. "This is a private space for the few guests I have who enjoy this sort of thing. Truth be told, Acme's rental is...well, it's in there." He points to a door on the back wall. Because it is also lacquered black and has no molding around it, I hadn't noticed it before.

He takes an old rusty iron key from the hook beside the door. "Follow me."

His tone seems to plea for us to do anything but that.

THIS SECOND ROOM IS MUCH LARGER. I'D GUESS IT RUNS NEARLY THE length of the mansion. There are no windows and it smells dank. The floor, hard-packed and dusty, slants slightly toward the middle of the room where five drains have been placed every thirty feet or so. Red streaks angle diagonally toward them, giving the effect of rays emanating from the sun. A bucket holding towels is stained a ruby hue.

It reeks of death.

One of the roughhewn stone walls is lined with wooden shelves that hold various tools: hammers, wrenches, screwdrivers, hatchets, knives, machetes, chainsaws, hoses, and scissors. On another wall, collars, neck high, are bolted above chains of varying lengths.

Jack wanders over to the tool wall. After scanning his choices, he picks up a hammer to measure its heft before setting it down again. The next thing that catches his eye is a handheld pipe vise.

"Yeah, I think this will do—for starters, anyway," he murmurs. "Donna, tell Abu to bring the guest star through Door Number Two."

Hearing this, Dominic drops onto a backless bench and buries his head in his hands.

Jack sighs as he drops the vise on the table. "Okay, listen: we'll start in your playpen first. But if she doesn't give up the ghost, I'll grab a few toys from Acme's side of the dungeon. Got it?"

Dominic nods miserably.

For once, I feel sorry for him and Lucky too.

17

Lucky

The open-handed slap across my cheek slammed my head to the left. The backhand from the other side launched it back to the right. I could taste blood as my lip swelled. I let my head hang, my chin on my chest, as I worked to unscramble the thoughts pinging around my empty skull.

Where was I? I moved—only millimeters to hide my returning faculties. Okay, someone had secured me to a chair, my hands tied behind me. My feet were free—an oversight I intended to punish him with...I knew it was a man. Large hand, controlled strength that left my cheeks stinging.

Okay, I was tied to a chair. But where? How had I gotten here? Last I remembered I was in a room at the club. There was red wine...bodacious red wine.

Dominic.

"No more." A female voice. "I think she's coming around."

Cold water hit me full face. I gasped against the cold. Slapping me I could forgive. But making me redo my hair? Unforgivable.

I blinked against the water dripping from tendrils of hair glued to my forehead.

As suspected a man came into view, but not the one I expected.

This one had brown curls, a cleft in his chin, and green eyes, I thought, but with the light shining from behind him and toward me in the best Hollywood interrogation manner, it was hard to tell.

I had walked into some British spy farce. That was the only explanation. Every man I'd met since arriving seemed to be trying to get in touch with his inner international spy. Not attractive. Not even on the nice specimen of the Y-chromosome set standing in front of me, his hand raised ready to strike again.

Rope burned against my skin as I moved my wrists and worked my hands. "I'm not sure I can feel my hands." I raised my head high and my gaze steady as it locked with his.

Green Eyes seemed unconcerned, but he dropped his hand.

Even though I couldn't see her, I knew a woman was there. I'd heard her, and, despite my scrambled brains, I hadn't imagined it. That made two against my one—odds I could live with. But there was someone else skulking in the shadows behind the light. I'd caught his stench.

Squinting against the light, I took stock of my surroundings. Glossy black walls. Enough bondage toys to stock a Great Expectations megastore. But what Green Eyes held in his hand wasn't the usual slap-and-tickle trinket but hardware meant to maim.

One thing I knew: if I screamed, no one would hear me. "So, whose little pleasure palace is this?"

"One of our colleague's family home."

Dominic.

At least he was consistent. But this latest revelation made my skin crawl.

I'd deal with him later. Right now, Green Eyes needed to be taught some manners.

"Hitting a woman while she's tied to a chair is hardly noble. Untie me and we'll let the best man win." I squinted one eye to bring him into focus.

He gave me a slow grin. "Playing fair isn't on my longevity plan. And, from what I've seen, it isn't a tool in your box either."

A tool in my box? He sounded American. Surely he knew better.

Cotton lined my mouth, but it couldn't hide a metallic taste. A headache pulsed in my left temple. Dizziness still lingered. I tried to move my feet but could only slide them a few inches.

I'd been roofied.

But I'd opened the wine and chosen my glass. "How'd you do it?" I asked the darkness.

"Syringe through the cork." The melodious tones of Dominic Fleming. Yep, I'd been right about the stench.

"You're a dead man."

"Lucky, I swear, I drugged you under grave duress. I have the utmost respect for you."

"High praise coming from a guy who has to roofie his conquests. You're still a dead man."

Green Eyes seemed to relish that idea.

"Same price for two, big guy."

"You'll have to go through me first." A woman shouldered in between us. Dark hair, intense, the woman's shoulders bowed a bit under the weight of worry, but a murderous look sharpened her features.

"Ah, the killer with nice taste in handbags." She didn't look like your normal killer, whatever that was. Ordinary, leapt to mind. The housewife next door. Women sporting the same look flooded through my hotels on a regular basis, bored despite the teenagers and requisite domesticated animals and husband, and now looking for adventure. Some found what they were looking for. Sometimes it killed them. "Why'd you do it? She was just a kid." I tugged at the ropes binding my wrists, ignoring the sting of raw flesh.

"*Me?*" Anger radiated off the woman and punched up the color in her cheeks. "She was dead when I got there."

Green Eyes stepped to the side. Nothing like a guy who deferred to a lady. He left me toe-to toe with the mystery woman, who loomed over me. "*You* killed her." The woman poked my shoulder.

I laughed, I couldn't help it. And didn't want to. It helped to control my anger. "I arrived in the Royal Suite after you left—I passed you at the elevator. You said she was dead when you found her. And you think I killed her? An already dead girl? To me, the facts support the theory that *you* killed her." When I'd found Aziza she wasn't fresh dead, but I went with what I could bullshit. Government types in the business of killing would see through me. Hired assassins, perhaps not.

"Her body had time to cool a few degrees before I found her."

I lean forward against my restraints. "Your word against mine."

"Don't be so smug. You don't even know what's going down at your club right under your nose." The woman vibrated with anger.

Dominic cleared his throat—a nervous habit.

"You won't rattle me, if that's what you're trying to do." A bluff, but not a big one. The lady was totally pissing me off. Anger focused me.

"Two of your desk clerks are sleeping with the members and trying to shake them down." She sounded triumphant. "Right, Dominic?"

Silence. But I could put the pieces together. He was such a cliché.

"Wouldn't be the first time." I worked to blink slowly, to appear unruffled. However, inside I was aching to wring a few necks.

"You had Aziza killed. Somebody like you wouldn't get her own hands dirty."

Somebody like me. Before this encounter I would've agreed with her. Now, as I contemplated homicide…her homicide…I was pretty sure getting my hands dirty would be worth the jail time. "Did she have something to do with the shakedown?"

"We haven't connected all the dots yet."

Simple answer: *we don't know.*

"How did she die?" My question seemed to throw her off.

"Heart attack."

I felt my eyebrows shoot toward my hairline. "She was all of what—twenty-three?"

"Heart condition." Donna eyed me intently.

I thought for a moment. The two marks on the back of her neck —I'd seen those before. "Taser?"

"Bad combination. But you would have known that, wouldn't you? Since it was in her employment records."

"You've got to be kidding!" Anger flared anew and I struggled against the ropes, rubbing my wrists raw. If I could just get my hands free I'd show them I was more than willing to kill when the situation dictated.

But, considering my current situation, today was a day to choose my battles wisely. I let it go. "Why would I kill Aziza? On my own property, no less? Other than angling for the top prize in this year's Stupidest Criminal." This show was getting old. If I could only get a hand loose. I worked my hand, but the rope only cut deeper.

"She was on to you. You were desperate."

"On to me?" My voice sounded shrill, even to me.

"Yep, the same reason you had Nigel killed."

"*Whaaaat?*" That knocked the stuffing out of me. "I didn't like the guy—much too priggish for me—but I can't see killing someone for being irritating." I angled a look up at the woman. "Although, I'm coming around. Want to tell me why you think I'm killing off my staff?"

The unmistakable ringtone of my phone split the tension. Green Eyes pulled it from his pocket, gave me a hard stare, then answered it. "Yo."

The thing was password protected and locked up tight absent the right word or my thumbprint. At my questioning look, he put his index finger over the microphone. "You'd be surprised how easy it is to lift a thumbprint."

"Who are you people? And why'd you steal my phone?" I said it loud enough for the person on the other end to have heard, but Green Eyes still covered the mic.

"Don't." His voice had a cruel edge to it.

No one answered my question as all eyes focused on the cute dude with my phone.

"Who is this?" The unmistakable irritation of only one person echoed through the line loud enough for all to hear.

Mona.

"Jean-Charles? Is that you? Where's Lucky?"

"She's tied up." Green Eyes clearly enjoyed this. "Who is this?"

"What?" Mona spluttered. The gravest sin imaginable to my mother was that someone wouldn't know her. "What do you mean 'who is this?' This is her mother. Where is Jean-Charles?"

"That I couldn't tell you."

"You put Lucky on right this minute!"

Green Eyes hung up.

I winced. Second gravest sin. "Not a good idea. That will piss her off. When she's pissed, she won't stop until she gets even."

The poor man ignored me. My phone rang again. This time he didn't even get a word in before my mother started. "Young man, your impertinence is a personal affront. Your mother would be disappointed. You put my daughter on the line right now!"

He hung up again.

The phone sang out again.

Dominic still lurked in the shadows. "You opened this can of worms, Old Boy."

Green Eyes smiled. "The caller ID came up as TERRORIST. Hard to resist."

The mystery woman, who had been watching this with amusement, weighed in. "We have her phone. Even though Tech Ops has masked the signal, it's still an open lead to us. Let Lucky mollify her mother, then she's off our backs."

I rolled my eyes. "My phone is a one-stop mayhem shop? If that were true, I really would be too stupid to live."

"You're laundering money through your casinos for various terrorist cells," Mystery Woman said. "I'd say that qualifies."

"What?" I spit the word at her. "I have billions of dollars' worth of properties around the world that are very good at converting money into entertainment for gamblers and profit for me. If there is even a whiff of money laundering, they'll jerk my gaming license so fast I won't have time to clear the tables and drain the slot machines. Do you have any idea what is at stake? If I'm laundering money, I really would be too stupid to live." I didn't even ask them if they had proof. They didn't. This was a fishing expedition.

"I think she's legit." Dominic, the lone voice of reason and my champion. I wasn't sure if that was a good thing or a bad thing.

"You're the good cop hiding in the shadows and Green Eyes here is the bad cop? Don't waste your time. I've played this game many times before, although I've never been the rube the cops were trying to break. It's interesting, but you're not very good at it."

A tic worked in Green Eye's cheek as my phone rang again. His gaze shifted to me. "Is your mother always like this?"

I shrugged.

"Jesus, I get the whole 'Terrorist 'caller ID thing."

"Yes, I console myself with the thought that she is penance for past bad deeds. Although, if I'd been that bad, I wish I could remember all the fun of it. Seems a bit harsh without that bit of quid-pro-quo. She's relentless; she won't stop."

"That maternal apple didn't fall far," Green Eyes said to the woman.

Normally any comparison to Mona filled me with indignation. Today, not so much.

"Take the call," Green Eyes said to me. "Play it straight."

I wanted to ask 'or what?' but at this point it didn't matter. No way in hell would Mona ride to my rescue. Why couldn't it be Detective Romeo, the ace-up-my-sleeve at the Metropolitan Police Department in Vegas, calling me about something grisly?

Green Eyes slid his finger across to answer the call, then held the phone to my ear.

"Hello, Mother."

"Lucky!" Mona adopted her how-could-you tone. "Who was that horrible man? Where are you? What are you doing? When are you going to Paris? You don't want to let that fabulous French chef wiggle off the hook now, do you? At your age, you don't have many options. You know what they say, a woman approaching forty has less chance of finding a husband than being struck by lightning."

For a moment I was at a loss, stripped bare like a mannequin in a department store window. "Thank you for that." I was years away from forty, but now was not the time to pick that bone. "I'd misplaced my phone. The man was returning it. I'm a bit busy right now. Can I call you back?"

"When are you going to Paris?"

"Mother, I can't talk."

"Well, you can listen then. It's very important."

We often had radically differing opinions as to what constituted "important" but I'd rather face a firing squad than take the fallout from ignoring the huff in her voice. "Make it quick."

"Okay," she puffed as if she was plumping verbal pillows then settling in for the story. "About the names for the twins."

"Seriously?" The squeak in my voice could shatter crystal.

"Lucky, this is very important. I'm setting the whole tone for my daughters' lives here. Their names could make or break them."

Overstating but she had a point, and I was its poster child. Naming me Lucky made me anything but. "Give them to me."

"Sugar and Spice," she announced with a triumphant gloat.

There was a collective sigh on my end from all of us in the room.

"Didn't they sing with Beyoncé?" Stupid, but that was the only thing that leapt to mind.

"No." Her gloat melted into a whine.

"I'd avoid pop culture references, if I were you, Mother. Too much baggage for two beautiful, vibrant young ladies to shoulder." I should know. My name always conjured Lucky Luciano. Not exactly the image my mother intended. Although perpetually well-intentioned, Mona almost always fell short in the execution.

"You think so?"

"I *know* so."

A sigh—her version of a verbal foot stomp—then the line went dead.

Green Eyes retracted the phone. "I get the terrorist thing now."

"Mona is an iceberg. What you see is dwarfed by what she's hiding." That shut him up for a moment, which I seized. "Who the hell are you people and what could you possibly want from me? And, for the record, you catch more flies with honey."

"My sentiments exactly." Dominic, who had stepped out of the shadows, glared at Green Eyes.

Looks passed between the three of them. An unspoken consensus was reached.

"Okay, if you're innocent, why didn't you sound the alarm and call the police when you found Aziza's body?" Mystery Woman asked.

"Her uncle, a prominent sheik, was due to arrive any minute. My staff would have escorted him to the Royal Suite. I needed to divert him. I never thought anyone would tamper with the crime scene." I leveled a gaze at her. "You took the body and cleaned the room, didn't you?"

She didn't answer, but that was really the only explanation.

"Which government do you work for? Please tell me so I can make sure I don't reside in the country you three are protecting. You drug an innocent citizen, slap her around, then ruin her hair. Hell of a thing."

Mystery Woman smiled at the hair bit. Either she was coming around to my way of thinking, or she'd figured out how she wanted to kill me. "What did you want with Aziza?" she asked.

"To smooth over a prickly family situation. Her uncle is our partner in this property, a minority partner. Her father is much more powerful. The Saudis take a dim view of the Royal family's females taking jobs."

"That was it?" My answer left her a bit slack-jawed.

"All the glamour in my job is in my title. I showed you mine. Now it's your turn. Which government?"

She glanced at the green-eyed dude. "Black ops, on hire to the CIA."

My turn to be a bit slack-jawed. "And Aziza?" What had the girl gotten herself into?

The Mystery Woman clammed up. "Need-to-know basis."

"Oh, I need to know. You need me to know. She was killed in my hotel. I have eyes and ears there who would never spill their guts to you." I stopped, worried I was overplaying.

"Okay. I'm Donna, this is Jack." She nudged Green Eyes in the ribs. "My husband."

"Lucky's taken," Dominic added. "Not to worry."

They both turned and gave him a long stare.

"Her fiancé?" He reddened under their gaze. "I'm sure you caught her ring," he stammered, looking oddly uncomfortable.

Donna turned back to me. Hooking a thumb over her shoulder, she said, "You know the comic relief. Former MI6, he's with us now."

"And Nigel?"

"Aziza's handler." Jack said. "She was supposed to pass some intel to Donna."

"Some info about a money trail, I'm guessing? And you thought it flowed through my property?"

"Still not sure it didn't." Donna stuck to her original theory.

"Gaming is the most regulated industry on the planet. If anyone wants to launder money through a casino, Macau is your spot. Not here and most assuredly not in the U.S."

She didn't quite let go of her theory, but my logic seemed to be prying her mental fingers from it. "So how do we know you're legit? Got anyone we'd believe who can vouch for you?"

In this little game of one-upmanship, I held the ace. "Would your Director do? Or perhaps POTUS?"

My merry band of government morons scoffed at me.

"Untie me. Give me the phone." If they bit, it would give me a chance to check their bona fides as well.

With only a moment's hesitation, Jack did as I demanded.

I circled my hands working my wrists, but it still took a bit for the blood flow to hit and enough feeling to return for me to keep hold of the phone.

The Big Boss answered on the first ring. "Lucky! What is going on? Are you okay? Sheik Ben is apoplectic. You were to keep him happy. No one can find you."

"I'm fine. Things are a bit out of hand. I need a favor." I cupped my hand around the phone and posed a question to the three in front of me. "Which will it be? The DIO or POTUS?"

18

Donna

"*H*ey, so, we have a wee bit of a situation." I applaud Jack's opening line to Ryan. Coupled with his calm tone of voice, it wouldn't set off any alarms for the average person.

However, Ryan knows us too well to hear this as anything other than "WE MAY BE IN THE MIDDLE OF A SHITSTORM."

Ryan sighs. "How can I help?"

"Can you arrange a conference call with DIO Branham? The prime suspect has indicated that he can verify her bona fides. We feel it might be useful before proceeding with the interrogation."

"That's a polite way of putting it," Lucky declares.

Jack holds up an index finger to silence her, but he's grinning too. She may think she's goading him, but she doesn't know him like I do. As an interrogation tactic, he always views torture as a last resort. That goes double in this sort of case, where there is a good amount of circumstantial evidence against Lucky but no hard proof. If she's involved in any way, he hopes to scare the information out of her before he turns the screws on her, literally.

"Of course. I'll contact him now. Stand by." Ryan puts the call on hold.

By now, Abu and Arnie have joined us here in Dominic's playpen. Everyone waits silently. Jack and Abu's faces are blandly unreadable. I'd like to think mine is too. Dominic purses his lips. His eyes, limpid with love, have yet to leave Lucky's face.

On the other hand, our prisoner shifts her angry gaze to each of us. When her eyes reach Dominic, they narrow. Disdain weighs on the corners of her mouth, pushing them downward into a grimace.

Even if she's cleared, I doubt he'll be able to convince her that he has always had her—and our country's—best interests at heart.

Lucky glances at Arnie, who is roaming the room. Every now and then something will grab his attention and we'll hear his low whistle or a shocked guffaw. But then his attempt to straddle a sex swing results in a back flip that entangles him in the leather straps, almost strangling him.

Lucky rolls her eyes. "Can someone help the pudgy guy out of that contraption? I'd hate to take the heat for yet one more agent's death."

Abu groans, but walks over anyway. After perusing the situation, he pulls a lever. Arnie falls to the floor with a yelp.

Seeing Jack's smile, Lucky allows herself a ghost of a grin.

She may not know it yet, but I pray that Branham will clear her. Having Lucky working with us may make all the difference in how quickly we find Aziza's killer, not to mention the cipher to break open her intel. That way neither Aziza nor Nigel will have died in vain.

"WHO ARE YOU HOLDING AGAIN?" DIRECTOR OF INTELLIGENCE Marcus Branham's question to Jack comes after a long pause and in a measured tone.

I can't tell if his question means he's never heard of her, or that it's a bad phone connection, or that he's incredulous that we'd do such a thing to Ms. Lucky O'Toole.

The first scenario gets her a bullet behind the ear and a burial at sea for being such an audacious liar. We'll know if it's the second one as soon as Jack repeats her name yet again.

If by some twisted fickle finger of fate it's the third scenario and

Lucky O'Toole is just someone who was in the wrong place at the wrong time caught on video saying and doing the wrong things, well then I guess Acme will get a verbal whuppin'.

I get my answer when Branham angrily sputters, "Is this some kind of joke? Ms. O'Toole is anything but a foreign agent! In fact, she was instrumental in alerting the FBI to a major money laundering operation in Macau. Not to mention that Ms. O'Toole's father, Albert Rothstein, is a valued member of POTUS's kitchen cabinet—*and* a generous donor to both political parties."

Oh…Shit. Our bad.

"Ah, good to know," Jack murmurs.

"That's putting it mildly," Lucky retorts.

"Ms. O'Toole, my personal apology. I only hope Acme is treating you with kid gloves." Branham's growl isn't just a warning. Inquiring minds—his and Ryan's—want to know if our interrogation efforts already crossed a line.

Gulp.

At the very least, Acme owes Lucky a spa day. Or a bottle of epic Champagne.

But from the gleam in Lucky's eyes, I doubt she'll feel that the Relax & De-Stress Lifestyle Programme at the Corinthia would even the score.

I hold my breath as Lucky replies, "Director Branham, albeit in a somewhat unconventional manner, Acme is pulling out all stops to find the killers of your operatives, who were also valued Babylon employees. I'm pissed as hell over Aziza's death." She pauses. "And Nigel's murder hurts too. My staff will feel the same way. We will do our best to pool resources with Acme and find the perpetrators." Lucky's vow is so adamant that the few droplets still clinging to her hair from Jack's bucket-in-the-face wake-up call fall as she speaks.

Branham says nothing. Finally: "Thank you for forgiving this, er, misunderstanding, Ms. O'Toole. To those with no more than a passing knowledge of covert operations, Acme's methods may indeed seem unorthodox. However, they are not unique, nor disingenuous, to field operatives in the intelligence community. The

Craigs' mission is sanctioned by me and by the President. That said, they're to use whatever tactics they feel necessary—without anyone's judgment."

The bluntness of Branham's declaration gives Lucky reason to wince.

"I appreciate your help, Lucky," Branham adds, "and I'm sure Acme does as well."

"Very much so," Ryan murmurs. "Thanks for your time, Director."

We hear a soft click as Branham hangs up.

"Ladies and gentlemen, you have your marching orders," Ryan warns us. "Now, play nicely."

The line goes dead.

I nudge Jack to untie Lucky.

He does so, quickly.

Lucky smiles sweetly as she nods her thanks—

But then punches him in the gut.

Jack doubles over. "I guess I deserved that," he gasps.

"You did," Lucky replies briskly. "Now, I'd like to clean up before I have to face my staff looking like an extra from the set of a zombie movie."

"Follow me," Dominic insists.

Lucky does so but swats away his attempt to lend her his arm. She takes a few steps but slowly, since she is still wobbly. She's determined to walk under her own steam, but after three steps, she stops. Her eye catches mine. She sighs resignedly, then beckons me forward. "Would you mind giving me a hand?"

"Not at all," I assure her.

With Dominic in tow, we take the elevator.

The rest of the men take the stairs.

"Is this where you sleep?" Lucky looks around the expansive bedroom that takes up the entire third floor.

The textured walls are painted navy, but the drop molding and tray ceiling are painted bright white. The platform bed covered with a simple gray duvet faces the three windows overlooking Regent's Park. A massive oak desk sits in the alcove opposite the room's ensuite bathroom.

I follow Lucky's gaze toward the bathroom. Its dove-gray veined marble walls are seamless, as if they were cut from one massive stone. The tub can hold two people; the shower can comfortably accommodate four. To make this point, vertical rain sticks have been placed every four feet, and four flat shower-heads hang down from the ceiling. Wishful thinking on Dominic's part? My guess is that such a foursome was an achievable goal.

The hardware and fittings are nickel. Lighting comes from a spiral chandelier.

Dominic motions toward the tub. "Let me run a bath for you."

Lucky shakes her head wearily. "If I lay down in that tub, I may never get back up."

Dominic nods. "Understandably so." He shoots me a cross look.

"Don't blame *her*. She was only doing her job." By Lucky's clipped tone, I can tell she hasn't forgiven me. Her head moves in Dominic's direction. "And so were you, so you can cut the suave suitor act, now that we're both on the same side."

Dominic's cheeks go ruddy. To hide this, he walks over to a wall that appears to be one long mirror. When he pushes a button, part of it opens to reveal a closet. Dresses hang in one compartment and blouses, skirts, and women's slacks in another. A floor-to-ceiling shoe rack holds a variety of heels, boots, sneakers, and flats.

"Feel free to choose whatever you wish to wear. I'm sure there's something in your size."

Lucky snickers. "Are you hiding a wife somewhere?"

"No, not at all," Dominic insists. "But one must be prepared for every occasion." Seeing Lucky smirk, he frowns. "Can I help it if I'm the consummate host?"

She laughs. "Dominic, listen—there is no shame in having a

fetish. And these days cross-dressing is out of the closet. One of my dearest friends is a female impersonator—"

"You think I like to…to…" Horrified, Dominic's back stiffens.

"There are two terrycloth robes on hooks beside the shower stall," Dominic tells her gruffly. "You'll find everything you need: Frette towels, Frederic Malle soaps, Phillip Kingsley shampoos. The vanity holds an assortment of cosmetics—"

"All the comforts of a great hotel," Lucky murmurs sarcastically. "I'm sure your guests appreciate it immensely. What's the monthly occupancy rate? I'm guessing seventy percent."

Dominic's head rears back. He closes his eyes as if that will allow him to contain his anger. "You've made your point, Ms. O'Toole. I'll leave you to freshen up."

On his way out, he slams the door.

"YOU KNOW, LUCKY, YOU'VE GOT DOMINIC ALL WRONG," I SHOUT through the steam rolling out of the bathroom.

At first, I think she didn't hear me because she's got all four showerheads pulsing at full force. A moment later the water stops. Through the door, I can see her hand pluck one of the plush towels from a shelf, and then another.

"Did you hear me?" I ask impatiently.

"I'm sure they heard you all the way over to Baker Street." She stares at me. "You've got to be kidding me, right?"

"Hardly. I've never seen him this way before."

Lucky comes out, tying the robe's sash around her waist. She pulls off the towel on her damp hair to rub it dry but groans softly when she lifts her arms.

I walk over. "Are you okay?"

She shrugs. "I've been better. For all our sakes, I'm glad it wasn't worse."

"We had to make sure you weren't feeding us bunk," I say evenly.

"I get it, okay? Trust me, you and your team of merry tricksters are forgiven." She pulls open the vanity and takes stock of Dominic's makeup offerings. "Are you sure Lord Lounge Lizard isn't a little light in his loafers?"

I tamp down a smile. "Worse. Dominic is a narcissist. As such, he doesn't like being turned down. So, tag you're it. And you have no one to blame but yourself."

"So, I'm attractive because I'm unavailable. High praise indeed." Lucky picks up a lipstick and opens it to examine its shade. "Even if I found Dominic Fleming attractive, and I don't"— she pauses, rubbing her lips together to even the lipstick application—"No, not completely true. I find him attractive, just not *appealing*." Satisfied, she applies it before adding, "But even so, I'm engaged."

"Yeah, the French guy. A chef, right?"

She stares at me. "How did you know that?"

I chuckle. "It's not a state secret or anything. And even if it were, we'd have found out."

Her mascara wand stops mid-air. "In other words, laws are meant to be broken? Are there any you haven't?"

"It depends on which country we're in," I reply casually. "Hey, it's a dirty job, but someone has to do it. Democracy comes with a price. Too many others around the globe play dirty. Organizations like ours provide enough assists to even the playing field. When Aziza put out feelers to the CIA, the agency couldn't follow up overtly because it didn't know if what she had would put us in Dutch with her country, supposedly a U.S. ally. If what she passed forward proves it isn't, all hell will break loose. Still, Aziza's information will have come to the CIA without it getting its hands dirty. On the other hand, if she stumbled across intel that will save her country from imminent peril, the CIA gets to play hero in the eyes of her people." My eyes meet Lucky's in the mirror. "I'm not ashamed of what I do and how I have to do it. And, frankly, I'm relieved we didn't have to do 'it' to you. You're smart, successful, and from what I can tell by how Julie reacted to seeing you with Dominic, a nice enough person to have someone like her concerned about you."

Lucky combs out her hair but says nothing. Finally, she mutters, "I'm angry about Aziza's death. Heck, I even feel bad about Nigel—and that says something, considering he was a total snob."

I nod. "Especially to 'Princess Maja.' But he was an excellent covert operative. And he enjoyed working at the club." I smile. "You certainly had him shitting bricks!"

"It's my job to crack the whip. It's not always fun," Lucky admits. "But it's why our casinos are respected around the world." She grins. "I'd sure like to know how Dominic won at baccarat."

"If you ask him sweetly, I'm sure he'll tell you." I bat my eyes. "Or better yet, show you."

"Ha! That's what I'm afraid of." Lucky moves into the closet. After rummaging through the hangers, she pulls out a simple little black dress. "Maybe this will get him to 'fess up." She holds it up against her torso.

It's so short that my giggle rolls into a snort. "Oh...I think he'd do more than that."

Lucky sighs. "Even if I weren't six feet tall, every item in that closet is specifically designed to truss up or hug tight."

She walks over to another part of the mirrored wall. With a tap of a button, another walk-in closet opens. It holds a man's wardrobe. She steps into it only to reappear a moment later wearing a white dress shirt and jeans that are snug in the seat but not the waist. To remedy that, she knots the shirt's tails at her waistline.

Lucky nods at her reflection in the mirror, satisfied. "As much as Dominic would love to catch a glimpse of my choochilala, he'll have to settle for knowing I wore something near and dear to his crotch: his jeans."

"He may never wash them again," I reply. "Hey, we better head downstairs before they think we fell asleep up here."

Lucky nods, but the way she's blinking, I realize she's still fighting off the after-effects of the roofie.

This time, when I hold her arm to help her to the elevator, she pats it as if to say, *Thanks.*

————

WE FIND THE MEN SPRAWLED OVER AN ENORMOUS U-SHAPED COUCH in the media room. They're munching on pesto pasta primavera and a green salad.

"Did you order in?" I ask.

Abu points to Dominic. "Chef Boyardee made it. Not half bad, either."

Dominic forks some onto two plates and walks over with it. Maybe he's praying that the old adage about winning a man's heart through his stomach works for the opposite sex as well.

I sink onto the couch beside Jack before digging into my food. I can't remember when I last ate.

Appreciatively, Jack kisses my cheek before plucking a few strands of my fettuccine with his fork.

Lucky waves off the food. "I'm still a bit queasy," she admits but her smile looks forced. "Dominic, would you mind terribly getting me a glass of water?"

He takes the olive branch and scurries off to do her bidding.

By the time Dominic gets back with the water, Lucky has migrated to Arnie's side of the couch. Arnie's plate sits on the coffee table while he taps away on his computer.

"Jack asked that I pull up the Underground camera footage of Nigel's murder so that you can see it, in case you recognize the killer," he explains to her.

Lucky watches intently as the assassin stabs Nigel and drags him into the elevator before slinking back toward the subway platform. The footage picks up as he strolls toward the exit stairwell. A third video shows me fighting with him.

Lucky must be somewhat impressed because she rewards me with a thumbs-up.

"Take a good look at the perpetrator," Jack suggests. "Do you recognize him?"

Lucky squints but shakes her head. "Arnie, do you mind playing it again?"

He accommodates.

Lucky leans in, but she's blinking as if trying to keep her eyes open. Finally, she mutters, "I do know him…I think." She closes her eyes for a moment. Suddenly, they pop open. "It's one of our butlers—Gerald."

"Are you sure?" I ask.

"Positive," she insists. "He's assigned to the sheik. Gerald accommodates him whenever he's in town."

"That can't be a coincidence," Jack declares.

"The way things are going, I'd guess you're right about that," Lucky replies.

"Lucky, as you saw on the tape, Gerald plays for keeps. The odds that he'll come with us quietly are nonexistent. So that we can exfiltrate him without any undue stress to your staff and guests, we'll need any address or cell phone you have for him."

"Of course," Lucky murmurs, but her eyelids are at half-mast. Slowly, she leans back onto the couch. "Donna, when you found Aziza, did she still have the information you were to get from her?"

"As it turns out, yes," I reply. "However, she coded it in such a way that the CIA can only see part of it. She was to give us the cipher when she was assured the perpetrators would be brought to justice."

"Nigel told us that Aziza warned him she was in trouble. Since Arnie never found the email, Nigel and Aziza communicated via inter-office correspondence, Lucky should be able to pull that for us," Jack suggests.

"What if it's in code?" I ask.

"They will have a simple one. Acme ComInt will be able to break it. Lucky, can you pull that for us tomorrow?... Lucky?"

Too late. She's asleep. Exhaustion has finally taken over.

"Let's not wake her. She's been through enough." Jack looks at his watch. "Dominic, do you mind if we camp out here for the night?"

"Not at all. You'll find three bedrooms on the second floor."

"Um…" I glance over at Lucky. "What about her?"

"I don't think we should leave her on the couch," Jack says.

"She'll sleep in my bed," Dominic insists.

Noting my warning stare, he quickly adds, "I'm not that big of a cad, Old Girl. I'll sleep here on the couch."

To make his point, he reaches under Lucky, picks her up, and strolls to the elevator. But before he reaches it, he grazes her forehead with his lips.

She sighs appreciatively.

Damn it, she's going to break his heart.

19

Lucky

*H*ow the hell had I ended up, fully clothed, in Dominic's bed? My memory was iffy. But I did know one thing: if I'd been naked, he'd be dead. And we wouldn't be pulling up in front of the club, the day barely underway.

I held the door to the club open for Donna, Jack, and the guy, Abu, who I recognized as the pickpocket who had lifted my phone. "After you." As I trailed after them, my mother's words about the company you keep, taunted me. The jury was out as to whether this group was a new high or a new low. People who do bad things for good causes normally got twenty-five years to life… or their own Hollywood movie. Jack and Donna didn't deserve either.

Julie's normal smile was absent, her eyes bloodshot, and her nose red, when we congregated in front of her at the reception desk. "Did you hear about poor Mr. Ahern?"

"So sad," I struggled for the right words—a never-ending quest that proved once again results are not always contingent on effort.

"Who would stab him at a train station?" She dabbed at the corner of one eye with a bedraggled hankie. "Where is Mr. Fleming?"

"No idea." The look of distaste on her face stopped me. "Why?"

"You seemed rather…fond of him…when you left." She leaned across the desk. "And weren't you wearing something else?"

My frown shut her down. I so didn't want to know how I'd humiliated myself under the influence of the roofie. Dominic Fleming should know paybacks are hell.

"The world is a vicious place." Donna jumped into the awkward pause.

Jack must've elbowed her in the ribs as she let out a whoosh of air and crumpled to the side a bit.

I reached across the desk and gave Julie's forearm a squeeze. "I'm sorry. Our family has lost a valued member. Perhaps we should arrange an employee gathering to honor his memory?"

She brightened a bit. "I could pull something together. Mr. Ahern would've liked that."

"When do Prunella and Lavinia come on duty today?"

She checked her screen. "They came on at midnight. Right now, they are on break."

"Have them meet me in security."

"Yes, Miss."

"Thank you." I stepped back to include Donna, Jack and Abu in our discussion. "Would we have two rooms available—both doubles? Something…understated?"

Julie gave me a long look, then the light dawned. A tiny smile tugged at one corner of her mouth. "Yes, Miss." She pulled out a drawer that contained the computer screen lying flat. The front of the drawer folded down to reveal a keyboard. "It'll take me a bit to prepare the accommodations."

"Very good. We'll go to my room for a bit. If you could, buzz me when the rooms are ready."

"Yes, ma'am."

Donna stepped forward. "A colleague of ours, Arnie, will be arriving sometime shortly. I'll tell him to ask for you. If the rooms are ready, would you mind giving him an extra key to Abu's room?"

"Not at all." Julie gave her a smile.

"Could you run the keys for them now?" I asked.

A minute, no more, and Julie had two rooms. She ran the keycards then pushed them across the desk. "First floor. In the back."

Near the kitchen—something she didn't add. Night would end late and the morning would start early—the perfect hours for spies. I handed one key to Donna. "For you and the mister." Then the other one to Abu, who I wasn't talking to yet.

He offered my phone for the key. "Sorry. Orders. Are we even?"

"You give me something that's mine and I give you something you don't deserve. No, not remotely even." I motioned to all of them. "We'll wait in my room."

I wanted to ask Julie about Gerald. Still grappling with the idea that one of our own was a murderer, I kept my mouth shut. Donna and Jack had been firm in their request—I was to let them handle him. Any indication I was onto him might spook him off. I got it, not that it set well. Somehow, I managed to keep my mouth shut—perhaps knowing it was three of them against my one tipped the scales in favor of compliance. Also, I figured there was reason not to piss off the pros—I'd seen their torture chamber.

While Donna, Jack and Abu organized their luggage, leaving it with the bellman, I gave them my room number.

"We'll be up in five," Jack said on his way to the car to get another suitcase.

Once in the elevator and out of earshot, I made a call.

Bree's brusque no-nonsense answer came immediately. "Security."

"We have a problem."

My last experience with wine being less than satisfactory, and the hour still quite early, I ordered a carafe of mimosas, three glasses, and a bucket of ice. I was just popping the cork when Donna, Jack and Abu arrived.

Donna headed for the windows, Jack for the booze and Abu for a chair.

"You have a nice view," Donna said, her back to the room.

I bolted down one flute of the happy bubbles, then thought I'd wait a bit considering this was my first nourishment of the day. "One of the perks of taking all the responsibility."

She looked at me over her shoulder. "And all the blame, too."

"For that I demand hazardous duty pay."

Once everyone had taken in the lay of the land and staked out their bit of my turf, we settled down to business. I broke the ice. "As I understand it, you have one dead informant and one dead handler. Someone is tying up loose ends. That would lead me to believe that you didn't get the information you hoped for from Aziza."

"We got it, but we can't read it," Jack said. "Clever girl. She encrypted the intel. Simple encryption, but virtually unbreakable without the cipher."

"Cipher?"

"The source document from which they built the encryption. Without it, we'd need a super computer and unlimited time, which the killings tell us we don't have. We need to find the cipher."

"Who else would know what she used?" After arguing with myself and losing, I poured myself another flute and forced myself to sip.

"That's where we need your help," Donna said from her perch by the window. "We're working the roommate and her Oxford connections. We need you to work the hotel. Who'd she hang with? Who'd she talk with?"

"I assume you have an in-house communication system?" Jack asked. "We couldn't find one to hack into."

"It's for internal purposes only. We keep all of it offline, no internet connection at all."

"Good, maybe you can see who she's been communicating with there?"

"I'm on it." Every now and then being the boss had its perks. "There is one thing I noticed. It's a long shot, but maybe just grist for the mill." Donna and Jack gave me their attention. Abu's had never wavered. "It's the flowers in the Royal Suite."

"Nigel told us they were a sign from Aziza," Donna said.

"Tell me *exactly* what he said. The exact words, if you can remember them."

Donna pushed herself off her perch and started pacing. I sipped my Champagne while she thought back. "Okay, he said if the flowers were different than the sheik's normal request—yellow roses, I believe?" She looked to Jack for confirmation. He nodded once, and she continued. "If the flowers weren't yellow roses, then that was a signal she was in trouble."

"So only if they were different? Not if they were a specific type of flower?"

"Nigel said they'd been changed from yellow roses to red dahlias.' Frankly, I was impressed he remembered."

"Why is that?" Jack asked.

"Because he was a guy." Donna looked like she regretted the comment the minute it was out of her mouth. She motioned for a mimosa. I poured it then held it out to her. She snagged it mid-pass.

"Sexist, but some truth to it," Jack said.

I was beginning to understand what Donna saw in him... besides the whole oozing virility thing.

"Yeah, just different, not a specific type. Why?" Donna stopped her pacing and faced me. "Do you think the flower she chose holds some special meaning?"

"I do. Red dahlias are very hard to find this time of year and come at a huge premium. I can't help but think she chose them on purpose."

Blank stares from Donna and Jack. Abu focused on his phone. When he looked up a smile split his face. "Betrayal."

I pointed at him. "Exactly. Red dahlias, in the language of flowers, mean betrayal."

"Someone close to her. That's who she feared." Abu stole my punch line.

I raised my glass.

We knew where to look. Now all we had to do was figure out who.

As I'd requested, Prunella and Lavinia were waiting for me when I arrived in Security. Bree had made them cool their heels standing in the corner. All that was missing were two dunce caps.

"You two have been busy little beavers, haven't you?" I smiled at the pun, which being young and too stupid to live, the girls didn't get.

"Our shift is over," Prunella said. "We want to go home. You have no right to hold us here."

I held my ground. Bree blew into her ever-present mug of tea as I shepherded the girls into her office.

"What did you find?"

"Enough." She took a sip and winced as she sat behind her video console. "Gather around girls. You're going to love the show."

The girls clustered behind Bree, huddled like the blindfolded in front of a firing squad, nervous, but knowing what's coming.

"You two have been busy." Bree kept her tone light. She cued the video then hit play.

We all had eyes glued to the screen and its montage of the girls going in and out of various rooms. Five separate instances—the Royal Suite twice, then three of our nicer rooms on the third and fourth floors.

"How long have they been doing this?" I asked Bree as if the girls weren't there. They wouldn't tell me the truth, so I didn't bother asking them.

"No more than a couple of weeks." Bree angled a look over her shoulder and up at Prunella and Lavinia and raised an eyebrow.

Prunella caved. "Our first was Mr. Smythe, ten days ago."

I spun them around to face me. "Let me guess how you wanted this to go. You arrange a three-way with one of our married members, or our political ones—anyone with a lot to lose if even a hint of scandal hit the grapevine, or worse, the media. You take a camera into the room in your purse or bag and position it so it will catch all the action. Then you mug for the camera, clean the video up a bit, and send a snippet to your mark."

The looks on their faces told me I'd dead-centered it.

"How much?"

"Ten thousand pounds each."

"Who else have you targeted?"

They gave me Dominic, who I knew about, and Sheik Ben, who I did not, and two other names, which were unknown to me. I had some apologizing to do—good thing sucking up was my super power.

Reading my murderous glare, Bree pulled the girls out of my reach, then held onto them, a hand around each girl's arm. Her knuckles whitened—the girls weren't getting away.

"Call the cops," I said to Bree, then I gave the girls my full attention. "You picked the wrong place and the wrong gal to be messing with. Please, I deal with pros in Vegas—you two are total pikers."

"Calling the cops is pointless." Lavinia skewered me with a haughty stare. "There's no one to charge us with anything. Do you really think these men are going to come forward to testify against us?" I admired her spunk. Unfortunately, she'd miscalculated.

She deflated as my smile widened. "I can think of one."

Dominic Fleming owed me big time. Time for him to pay up.

EVEN THOUGH IT WAS STILL EARLY, SHEIK BEN OPENED THE DOOR TO the Royal Suite when I knocked. No Gerald—a pity but not a surprise. Besides, thinking this would be a "piece of cake" as my father said, I'd arrived in country still dangerous, but unarmed. If I met Gerald in a dark alley or a bright hallway, I wanted a gun. Sheik Ben turned his back, leaving me to fend for myself. "Ever since you showed up, the level of service here has declined precipitously."

I followed him into the great room, shutting the front door behind me. "I'm so sorry. What have we done wrong?"

He poured himself a cup of coffee. The aroma was tantalizing. When he turned back around his face was a mask. A five o'clock shadow darkened his cheeks, his white cotton shirt looked like he'd worn it since yesterday. The club wasn't the only thing that had slipped a notch or two. "For starters, you've misplaced my niece."

"I didn't know I was in charge of her whereabouts." She was dead, but I had no tangible proof. The CIA, through Acme, had her body. Presumably, at some point, they would return it to her family, but who knew with the spooks. They could pull a *Raiders of the Lost Ark* thing and Aziza would simply disappear. That would not sit well with me. I might not have power, but I had connections. Hopefully I wouldn't have to use them.

"She worked for you."

"She belonged to *you*." I didn't mean that in the Arab sense, but he could take it any way he liked. "What else is not to your satisfaction?"

"Gerald did not show up today. No phone call. No explanation." He eyed me over the lip of his coffee cup as if measuring my response.

"First I've heard of it. Did you alert the staff?"

"Mr. Ahern is not here either."

"Mr. Ahern is dead."

Sheik Ben lowered his cup slowly. "How?"

"Knifed in the underground."

"Terrorists." A catch-all for groups the UAE funded, and others they fought. Hard to keep it all straight.

"How do you know?"

He shrugged. "They're everywhere here."

"Maybe. More than likely a mugging gone bad. The police haven't said." I wanted to spill it all: Gerald, Nigel, Aziza, but I'd only forestall our ability to catch the killer. "How well do you know Gerald?"

"Not well. Why do you ask?" He tilted his head as if measuring me, my questions, and my responses.

"You request Gerald each time you stay here." I felt uncomfortable standing in the middle of the room. He hadn't offered me a chair or a drink, so I grew roots, crossing my arms against what, I didn't know, but it made me feel better.

"Gerald keeps his nose out of other people's business." The implication was clear. His words carried a veiled threat.

Surely, he knew a threat was a red cape to this bull? "What had he done that made you so angry with him when I saw you two at the bar?"

A moment of hesitation. "The flowers."

"Not your normal yellow."

"Red is not a good omen." He flicked a glance over my shoulder to the foyer and the spray of red dahlias.

I followed it. The dahlias had begun to wilt—death was everywhere in this suite. "I'll have them changed immediately. Anything else?"

"No." He took a sip of his coffee, holding the liquid in his mouth before swallowing it.

I stalled for a bit then dove into indelicate waters. "I do have something I need your help with." There was no delicate way to broach the sex subject, so I dove in. "It has come to my attention that two of our female employees are shaking down some of the members. I have reason to believe you might be one of their potential victims."

"Did they tell you that?"

"Has anyone tried to blackmail you for behavior that would be…an embarrassment…should it get out?" The girls had named him, but I needed to be sure.

He turned to look out the window. "No."

The anger in his posture told me otherwise.

I SAT AT NIGEL'S COMPUTER AND TYPED IN MY CREDENTIALS. WITH

too many questions and not enough answers, I needed to do some digging.

As I waited for authentication, I thought through what I knew already. Aziza apparently had some intel on money machinations —for whom and for what purpose, I didn't know. She'd hit the CIA's radar enough to have a handler: Nigel Ahern. I still couldn't get my brain around that one. The intel transfer went south. Someone was onto her and eventually killed her. As a clever young woman, she'd not trusted even the good guys, encrypting what she'd given them. Now the CIA needed the cipher to break her code. Meanwhile, I had a couple of rogue idiots trying to shake down club members, including Aziza's uncle. Gerald, the uncle's butler, killed Ahern, the handler. What was the connection, CIA intel or hush money? Did Sheik Ben have something to do with his niece's intel? Did Nigel Ahern have anything to do with Prunella and Lavinia's plot?

And where was the cipher?

Someone had to know.

The computer dinged its approval—the only approval I'd gotten since I had landed.

One of the security precautions we'd taken was to assign employees discrete identifiers, so they could report incidents, complain, and point out problems without fear of retribution. Only a few people had access to the file, which we kept on this, the manager's computer, that was not ever connected to the internet. As one of the great Technologically Challenged, I needed a few more minutes to work through several security walls, but then I was in.

First to email Gerald's address to Donna. Piece of cake. Done.

Now for Aziza.

She wasn't particularly communicative with her fellow employees via email. Several were between she and Nigel, which made sense. I pulled the emails and collected them in a document for the Acme team. A cursory glance told me Nigel and Aziza employed some special sort of code words that, on the surface, didn't make sense.

Best left to the pros.

I continued searching. Who knew our employees were so chatty? Thirty minutes of scrolling and searching, I found a thread —there was someone else Aziza communicated with.

I cross-checked the identifier.

Adam Kalb—the dealer tossing cards to Dominic Fleming at the baccarat table.

20

Donna

"This isn't a room! It's a broom closet with a peephole." Jack stares out the narrow window over the tiny bed stand positioned between two twin beds. The view looks out onto an alley. The buildings around us are just as tall, so very little light filters down to the very bottom floor. What does come through halos the snow flurries drifting down.

I look down at what I'm wearing: yesterday's barely-there party-hearty dress. "I'm going to take a shower. Thanks to Dominic's guest room sheets, I reek of lemon verbena."

There is a small shower stall and no bathtub. I flip the water handles. After ten seconds, I hold my hand under the water raining down from the showerhead, but then I leap away because it's so frigid.

Four minutes later, even with just the hot spigot on full blast, the water is still chilly.

I walk back into the bedroom. "The water is as cold as a witch's tit! I'm just going to let it run."

Jack nods. Shifting his gaze to the twin beds, he scowls.

"You know, this is Lucky's payback," I reply.

"What I know is that this is bullshit," he grumbles, "But I also know how to make it infinitely more pleasurable."

To make his point, Jack grabs hold of the bed stand to push it out.

It doesn't move.

Incredulous, he stares at me. "The damn thing is bolted down!"

I flop down on one of the beds. "Since we spoon anyway, it's a minor inconvenience." My invitation to join me is a pat on the mattress.

He drops beside me. Pulling me into his arms, he mutters, "It isn't the 'spooning' part that concerns me. It's how we handle the pre-spooning activity."

I laugh. "Necessity is the mother of invention. I'm sure you'll figure something out."

Have I thrown down the gauntlet? Jack must think so by the way in which he leans me onto the bed with one hand while the other inches up my thigh.

It doesn't stop there. A finger hooks my panty and slowly tugs it downward. To help it along to its final destination—anywhere but on my body—Jack lifts me gently at the waist before sliding it down my legs and off my feet. Smiling, he lifts it over his head before tossing it onto the floor.

He then pulls me up again and into his lap.

I feel the zipper of my dress inching down my back. When its bodice drops to my waist, he pushes me forward onto my hands and knees. With me in that position, he has no problem inching it off my hips. I have no issues with what he does next: gently following the half-moon curve of each ass cheek with a hand.

He sighs happily.

"Having fun?" I taunt.

"Immensely," he murmurs.

When his thumb and finger enter me, I gasp at the pleasure.

"I suspect you are too?" he asks.

"Immensely," I whisper.

Jack's next move—to drive me insane with his mouth on my face, my neck, my breasts, my abdomen—is barely hindered by my determination to strip off his tux jacket and shirt, buttons be damned.

With a quick zip his pants are ready to come off. My hint to him that I'm to do the honors is to push him flat on his back. By straddling him, I'm able to tug off his pants and boxer briefs, inch by inch, all the while allowing him the view he so admires. Still, it's not easy because he is already erect.

The second I've thrown his pants on the floor he pulls me back toward him—

And onto him.

Our mutual pleasure grows with each thrust, at first slow and steady. But as I rise and fall, our rapture builds. Each time I clench, Jack seems to grow larger within me. Soon, I am aching—not from pain but ecstasy.

When finally Jack explodes, my own bliss catapults me beyond this sad little room and even the whole of London. I am somewhere between heaven and earth...but where?

Jack cradles me to his chest.

Feeling his heartbeat, I know I'm home.

MY CELL PHONE BUZZES.

With a sad sigh, Jack lets go of me so that I can look at the screen.

Caller ID shows that I've been pinged with emails from Lucky. The first one reads:

BUTLER GERALD MORTEN IS NOT HERE TODAY. ADDRESS: **23A Edwardes Square, Kensington, London W8 6HE, UK**

"AS YOU REQUESTED, LUCKY SENT US THE BUTLER'S ADDRESS," I SAY to Jack.

"Pull it up on GPS," he replies.

After doing so, I frown. "This can't be right." I show him what I see: a single-story pub adjacent to a residential green."

"Not surprising," Jack says. "The butler gave a false address to the club. Well, we know he was in the club yesterday. Call Arnie. I know just how he can track our missing butler."

I tap in our tech op's number and put the phone's microphone on speaker.

"Hey, guy, do us a favor. Pull up the personnel file of the Babylon London butler, Gerald Morten. He may be going under an assumed. Scan his photo through Interpol's facial recognition program. We'll also need you to hack the city's CCTV video feed in front of the club, starting at eleven-thirty yesterday. We want Gerald's final destination," Jack says.

"How long do I have?" Arnie asks.

"We need it, like, yesterday." Jack explains.

Arnie chuckles weakly. "I'll give it to you in, say, fifteen." He rings off.

"What's in Lucky's second message?" Jack asks me.

"Attachments of the employee correspondences sent between Nigel and Aziza...Oh, and here's something else of interest! Aziza was chummy with another club employee: a baccarat dealer named Adam Kalb. Lucky attached those emails as well."

"Go ahead and forward all of Aziza's correspondence to Emma so that the ComInt can assess them for hidden codes. She should also pull up the club's personnel photo of Adam, run it through Interpol and facial recognition, then track Adam's movements these past forty-eight hours within the club via its security archive."

"Sir, yes sir!" I say with a mock salute.

Jack grins supremely. "I could get used to that."

"Don't bother," I mutter as I forward Aziza's emails to Emma. "Done! And we have just enough time to clean up before Arnie gets back to us."

As I get up and stroll toward the bathroom door, Jack gives an appreciative whistle.

By now the running water is tepid. That will have to do. I stick my head through the bedroom door. "Care to join me?"

I don't have to ask twice.

By the time Arnie has called back on my phone, we've showered, dressed, and are anxious to leave our scullery closet. "As you suspected, Gerald is an alias. His real name is Edgar Black. He served in the U.K.'s Special Reconnaissance Regiment."

"The regiment that handles counter-terrorism for the United Kingdom," Jack declares.

"Yep," Arnie says. "His tours of duty included Afghanistan, but most recently—just a few years ago—an attachment to MI6 in Yemen, where he trained Yemini forces against Al-Qaeda. Interesting note: his file indicated a dishonorable discharge."

"Does it say why?" I ask.

"No," Arnie replies.

"We'll have to ask our friends at MI6," Jack says. To start the process, he taps out a text to Ryan.

"Gerald—or Edgar, if we're to start calling him that—was last seen leaving the club yesterday before noon," Arnie says. "He took a circuitous route but ended up at the Green Park Underground Station when Nigel was killed."

"And he knew where the cameras were placed so that Nigel's extermination wouldn't be caught on the security cams. He's certainly our man," I reply. "Still, he would have walked out a side entrance between twelve-ten and twelve twenty. That should have been grabbed by a camera."

"On it," Arnie replies.

We wait a few minutes. Finally, he says, "Got him. From there, he walked west on Piccadilly.... and turned right on White Horse Street.... until it ends on Curzon Street, where he took a jog to the left, for a quick right onto Queen Street...and into a building of flats. The street number is three-twelve."

"Fast-forward until you see him leaving again," Jack requests.

We wait for what seems like an eternity. Finally, Arnie says. "I'm up to about fifteen minutes ago, and he's stayed put all this time..." Suddenly Arnie whistles low and slow. "Hey, guess who just walked into his building?"

"Don't leave us in suspense," I retort.

"Aziza's roommate—what was her name again? Roxanna?"

"*Her*? Well, that's got to be more than a coincidence," Jack says. "Arnie, tell Abu and Dominic to meet us with the car in the alley next to the club. Tell them to wear eyes and ears, and to be armed. And please keep up surveillance. If Gerald and Roxanna leave, we want to know where they go."

"On it," Arnie assures us.

THIS TIME OF DAY, TRAFFIC IS SLOW THROUGH MAYFAIR'S NARROW streets.

The short trip is made even more interminable with Dominic's inconsolable moaning over Lucky.

"Just look at me!" Although Dominic is sitting in the front passenger seat, he's able to make eye contact with Jack and me through the mirror on his sun visor. "I've got the profile of a Greek god! What is wrong with that confounding woman?"

"Maybe you opened your mouth." Jack mutters.

Dominic takes his aside as a knock against his teeth. He smiles wide into the mirror to assure himself that they are as Chiclets-even and spotlight-white as ever. Satisfied, he winks at his reflection.

Jack feigns gagging by sticking a finger in his mouth.

"Lucky strikes me as the type of woman who is more impressed with brains than beauty," I suggest.

"Don't try to make that scintillating siren over in your own dull, dour bluestocking image, Ducky," Dominic scoffs. "I won't have it!"

Jack's guffaw turns into a choke when I poke him into silence. I don't know why I give a hoot that Dominic's heart is breaking. I guess it's because I'm shocked to discover he had one in the first place. Frankly, the fact that Lucky is completely immune to Dominic's innate sensuality is admirable.

Still, he's my teammate. And right now, we need him on his A-

Game—at least, until this mission is over and Lucky is out of range. "My guess is that she just needs a little warming up," I say brightly. "Perhaps less of your always flattering hard-court press and more of your indomitable silent-but-noble presence will be more to her liking."

"Ah! I see." Dominic leans back thoughtfully.

Jack stares at me as if my hair is on fire.

Abu pulls to the curb. "I hate to interrupt this truly insightful Mars-Venus moment but we're here." He points to a four-story townhouse a block up and across the street.

Through our earbuds Arnie adds, "I've turned on everyone's video lens feeds. There has been no movement from either of the targets, via the front door or back. The building holds four tenants: a young couple on the top floor—Betsy and Ronald McInnis—who have been there for two years. An eighty-year-old widow—Brenda Coyle—rents out the first floor. She's been a tenant for over two decades. Right now, she's on holiday in Spain. A single woman in the basement studio—Liz McNamara. She and the couple should still be at their day jobs. My guess is that our target is the recent rental on the second floor: someone under the name of 'James Jones.'"

"You're right, that's got to be him," Jack reasons. "If Roxanna is there under her own free will, we may get resistance from both of them. Since we need to question them, any shots taken should be non-lethal. That way, we can exfiltrate them to Harrington Hall and do the questioning there. As for your positions: Abu, keep the engine running. Dominic and I will take the front entrance and go up to the second-story flat." He turns to Dominic. "We'll walk quietly. When we get to the door, you do the talking. Pretend you're the leasing agent and that there's an emergency that needs your immediate attention." Jack now looks at me. "Donna, you hang out back in case one or both of them exit from that direction. Arnie, if by some chance they escape us, keep monitoring the real-time CCTV feed."

And we're off.

A BACK ALLEY RUNS THE FULL LENGTH OF THE BLOCK BEFORE OPENING onto a side street that intersects Queen Street. There's a tall wrought iron gate in the high brick wall behind the townhome. I position beside it, next to a row of aluminum trashcans. From here, I'm still able to see the backstairs on the exterior of the building.

"In position," I murmur into my microphone.

"Roger," Jack mutters back. Through his lenses to mine, I see what he sees: the second-story flat's front door.

Dominic knocks politely on it. "Hello? I say! I say there, Mr. Jones! 'Tis the estate agent, O'Dooley. Please open up! I have an emergency of the utmost importance and must get into your flat! We've found a leak in the gas line upstairs and we think it's seeping into all the units."

Silence.

Dominic again: "Mr. Jones! It is imperative that you open the door!"

Finally, a man shouts gruffly, "Busy, now! Come back, say, in an hour!"

"As I said, Sir, it is imperative that I get in *now!*"

"We have a visual," Abu reports to us. "A man has pushed aside the shade in the front window to look out at the street."

"I see it through your lenses," Arnie replies. "That's Gerald alright. Spitting image of his employee photo."

A woman's screams: "Help me! He's—"

She's interrupted by the faintest bang, immediately followed by a thud.

I hear more shots and a bang: from Jack and Dominic, who have shot through the lock on Gerald's front door—

Gun drawn, Gerald rushes out the back door. With lightning speed, he descends the metal staircase. In no time, he runs to the gate.

As he opens it, I leap up, gun drawn. Dammit, the gate opens out instead of in and slams into me, tossing me against the cans and knocking my gun out of my hand.

Gerald turns around. Seeing me, he aims in my direction.

Finding my footing, I grab a lid off one off the cans. With both hands, I swing it broadside, at his head.

Stunned by the blow, he falls against the wall.

But when he staggers to his feet, he's still holding onto his gun.

His face is etched in anger. He wastes no time putting me back in his sights—

I also move quickly. This time the lid hits his gun—

Just as the shot goes off.

The bullet pierces the lid and misses my head by mere inches.

From behind me, I hear Jack shout, "Donna—*down!*"

So that I'm not in the line of Jack's fire I hit the ground with the lid still shielding me from Gerald, just in case he wants to get off one last shot before turning the corner.

He doesn't. Instead, he makes a beeline for the street at the end of the alley.

Jack runs past me, but by the time he turns the corner, Gerald has disappeared.

"Arnie, which way did Gerald go?" Jack shouts.

"He ducked into Kingsbridge Mall," Arnie informs us. "I'll see if I can pull up footage there before he disappears into a store, or catches an Underground train from there. But it'll take a while."

In other words, we've lost him—for now, anyway.

The shrill singsong trill of an ambulance comes closer and closer before stopping abruptly on the opposite side of the house.

Jack trots back to me just as I get back on my feet. "What happened in there?" I ask.

"Gerald shot Roxanna before he ran. By the time we shot off the lock, she was unconscious and bleeding out. Abu will ride to the hospital with her."

"I thought Gerald and Roxanna were in cahoots! Why did he want to kill her?"

Jack shrugs. "Another loose end? I don't know. And we won't know those answers until Roxanna pulls through—or not. If she does, he'll call us so that we can question her. Dominic is driving us back to the club for now."

I'm on Jack's heels as he heads back down the alley and toward the car.

WE'RE DRIVING BACK WHEN EMMA CALLS. "OKAY, I'VE GOT BAD NEWS and good news."

"Save the best for last," Jack and I say in unison.

Emma chuckles. "Works for me. Okay so, Aziza's texts with Adam are pretty much run-of-the-mill: weather, club gossip, employee griping, blue-skying on their hopes for their future, some flirting. Which leaves me to think they must have worked out a few code words in advance. But because there's no evidence here of a monoalphabetic substitution cipher, more than likely the words were changed on a daily basis. Heck, even the emojis they used might have been part of the code."

"Ouch," I murmur.

"As for Adam's movements within the club on the day in question, other than going from his employee locker to the casino or employee break room, he did nothing out of the ordinary if in fact employees are allowed to borrow books from the club's library."

"I know that staff is encouraged to do so, as long as they read and return," Dominic explains.

"Even so, why would he put one on the library's shelves in such a strange manner?"

"How so?" I ask.

"He pulled out several books first and then mixed them around before putting them back on the shelf—along with his, I assume," Emma explains.

"Why do you say 'assume?'" Jack asks.

"Because he made sure that the security camera couldn't see the name or spine of the book in his hand when he walked in."

"He must have known the camera would catch his shuffle game," Jack deduces.

Strange.

Suddenly, it hits me. "He did it because he knew Aziza would watch for it."

"If so, we have to get back and tell Lucky," Dominic exclaims fervently. "She'll be intimately familiar with the library's collection." He lingers on the word, *intimately*.

Jack catches my eye and shakes his head: his way of signaling me to take the lead on the book retrieval task.

I hope he doesn't have to taze Dominic to keep him from joining me.

21

Lucky

*D*esperate to wash off the previous day, especially the horrible night, and sitting on go waiting to hear from Donna and Jack, I repaired to my room. As I stepped out of my shoes and tugged off my earrings, I called for some lunch. My order of something edible and hot with a full pot of American coffee, left the room service guy a bit perplexed. I didn't care.

Peeling off clothes as I headed toward the bathroom, I'd dropped the last of them by the time I reached and opened the tap. Scalding would do the trick on yesterday's grime.

While the steam billowed, and the tub filled, I checked my phone. Jean-Charles had given up. I hadn't received a text from him since the last one I ignored. Was it yesterday or the day before? At some point I'd have to throw the man a bone...or he'd have to offer me one.

I wondered how we'd be at make-up sex.

Should I text him? Call him? What would I say? We had so much to hash out that it stifled even the simplest connection.

I dipped a toe in the water, then slowly lowered myself to chin level. I felt time slipping away. Why didn't Donna call?

I'D JUST STEPPED OUT OF THE BATH AND DONNED A THICK TURKISH terry cloth robe, winding the sash around my waist twice, when a knock at the door announced the arrival of my food. Copious amounts of caffeine would do my body good, and maybe get my brain in gear. The food wouldn't hurt either.

The room service guy left the door ajar as he set the tray on a table by the window. He nodded then vanished, leaving a large silver pot in a quilted cover, a delicate porcelain cup with matching creamer, no sugar, and a small plate holding a perfect omelet and two perfect croissants I'd forgotten to order. An oversight my well-trained staff would never tolerate. Now if they could just save me from myself in every other aspect of my life…

My phone pierced the blissful quiet, interrupting my first delicious sip of the steaming brew. My cup clattered on the tray as I ran to find the offending device. I shook out my clothes that pooled on the floor where I had discarded them. Nothing. Then I dashed into the bathroom. Still nothing. Four rings so far. The call would cycle to voicemail soon. Then I unfolded the crumpled towel. Bingo! I squinted at the caller ID as I swiped to answer.

Of course, it would be Mother.

"Isn't it late there," I asked before she could launch in. The weather outside was half-gloom, London's everyday version of our full brightness at home. Early yet, but the traffic hummed and honked below. The day was well under way. Friday. My French fish-or-cut-bait day.

"When you have babies, day and night are irrelevant. Time is separated into asleep and awake." She sounded tired and more than a little bit frazzled. "Right now, they are asleep, I am awake. I'm working on it."

"I assume we have more names?" I regained my cup and stared out the window into another gray day. As much as I found the constant sunshine in Vegas monotonous, places like London made me realize I couldn't live without feeling the warmth on my skin. Was Seasonal Affect Disorder environmental or inherited? Who knew? Either way, sunshine mattered. That whole Vitamin D thing probably played into it. If we didn't need sunshine, then why did the Powers That Be make a critical vitamin sunshine-dependent? And why did my thoughts roll off down that hill today?

Probably because I didn't want to think about anything else.

Aziza. Nigel. CIA operatives in my club. Employees running a sex-tape extortion scheme. A demanding fiancé. Hell, my mother looked like a minor distraction.

Mona sighed, her weariness feeding mine. "Naming someone is more responsibility than I remember."

Or want, I thought, but kept my mouth shut. Poking her was bad form and no fun.

"Nobody ever likes their names, so I wouldn't give it more thought than it's due. What are you thinking?"

"Blackjack and Roulette. We'd call them Jackie and Rou."

I could picture my mother, disheveled, exhausted, desperate to do the right thing but totally unsure how, as she white-knuckled the phone. "Closer. Much closer. I do like Jackie and Rou. The whole Vegas tie-in works. But having their given names, the ones the teachers will be calling out in front of the class at the beginning of the school year, being Blackjack and Roulette, that might be a little hard."

"But if I just name them Jackie and Rou then I lose the impact."

"I get it. Could you maybe give it one more shot? You're really close."

"You think?"

"I know so, Mother." I held the phone to my ear with my shoulder so I could pour more coffee. Somehow, I knew today would require full caffeination. "How's Father?" Even though I wanted to shoot him, I loved him. His recovery had been slower than everyone had hoped.

"He's not himself. I don't know what to do."

My heart sank. "Has he been back to the doctor's?"

"You know your father."

That meant no. One more problem without a ready solution. "I'll see what I can do."

"Lucky, go to Paris then come home," she whispered then the line went dead.

Problems were my specialty, yet I stood there transfixed, as if concrete encased my feet, while I pressed the phone to my ear even though my mother had severed the connection.

Desperate for a problem I could solve, I hit a familiar speed dial.

Detective Romeo answered on the first ring. "Yo."

"You sound rather perky." He also sounded awake. I was glad I hadn't awakened him. Well, sort of. The kid got far too little sleep as it was.

"The mischief turns serious here after dark."

"I know. Do you have anything pressing at the moment?"

"No. Whatcha need?"

"I need you to go get my father and take him to the hospital. Use your gun if you have to."

"Oh, that'll be fun." His tone told me the exact opposite.

"Please."

"What, no threat? No 'I'll owe you big time.'"

"No. This is serious."

"You got it."

"Thanks. Just add it to my tab."

"Ah, there you are." I could hear the smile in his voice. "Heard your trip went to shit. Anything I can do?"

"Just take care of my father. Please."

I pocketed my phone and stared once again, lost in the gray. Friends. So important. That intrinsic trust. I wondered about Donna, Jack, and the Acme group.

Could I trust them? Or would they leave me dangling?

Worse, would I regret giving them Adam?

A TEXT BUZZED THROUGH AS I WAS PUTTING THE FINISHING TOUCHES on what was determined to be a bad hair day. My heart leapt.

Jean-Charles.

No, Donna. *Meet me in the library when you're decent.*

As I stared at my reflection, I wondered what her definition of decent was. My standards were pretty low. I'd tamed the hair, slapped on some war paint—nothing I could do about the dark circles hanging like hammocks under my eyes. They did offset the blue rather well, though. Small consolation for looking like a member of the zombie apocalypse. I brushed down the brown cashmere sweater and adjusted the collar of the matching silk shirt underneath. My slacks were khaki and the Ferragamos with kitten heels were two-toned to pick up both the dark and the light brown. Mona always told me, no matter what, I should dress and put on my face. That way the day would never be a total loss. As I checked my teeth then turned off the light, I wasn't buying it.

The library was tucked in beside the room used for breakfast, which fronted the building. They were clearing away the buffet or I'd have been tempted—the omelet and croissants, while brilliant, did little to fill the hole in my belly.

As I passed the larger room we used for state dinners and that sort of fanciness, I noticed two of the three rugs had been returned. The third one was still missing. I detoured to the front desk to inquire. Julie was still manning her post—and probably would for a bit since we were now understaffed due to the hasty departures of Prunella and Lavinia.

"Miss O'Toole." A wariness replaced her normal warmth. The change in her demeanor had appeared this morning after Dominic and his friends had walked me out of the club, drugged to the max, the night before. I wanted to ask Julie what I'd done, but I didn't. I wasn't sure I could handle it.

"Good morning. The third rug?" I hooked my thumb toward the room.

"It'll be back today. In time for the party tonight."

"Thanks." *The party tonight.* If I wanted to have some choice in my future, I had a party I needed to get to. Eight-thirty sharp, Jean-Charles had said. Avenue Kleber near the Hotel Raphael. I glanced at my watch. Make-it-or-break-it time. Six hours max and I'd better be racing for the airport.

Donna fell into step as I strode into the library. "Good to see you've pulled yourself together."

"Outsides can be deceiving." I stopped in the middle of the room and did a three-sixty. Something about libraries with their walls of floor-to-ceiling books soothed my soul. This one was octagonal and two-storied with a brass ladder on rollers attached to a railing that could be positioned exactly where one wanted it. As a little girl I lusted after Professor Higgins's library in *My Fair Lady*. Now I had one—if I was willing to travel to London to partake. A bit of a commute but worth the experience. "It's something, isn't it?"

Even Donna seemed affected as she drank it in.

"Why are we here?" I asked after we each had taken a moment. Thankfully, we had the room to ourselves.

"A couple of reasons. First, we tracked Gerald. He'd given the club a false address, but we were able to track his movements from his last day here. In fact, he has a deeply buried original name and background. Once upon a time he was known as Edgar Black. He served in the U.K.'s Special Reconnaissance Regiment in Afghanistan and Yemen. Dishonorable discharge."

I winced. So not good. "We vet our people very well."

"Whatever he had his fingers in, he knew enough folks to scrub his identity. We had to dig deep, and our resources are far beyond those you have access to."

I didn't know whether that was a good thing or a bad thing.

"We've got feelers out to MI6 to find out exactly how and why." Donna touched my arm. "And here's another piece of the puzzle: Edgar aka Gerald had a visitor: Aziza's roommate from Oxford—Roxanna Marmaduke."

"Interesting."

"We thought so too." Donna shrugged. "So, we crashed their little party, and just in time to save her life. She's comatose but the doctors say she should make it. If she comes out of it, Abu is there to grill her." Donna glanced into the lobby. "However, Gerald got away."

"A shame." And a shit storm. "I guess we have our murderer. I'd just like to know why. Why did he kill Aziza?"

"I've seen all kinds of reasons." Donna returned her attention to the books surrounding us. "On another note, after you told us about Adam Kalb, we did some digging. I put our team on your security tapes. The day Aziza died Adam came in here with a book —one he put back in the collection."

"You've been up in Security?" I felt a bit of a huff coming on. "Why wasn't I consulted?"

"No. We tapped in." She seemed rather nonchalant.

"You hacked our system? Do I really need to know this?"

Donna shrugged. "I'm being honest. Thought you'd want to know. And I invited you here. I could just as easily have bypassed you altogether."

Not much I could argue with there. "Was he here for a shift?"

"Yes, he was working the baccarat table. The detour came during his only break."

"Okay, a book you say?" I looked around at the thousands of volumes. "Needle in a haystack or do you have something to go on?"

"He was rather clever, as if he knew he was being watched." Donna wandered over to stand before a section of books on the far wall.

"He worked here. He knew where the cameras were." I stepped in next to her. "But the fact he came here at all meant he was spooked or out of time."

"He moved several of the books, then replaced them all, including the one he walked in with. We didn't get a good look at that one—he kept it hidden until he shuffled it with the other books. I wish I knew exactly what we were looking for, but, whatever it is, it'll be right in here." Donna indicated a small section on the two middle shelves.

"Something that doesn't fit would be my bet." I scanned the spines. Old musty leather splitting and cracked by time and attention. English history. Some of the great English writers. I made a note to redo the collection to reflect the diversity of our members who hailed from the far corners. I let my gaze drift and wander, engaging my subconscious to identify what looked out of place. I'd been down the rows twice before I saw it. A thin white spine.

Letters to a Young Muslim. "Here." I pulled it out. I was familiar with the book. Letters from a UAE Ambassador to Russia written to his son, the collection was billed as a take on what it means to be a Muslim in the modern world. My guess was Aziza struggled with that as well.

As I held up the book, Adam Kalb rounded the corner and burst into the room. His eyes widened when he saw what I held.

Bingo.

His attention flicked to Donna then back to me.

"We know, Adam." Total bullshit. We knew nothing, but over-playing was my strong suit.

His expression hardened. His voice went flat. "What do you know?"

"I know Aziza is dead."

The news sucker-punched him. He crumpled into himself, then straightened, his eyes bright with tears. "She didn't come home. I couldn't find her. I feared the worst. She never told me, but I could see she was scared."

"Home?"

"To her place in Oxford. Or to my flat." He swiped at his tears with the back of his hand. "She was mine. This is all my fault. I loved her so. My heart, it is gone."

I reached toward him, but he pulled back. "Adam, we've known each other a while. Have you ever known me to go back on promises, to not play fair?"

He shook his head. "You are very good to us. I heard what you did in Macau. We all did."

"Why do you think this is all your fault? Aziza was a young woman with a wide independent streak. She made her own choices."

That got a flicker of a smile. "She wouldn't listen." He pulled in a ragged breath. "I told her about the group I am a member of. We want our country back."

His last name was Kalb. "Country?"

"I too am Arab. The Royal family, they run the country with an iron hand. They repress their people and they lie to the world, one minute smiling at the United States and the other Western countries, while sending huge sums of money to terrorist organizations whose sole purpose is to bring down the West. The people, we want more freedom. We want the truth." He pulled a sleeve back to reveal a tattoo on his forearm. I'd seen one just like it...on the back of Aziza's thigh. "This is our symbol. We added an extra character of our own to signify our love." He colored a bit as sadness flattened his features.

Donna leaned in. "The amulet the girl had around her neck had the same inscription.

"As did her thigh." I could tell Donna had made the same connection.

"We want to be a part of the world working together for the greater good." Adam sounded like a true believer.

That last part I thought was a bit idealistic, but I was old. I'd earned my cynicism. Perhaps the kids could change the world. God, I hoped so. We'd sure made a muck of it.

"Aziza wanted in?"

"Not only wanted in, she went after the gold."

"The proof." My stomach knotted. "Her family is involved?"

"Very much so." Adam looked pained. "At least some of them. I let her do it. Such a high price to pay."

And she doubled-down with her life. "You both are very brave. She obviously felt the risk was worth it, even given her health and all."

Someone close. Adam was close. I watched for his reaction.

Confusion. Not what I expected. "Her health? She was as strong as a horse!"

He didn't know. "Sorry. I must be confused. Let's finish the job. We don't want her to have paid the ultimate sacrifice for nothing."

He straightened his shoulders. "You're right."

"Who was after her?"

He glanced at the book; his tears drying. A man remembering his mission. "You have the book, but it's worth nothing without the page number and specific line."

I shot a side-eye at Donna. She nodded.

Damn.

"Adam, we can help you." Jeez, I sounded like some cop spouting fake promises to talk someone off a ledge. Since I had no idea what he and Aziza had really been up to, I had no idea how to help. My toolbox was limited. Acme's, politically constrained.

A conundrum but we needed the truth.

"Who's 'we'?" Adam shot a quick glance at Donna.

Donna stuck out her hand. "Donna Craig, Covert Operations for the CIA."

Adam crossed his arms, ignoring her. "We don't trust the American government. That's why the encryption. We've seen you make promises then leave those who helped you once you got what you wanted. The promises, the human suffering, they meant nothing."

Only one weapon effective against the truth. "I don't blame you. I think you'll find Mrs. Craig to stand by her promises, but maybe you could get a show of good faith or something from the CIA? Would that help? We've got to do something to move forward."

Donna looked at me wide-eyed. I ignored her. She navigated a den of snakes on a daily basis.

Adam weighted my words.

"Who else can you turn to, really?" I was so far out on the limb I felt it would break any minute behind me, plunging me into the abyss.

"Okay. What did you have in mind?"

Donna stepped in. "Can you de-encrypt one name, one Saudi of some importance, who has been funneling money to a terrorist organization?"

"And then?"

"We'll need the proof."

"Okay. And then?"

"What do you want to happen, Adam?" I asked.

"We want them eliminated. We want our country back. The monarchy is corrupt. They play two ends against the middle. They fund unrest and war around the world to keep the oil prices high. It hurts all of us." His passion was clear.

"Okay," Donna said. "You give us a name and proof. And we'll do as you ask."

"I will text it to you."

Smart boy. Acme was great at hacking computers.

Donna gave him her contact info. Within a minute her phone dinged the arrival of a text.

"Wow. Okay. Where is this man now?"

"Athens. Meeting with the Russians—in an hour, in fact. Aziza knew this."

"Then I better get moving." She brushed by Adam on her way out the door.

Adam and I watched her go.

"Do you think she'll do what she said?" Adam asked. The hardness had left his voice. Hurt replaced it. "It's all on me now and we are running out of time. They killed Aziza, I know they did."

I watched the empty doorway long after Donna had disappeared.

"She'll make good."

If she didn't, I'd kill her myself.

22

Donna

"So, what you're telling me is that the only way the CIA gets the full list of Saudi terrorist funders is this supposed show of faith? Extermination photos of a couple of Saudi operatives as they purchase arms from the Russians?" Ryan asks.

"Yes. Frankly, I can't blame Adam for asking for some sort of assurance," I reply. "The CIA is notorious for giving with one hand and taking away with the other."

Because I've got my phone on speaker mode, I can pace the room as I speak. Jack is propped up on one of the twin beds. His way of showing his concern about our time crunch is by flexing his fingers.

"Our largest employer has its reasons for what it does. And it always does what is best for our country, first and foremost," Ryan counters. "Okay, so from what I'm reading, in less than an hour the munitions sale is to take place in a warehouse located on the outskirts of Athens' Metaxourgeio district."

"Affirmative," Jack says. "You've just received the warehouse's address as well as the video of the two Arab businessmen in question. We also know that arms and ammo are being given to a Yemeni-based Houthis terrorist cell."

"Once the CIA provides us with photos of the dead men, Adam

will release their identities to us, along with Aziza's cipher for the rest of her intel. It includes the full list of the UAE traitors along with the bank accounts that trace all previous munitions purchases from Russia, and the traitors' sales to the UAE's enemies," I add. "Adam also wants the CIA to feel free to pass the success of this operation forward to the Saudis. Or, as he put it, 'the sooner the UAE knows it has a bed of snakes in its midst, the better.'"

"It'll be a feather in the CIA's cap," Jack points out.

"Something DIO Branham will greatly appreciate," Ryan agrees. "I'll send this over to him now. As you're already aware, the CIA has a strong presence in Athens. Hopefully, a couple of exterminators can be deployed quickly enough to catch the operation in action. As soon as I have the kill photos, you will too."

THE SECOND RYAN RINGS OFF MY PHONE, ABU'S NUMBER LIGHTS UP Jack's caller ID.

When Jack responds, Abu appears on the phone video app. "The bullet missed her lung. Roxanna is out of surgery," Abu assures us. "And she's willing to talk." He turns the phone so that we can see her.

Roxanna's lids are barely open, but her eyes and mouth open wide when she realizes she may be taking a different and much less desirable tumble with the mystery man who she almost took into her bed.

"Roxanna, my name is Jack Craig." Jack doesn't smile, and his tone is severe. "You're a person of interest in the death of your roommate, Aziza Halabi."

She bows her head. Tears fall from her cheeks onto her hospital gown.

"You knew she'd been murdered." Jack's tone dares her to deny this.

Roxanna nods slowly.

"In fact, you played a role in her death." We don't know this for sure. Still, Jack wants to see if she denies it.

Roxanna responds with a torrent of grief. "I didn't know that was what he'd planned! When he approached me, he said he was concerned that she'd fallen in with some terrible people. He asked me to keep an eye on her—you know, report back daily to him, about anyone who came to visit her. Men, women, it didn't matter. He insisted on knowing about it. He even offered me money—a lot of it." Roxanna shrugs. "But crikey! Aziza was the closest thing to a hermit I've ever known!" She stares into the camera's eye. "He thought I was lying, so he upped the ante. I was to get a bonus if I...if I ..." Roxanna's voice breaks under the weight of her guilt.

"If you what?" Jack asks.

"If I broke into her computer or her mobile. But it wasn't as easy as he thought. If she didn't have her devices on her, she locked them in her desk. The few times she left them alone I couldn't open them because they were password protected. Still, I needed the money, so I had to try! The last time I saw her, she was taking notes as she talked to someone on the phone. Then she hurried out. I got the bright idea to run a pencil over the pad and see what letters came up."

"What did you find?" Jack demands.

"'Vulture.' A few other words or phrases as well. But because she'd written them in a row, it certainly didn't make any sense to me."

"Do you remember what they were?"

She grimaces as she thinks. "'Royal S.' Tuesday's date. 20:10, and..." She pauses in thought. "Oh yes—Hermès!"

Roxanna can see that Jack is now staring off-screen, but not at what, or whom.

Me.

Aziza was writing down Nigel Ahern's instructions on whom the CIA would send for the intel, and where she was to meet me.

So yes, Roxanna was complicit in her murder.

"And this is the information you passed along to Gerald."

"Who?" Roxanna stares quizzically at Jack.

He shakes his head. "The man who tried to kill you—Gerald Morten. Or perhaps you know him as Edgar Black."

"That man?" Adamantly, she shakes her head. "No! I was talking about Aziza's uncle—Sheik Mohammed Ben Halabi."

I'm stunned, as is Jack.

Finally, Roxanna adds, "That man—Gerald, you say?—He was...well if you must know, sometimes I must sell my services as...a private escort." She buries her face in her hands. "He must have seen my ad somewhere."

"That's too much of a coincidence," I whisper to Jack.

He nods in agreement, but he's smart enough to keep this to himself.

"But I don't like the rough stuff, and I refused to be tied up. That's when he pulled out his gun. If you and that other hunky toff hadn't broken down the door, I'd be..." Roxanna's voice trails off.

"As dead as Aziza," Jack tells her.

She buries her head in a pillow and sobs.

To talk further in private, Abu walks out of Roxanna's room. "At Ryan's behest, MI6 was kind enough to have a police officer stationed outside Roxanna's door," Abu explains. "I'm heading back now."

"Is Ryan worried that Gerald will come back to finish the job?" I ask.

"No. The security is just a precautionary measure. Ryan feels Edgar Black may be long gone. And believe me, he's not happy about that."

Of course not. And there will be hell to pay for letting Black slip from our fingers.

"Arnie is trying his damnedest to pick up his trail again," Jack points out.

Here's hoping he succeeds.

In the meantime, I pray the CIA doesn't blow Acme's one chance to pull its fat out of the fire: bringing down the Saudi traitors who wish to keep the Middle East in constant turmoil.

I AM BACK TO PACING, WHICH IS BETTER THAN JACK'S CURRENT activity: staring at me while I pace.

Okay, maybe having his eyes follow me around this oversized closet of a room isn't so bad. If I weren't in such an anxious frame of mind, I'd do something to make it worth his while. I don't know, maybe a striptease or something.

The thought of this makes me smile.

Seeing me smile puts a grin on Jack's face. "What are you thinking about?" he asks.

"You."

His smile widens. He pats the bed.

But then these few seconds of diversion are cut short by the muted hum of my phone.

I look down at the caller ID: "It's Ryan."

Jack nods resignedly. Back to battle stations.

"The exterminators got there in time and made the kill." There's a satisfied lilt in Ryan's voice. "They took down the two buyers and their bodyguards—two of them—along with three Russians. The ops team collected the munitions cache too. Video taken from a surveillance drone is coming in now."

The footage looks as if it's happening in real time:

Despite January's early nightfall, the video from the drone—the shape and size of a mosquito— is crystal clear. We watch as the targets, driving a panel van, pull up to the roll-up cargo door of a one-story unmarked windowless warehouse that sits in the middle of a block filled with other nondescript buildings.

A man—buff, chrome-domed, and unshaven—walks out from the warehouse's security door, solid metal except for a peephole and knob. Chrome Dome glares hard at the driver and his passenger before nodding, at which point the cargo door rolls up and the van backs into it before the door goes down again.

Three blocks away, the CIA ops team—two men and a woman —stroll nonchalantly toward the warehouse. In dress and coloring —olive complexions, casual jackets, and jeans—they could easily pass for Greek natives.

Security cameras are placed around the warehouse, but no doubt the CIA had hacked the feeds and looped them.

When the operatives are two blocks away, the older of the two men breaks away from the others to enter the yard of the warehouse next door. After leaping over the adjoining fence, he positions himself behind a dumpster. From there he has a bird's eye view of the back door.

The other man and the woman cross the street. They have now taken on the role of entwined lovers out for a walk. Acts of adoration—stroking fingers, furtive kisses—are mimed as they make their way past the warehouse. In case anyone inside the warehouse is looking out through a peephole, they walk another half-block before doubling back around. When they reach the two-story building on the far side of the warehouse—a book depository—the man ducks behind the leafy bushes against the fence closest to the targets' warehouse. He is in position to shoot anyone who goes out the front door.

As for the woman, she makes her way up the book depository's back staircase to its second floor. From there she's able to leap onto a small balcony, where she climbs up on its railing to pull herself onto the roof. She then runs to the side closest to the targets' warehouse and leaps onto its flat tar roof. She lands low and tucks into a roll. When she stops, she lies flat.

The team waits for someone to come out to investigate.

No one does.

The woman crawls toward a vent on the roof and drops something into it.

In less than a minute, six men are running out the back door followed by a gold cloud of tear gas. The first one takes a bullet to the head. By the time he falls, the man behind him is shot in the chest. The third man tries to sidestep his fallen friends, but he can't outrun the bullet meant for him.

By now the woman has rolled to the back of the roof. She aims down from above, taking out the next two of the men with shots to the back of their necks.

The last man comes out the door coughing, sputtering, and with his hands up, only to get a bullet to the chest.

A moment later all three CIA operatives are in the back of the warehouse. After the woman takes a picture of each kill, the men take turns dragging the bodies back inside the warehouse.

Six minutes later the cargo door rolls up, and the van pulls out. After it closes again, the van drives away.

The drone video ends. The still shots of the dead men's faces are attached in a separate file.

"Text Lucky," Jack says. "Tell her we have what Adam needs to see, and we'll meet her in Nigel's office. In the meantime, I'll call Arnie and Emma. We can send her the cipher, page by page, when we get in. Still, she and her team will need to move quickly."

Even as I nod, I'm already texting:

Proof is here. Meet you with AK in manager's office?

Lucky immediately texts back:

We'll be waiting for you.

Glancing over at my phone screen, Jack smirks, "What, no happy face emoji?"

I sigh. "Does Lucky strike you as the emoji type?"

"No more than she strikes me as Dominic's," Jack retorts.

"Where is Casanova anyway?"

Jack rolls his eyes. "Picking up flowers for Lucky. He thinks that will woo her away from her Frenchman."

"He'll have to do better than that," I acknowledge. "Like, say, crack a book or two. Or maybe get the words 'I' and 'me' out of every sentence. And it wouldn't hurt if he could look a woman in the eye as opposed to her chest."

Jack laughs. "You've enjoyed watching her put him in his place, haven't you?"

"At first, yes," I concede. "But now I can't wait to see him back to his old pompous, narcissistic self."

"As soon as Adam gives us what we need, Lucky takes off for Paris," Jack replies. "All the more reason we should head up now."

As PROMISED, LUCKY AND ADAM ARE WAITING FOR US IN NIGEL'S office. While I play the video, Adam's face shifts through a kaleido-scope of emotions. His initial wariness as to whether his wish was granted softens to fascination as the agents take their positions. Watching as the targets are shot as they run out, he smiles approvingly.

And yet, when the van finally drives away, the sadness returns to Adam's eyes. "I wish Aziza was here to see this."

Lucky puts her hand on his arm as if to comfort him.

Jack says softly, "Adam, we now need the cipher."

Adam nods and pulls the book from his satchel. "Page 156, line 17."

Arnie takes it. Immediately he photographs the page and trans-mits it to Emma.

Emma answers, "Got it. Give us a few minutes."

While everyone waits in silence, Lucky looks down at her watch and frowns. No doubt she's worried about making her flight.

"Hey, listen, if you need to get ready for your departure, no worries. The second we break the code I'll call you. I know how important it is to you that Aziza and Nigel's deaths weren't in vain." I place a hand on Lucky's arm. "Again, I want to apologize about our earlier misunderstanding. And I'm sure I speak for all of us at Acme when I say your assistance was invaluable."

Lucky smiles. "I'm just glad I was able to convince you I was one of the good guys before I lost a few knuckles."

"Well, if you had, it might have been just the thing to smother the flames of Dominic's ardor," I reply slyly.

She laughs all the way out the door.

23

Lucky

*F*or once I decided to leave the clean-up to the pros.

We didn't yet have Aziza's killer, but we had everything else. And Donna and Jack had promised—Aziza's murderer would be brought to justice. They'd delivered on their promises so far. Trust wasn't my best thing, but I trusted them to finish the deal.

I had to.

It was Paris make-it-or-break-it time. If I planned to arrive at the party before cocktails were served, wheels up had to happen within the next hour. Even then it would be tight. So, the sooner, the better. Hence the packing thing.

Even though the murderer was no longer my problem, something niggled at me. Something I knew.

The call came in just as I was sitting on my suitcase trying to force it closed. Just out of reach, my phone taunted me, dancing as it vibrated. I tried to see the caller ID. The angle was wrong, the distance too far. Should I, or shouldn't I? If I released the pressure on my suitcase, the thing would explode, clothes popping out like a clown from a wind-up box. And I'd have to start over. Short on time, that was not my best option.

Ignore it, Lucky!

Gerald killed Nigel and Roxanna. The flowers…someone close. Adam was close to Aziza. But he was working when Aziza was killed. Sheik Ben? Gerald.

Would Ben order a hit on his own niece? But he was family…

I worked the zipper, tugging, stuffing, tugging some more as I tried to ignore the Siren call of the phone. It could be a problem needing my attention—a drug to my inner do-gooder. Resistance was almost futile.

Ben knew the door to the Royal Suite was open. He made a beeline for the master suite. He knew.

Finally, I managed to get a latch into its slot, then lunged for my phone. I caught the call on the verge of rolling to voicemail. "O'Toole."

"Emma's team cracked the cipher," Donna said. "The boss is out, but when he gets back he'll be quite pleased."

"That's great, Donna, but I've got to run. Ball is in your court now."

"There's something you should know."

Her tone brought me up short and my heart flopped over like a dying duck. "What?"

"The ringleader?" She left it hanging.

The truth sucker punched me: "Sheik Mohammed Ben Halabi."

"Bingo." Donna didn't seem surprised.

I sank into a chair as my one fear was realized. Sheik Ben. Family. Someone Aziza should have been able to trust…

"She'd been a sick child," he'd said. The son of a bitch!

"Donna, Ben knew she had a heart condition." I paced the floor. "Gerald must be killing on Ben's orders."

"If so, Gerald may have put two more scalps on his belt since this morning," Donna replied. "Emma pulled up a Scotland Yard alert about a mysterious double homicide that took place early this morning. You know them: Prunella and Lavinia. Their bodies were found in the locked bathroom stall of a local pub just a couple of blocks from the Babylon, so it may have been after their shift. Their throats were slit."

Holy shit! My hands shook and tears stung my eyes as I

fumbled with my earphones, jamming them in my ears, then dropping my phone in my pocket.

Aziza, Nigel, Roxanna, Prunella, Lavinia...

Adam! *Shit!*

I bolted out of my chair, grabbed my suitcase and headed toward the door. "And we need to find Adam. He's the last loose end to tie up, at least that we know of."

"Hey, I need to jump on a call here," Donna replied. "It's the boss man!"

"I'll work on corralling Sheik Ben on this end." I'll probably kill him when I find him. I left that part out.

"We'll get there as soon as we can." Donna sounded worried, as if she thought I might do something stupid. "Be careful."

Silly woman. In situations like this, stupid was my go-to.

My next call was to Security. Bree still manned the phones. "Can you get a visual on Sheik Ben?"

"Thirty seconds." Bree's voice dropped into all-business mode. I'd almost made it to the lobby when she came back. "His limo just pulled away. He has luggage."

My best guess is he'd be heading to the heliport on the river. "And Adam Kalb?"

"The dealer?" Part of her job was intimate familiarity with our staff.

"Yep." The elevator doors opened, and I bolted toward the front door. Dodging and darting I ignored the stunned looks as I raced by.

"Hang on." Another pause. "Odd. He followed Ben out."

I skidded to a stop at the curb, then scanned the street to my left—that's how they'd have to go to get to the river. A black limo, it's brake lights blinking red, turned right at the corner. The revving of a motor to my right made me jump back. A motorcycle flashed past, its driver hunched over the handlebars. No helmet. No jacket. In a hurry.

Adam Kalb!

Shit!

He'd put two and two together one step ahead of me and was

now most likely hell bent on revenge. At least, with my limited understanding of men, that's what I assumed.

I shoved my suitcase at a bellman—the other two I'd arrived with, I'd sent ahead. "Have this delivered immediately to my plane at the FBO at London City airport. Tell them to be ready to go."

I didn't wait for a reply. Instead, I worked on a solution. No cabs. No limos. The street choked with traffic.

As if the Fates wanted to give me a fighting chance, a courier on a Ducati bumped up the curb to my right. He left the engine running as he dashed inside with an envelope.

After only a moment of indecision, I straddled the machine, pushed it off its kickstand, then rolled throttle and popped the clutch. A car screeched to a stop. The sound of metal crunching. I didn't look back as I darted, squeezing through the knotted traffic, cars jammed together, the drivers aggressively claiming every inch.

At this time of day, the traffic would slow down the limo, but I had a small footprint and could wiggle through. If Ben didn't know we were onto him, that might give me the time I needed to catch up and save Adam from himself, and the rest of us from the likes of Sheik Ben.

If Adam didn't do something stupid before I got there.

I shouted at Siri to call the last number that had called me as I worked through the gears. The wind whipped past, bringing tears to my eyes as I shed the rust of having traded a Harley for a Porsche a decade or more ago. Amazingly, Siri did as I asked, and I heard my call ring through. When I came to a straight stretch, I lowered myself over the handlebars, shut my eyes, and opened the throttle, splitting lanes. At one point I think a side mirror grazed my elbow.

The shouted epithet riding the wind behind me confirmed my suspicion. I raised a hand in apology, not that it would do anything more than add fuel to the fire of his road rage. But I tried.

Donna answered, and I gave her the high points, adding, "My

guess is Ben will be flying out of the London Heliport on the river."

"Got it. We're heading out now." The line went dead.

Feeling the call of longevity, I opened one eye to a slit—just enough to avoid cracking my skull like a melon on the car in front of me. A flash of brake lights. A quick glance to mark Adam's progress. Then I swerved to my left, bumping up the curb. I let the speed bleed off, but not much as I darted around startled pedestrians. One lady, her arms filled with packages, grew wide-eyed and made like a deer in the headlights, stopping stiff-legged in the middle of the walkway.

Instinctively, I yanked the handlebars to the right, throwing my weight to the left. A dodge, then a dart. No blood spilled. But ten years erased from my future. Sort of a good trade.

I wiggled off the curb, then into the crush of cars. I had to tiptoe the bike through, then balance at a slow speed until I had an opening. I put a foot down, steering, ignoring the epithets. Muscle memory overriding fear.

Finally, in the clear, with a narrow slot, I twisted the throttle. Adam had disappeared.

Shit!

My phone rang in my ear.

Donna and Jack, I bet. I had to answer. Risking death, I let go with my left hand and found the tiny place to squeeze on my earbuds to answer.

"Lucky?" A familiar voice, but not the one I expected.

"Mother?" Seriously? If there was a bad time to call, that woman could find it.

"Where are you?"

"Risking death."

"You are always one for the drama."

I didn't argue. That would take brainpower I needed right now to avoid killing myself. I swerved to the right, then took a right at the next corner, trying to wind my way toward the heliport. Worrying about losing Adam was pointless. I knew where he was going.

Okay, worrying was pointless only if I arrived first.

"Mother, I can't talk," I shouted over the wind.

"But I've finally come up with good names for the girls." Even with the engine whining and the air shouting past, I could hear her whine.

"Not now." I slammed an open palm against my chest, hoping I disconnected the call somehow.

I flew past a cop writing a ticket and thereby adding to the bottleneck. I never understood why cops did that. Rush hour, and the guy wants to take a lane to make a point. As I gunned the engine, his head swiveled my way. But, already busy, he didn't give chase.

Too bad—if he'd followed me, he could've made a murder bust instead of dropping a few pounds into the local coffers. His choice.

Up ahead, I could see a figure on a motorcycle also weaving in and out of traffic. Adam! Either I guessed right as to the shortest path to the river and the heliport, or we both were lost. Either way, I had the kid. Donna and Jack could take care of Sheik Ben, which was a good thing. Frankly, I didn't trust myself not to wring his neck, which would be awkward.

I kept Adam in sight but allowed some room between us. He didn't need to know I was there.

Up ahead the kid weaved in and out of traffic, his speed increasing. To keep him in sight, I did the same. We had to be getting close. I could smell the river—that disturbing smell of nature carrying the load of industry and the hopes of mankind. A heavy load the river often suffered.

Adam banked hard to the left across traffic. A car swerved to miss him. I cringed, then leapt into the fray. The Fates were still playing fair. I popped through and onto an expanse of concrete, hot on the kid's tailpipe.

A guard had stopped the limo at the heliport's gate then stepped back from the driver's window. A single wooden arm rose up, allowing the car through. Adam and I both seized the opening. I twisted the throttle to the stops, laying my chest on the gas tank and flattening myself against the machine.

The arm lowered as we raced toward it. Ten yards to go.

Lower.

Side by side now, Adam's knee touched mine. He glanced at me, his eyes wide.

Five yards.

The guard stepped into our path, waving his arms.

At least he didn't have a gun.

I never wavered.

Keeping my weight centered, the bike upright, I leaned off to the side.

The guard dove out of the way.

The arm came down.

I cleared it by inches. Then slammed on the brakes to miss the guard's ankle and foot that stuck into my path. Adam was twenty yards ahead when I returned to the chase.

A car screeched in from the other direction. Donna, Jack, and Dominic piled out and ran for the helicopter.

Sheik Ben grabbed his valise from the porter and rushed to the chopper, which was already spooling up. A black beast with Arab markings—the Sheik's personal aircraft. At the open door, he turned.

He centered a gun on Adam. Almost abreast, I leapt off my machine, hitting Adam shoulder high. A sting blazed across my upper arm as we both fell. Adam absorbed the brunt of our landing. On the bottom, he hit the ground with a thud, breaking my fall with his body. His breath rushed out of him in a whoosh.

The bikes wobbled then laid down, gouging the earth, mud flying, until their momentum was spent. Then engines idled as if awaiting our next stupidity.

I stayed where I'd stopped. My bulk and Adam's lack of air would hold him at least long enough for Donna and Jack to get Sheik Ben.

While Adam gulped air, I swiveled to watch Donna and her team. The three of them surrounded Sheik Ben. Dominic took his gun, which he relinquished more easily than I would have in his position.

I rolled off Adam, then extended a hand and pulled him to his feet. "You look a little green." And covered with mud, which he didn't try to wipe off.

"He must die." Adam's tone was flat with finality.

"Kid, there are worse things than death. Let's serve him up one of those experiences. What do you say?" The image of Sheik Ben being the pretty play toy in a Federal pen captured my imagination. Justice most divine...and deserved.

Adam swallowed hard but didn't look convinced. Revenge, a powerful emotion that gave rise to so many foolish acts.

"He's not worth the jail time."

"But Aziza..." Adam's pain etched deep grooves around his mouth. He'd aged ten years in two days.

I tugged him toward the gaggle that now surrounded Sheik Ben. "Aziza would want you to finish the job, to restore her country to her people."

That seemed to do it. I felt the anger leave him. Once I was sure Adam wouldn't go running off like an avenging angel, I let go of him.

The noise of the helicopter as it beat the air into submission pulsed through us. The jet engine whined.

I bent at the waist, ducking under the blades as they gained speed, and motioned Adam to do the same. The downdraft whipped at us, tugging at our clothes, sending grit into our eyes.

We joined the group just in time to hear Ben shout, "I don't give a fuck who you are or what authority you think you have. I'm a member of the Saudi Royal Family and an official emissary to the UK. As such, I have complete diplomatic immunity."

"That's bullshit!" I raised my voice to be heard. Subtlety and diplomacy were not tools in my toolbox. "You knew about Aziza's heart condition, didn't you?" I pointed at Sheik Ben. Somehow, I managed to resist grabbing him by the throat and squeezing until he turned blue. God that would feel good.

His dark eyes locked on mine. He smiled pure evil. "She was a sick child."

I turned to Donna. "There! He just admitted it. He killed her, or ordered it done. Immunity does not extend to charges of first-degree murder." I looked to Donna for confirmation.

She backed away, one finger pressed to an earpiece. "Let him go," she mouthed then motioned to her team.

"What?" I shouted as I grabbed her arm. "You can't just let him waltz out of here!" I considered the penalty for killing him myself. Like I said, stupid is my go-to and the sheik's smirk was goad enough.

Donna peeled my fingers off her arm. She gave me a long stare. "Lucky, it'll be okay." I couldn't quite catch her tone, but her words were clear.

Adam must've sensed my give-in. He leapt toward Sheik Ben. "No!"

Jack coldcocked the kid and he dropped like a sack of potatoes.

Ben brushed his hair into place, then tugged on the tail of his shirt. He gave me a nod, then turned and climbed into the chopper.

Jack and Dominic each grabbed an arm and pulled Adam away from the chopper. Donna and I joined them a safe distance away. We watched as Ben secured himself into the aircraft, then turned and gave us a salute as the craft lifted.

The blades kicked up a cloud of dirt and we all flinched away from it, shielding our eyes. At about fifty feet, the pilot—one of Ben's pilots—eased into forward flight. The dust settled, and we watched the chopper bank sharply over the river, still climbing.

I was just about to turn away when an explosion ripped the air.

The helicopter burst into a fireball.

We all hit the deck. Pieces of the blades whirled by, peppering the earth. I covered Adam with my body, then held my arms over my head as pieces of metal rained down.

QUIET FILLED THE AIR AROUND US AS IF THE WORLD HELD ITS BREATH after the explosion.

Donna was the first to speak. "An eye for an eye."

I pushed myself off of Adam who was beginning to stir. Sitting on my heels, I took a quick appraisal—all body parts attached and functional. "Did you do that?" I asked her as I looked at the hole in the sky where the chopper had been.

"I can neither confirm nor deny," she said as she stood, looking sad and satisfied at the same time.

I so got that. But still, something about being judge and jury bothered me. Not my universe, I guess. And I was glad there were folks like Donna and Jack who could exact justice. Right now, I envied them, but I knew their shades of gray would not be a comfortable place for this black and white gal.

"What happened?" Adam sat up, working his jaw.

"You can thank the gentleman there," I pointed to Jack, "for saving you from yourself."

Jack offered Adam a hand. "If you have to give up yourself to gain victory, the price is way too high, kid. Wait for a better opportunity."

"In my culture, it is considered holy to martyr oneself for the greater good." Adam scanned the sky.

"In my culture, it's a waste of resources." Jack said exactly what I was thinking.

That seemed to get Adam's attention. "The sheik. He is gone?"

I jumped in, letting Donna and her crew off the hook. "In a manner of speaking." I filled Adam in.

Incredulity hiked his eyebrows toward his hairline. "It exploded? Does that happen often?"

Now it was my turn to join in the group shrug.

Dominic brushed himself off then helped me to my feet. I looked at the three of them: Jack, Donna, and Dominic. "Gerald?"

"We'll get him," Donna said with a conviction that left little doubt.

"You kept your promise. Not sure I agree with your methodology." I looked at a few of the larger metal parts littering the area around us. They still smoldered. "But I'm not going to quibble."

Sirens sounded in the distance. The guard had taken refuge in his shack, keeping his distance from the mayhem. People drifted toward the bank of the river. No one jumped in to swim around looking for survivors. There wouldn't be any.

Suddenly the day turned cold—or perhaps the chill of death filtered past.

Regardless, the warmth of the chase was gone, leaving only emptiness. I tugged my sweater closed, not that it would be any protection against the kind of chill I felt.

Dominic touched my elbow. "I understand you need a ride to the airport?"

"Damn!" I glanced at my phone. I could still make it, but everything would have to go without a hitch. "Shouldn't I stay? The authorities will have questions."

"We'll have the right answers," Donna assured me. "But we can't cover you. You were never here."

I nodded.

She scanned our little group. "Lucky was never here, right?"

"Right," everyone chorused.

"The motorcycle?"

"I will return it to the club and pick up mine later," Adam said, a hint of awe in his voice. "You really can solve problems."

"These guys made me look good. Always remember it's critical to play for the right team."

"You need to go." Donna said to me, then glanced at Dominic. "Did you bring what I asked?"

"Right here." He pulled a paper-wrapped parcel from under his shirt. "I've been keeping it next to my heart."

Did the guy ever quit?

I unwrapped the package.

The vintage Hermès Kelly bag.

"And something that belongs to you is inside," Donna added.

I opened the bag. The vintage Chinese vase from the Royal Suite! "You saved me one hell of an insurance claim." I took the vase out and held out the bag. "Thank you."

"Keep the bag. Mind you, it's just a loan," Donna said, pink coloring her cheeks. "I figure it might impress your future mother-in-law. Maybe soften her up a bit to see you have some class."

I ignored the 'some' thing—in Vegas, we didn't put a premium on class—and wrapped her in a bear hug.

"I've had my share of bad men," she whispered in my ear. "Don't settle. Listen to your gut. Your heart and your brain can't be trusted." She pulled away.

"How will I know how to get the purse back to you?" I nestled the vase back inside the protection of the bag.

The sirens grew louder.

Donna smiled. "I'll find you."

"Allow me?" Dominic touched my elbow. "We need to leave." He wouldn't take no for an answer, that much I could tell. "I have a friend who works on fine automobiles just around the corner. From time to time he lets me borrow one."

"Something wicked fast, I hope?" I asked half in jest.

"Is there any other kind?" He steered me away from the group. "How fast can you drive?"

"I'm a past winner at LeMans." He said it without his usual conceit.

"Of course you are. I'd be delighted, but this time I'll be very receptive if you want to show me your skills."

24

Donna

*a*s we watch Dominic and Lucky drive off, Jack heaves a sigh. "Don't they make a cute couple?"

I laugh. "I'm glad Lucky didn't hear you say that. She may have suckerpunched you again."

"No shit. And she packs quite a wallop." He winces at the thought.

I give him a sidelong glance. "Now that she promised to let Dominic down easy, don't you get him revved up again about her."

"Scout's honor." Jack crosses his heart before holding his hand in the official three-finger salute.

As he does, his cell rings.

I reach into his pocket to retrieve it.

"Feel free to do that more often," he murmurs.

So that I don't encourage him, I suppress a grin.

The Caller ID shows Arnie. I tap speaker mode. "Make me happy," I command him.

"I'll—I'll try my best," Arnie stammers. He knows it's a demand I usually reserve for Jack.

Jack clicks his tongue at my quip at our tech op's expense. "Donna's just being cute, Arnie. What's up?"

"Two things. Ryan already has MI6 fielding all police inquiries over Sheik Ben's untimely demise. No need for you to hang around."

"Works for us," Jack declares.

Three screaming cop-mobiles are careening onto the tarmac. Suddenly, they screech to a halt, make U-turns, and follow Adam as he drives off the heliport's tarmac on Lucky's stolen motorcycle. Whereas Adam turns right in order to go north and over the Battersea Bridge, the coppers are routed south.

"I guess they just got the memo," I say.

From the tarmac we can see police boats circling the burning debris. "It's the Thames River Police," Jack explains.

"I guess the Saudi prince was pretty pissed to learn that his brother not only had his daughter murdered but was a prime funding source for jihadi terrorists and Islamist populists," Arnie muses. "Talk about making the UAE look bad to its Western allies!"

"'Pissed?' Considering the payback he requested be made by the CIA, I'd say that's an understatement." Jack nods toward the burning wreckage bobbing just above the river's wake. "The Prince would have much preferred that any funding of radicals stay its family's dirty little secret."

"What with all the turmoil currently happening throughout the Middle East, I guess POTUS was glad to accommodate the UAE's request to make Ben's death look like an accident," I add. "If word of Ben Halabi's role in this had gotten out, Saudi civilians may have revolted against the monarchy."

"That's funny," Arnie muses. "News outlets are already calling it 'an act of terrorism.' And the source being quoted is the UAE's Federal Supreme Council."

Frowning, Jack glances my way. "I guess the council felt it needed a boogeyman after all."

"Anything to keep its citizens in line, right?" I reason. "The monster you know is better than the one you don't."

"I imagine POTUS assumes it's better to shore up an autocracy with a lousy civil rights track record than to bet on the alternative," Jack mutters.

"But who's to say a democracy in the Middle East wouldn't work if we don't let the chips fall where they may?" Arnie wonders aloud. "Adam seemed to think change would bring about democracy."

"Feel free to bring that up with POTUS," I snap. "What other great news do you have for us, Arnie?"

"Trust me, you'll love this!" Arnie pauses for emphasis: "I found Gerald."

"I'm impressed!" I exclaim. "How did you do it?"

"Ryan got permission to tap into MI5's new crowd scanning facial recognition system—doable since we stole it from the Chinese and shared it with the Brits in the first place."

Jack snorts. "It's a small world after all. Where is Gerald now?"

"I found him in the thick of the underground rush-hour traffic," Arnie boasts. "He jumped on the Piccadilly Line from the Knightsbridge Station. Rode it up to the Kings Cross station. From there, he walked the couple of blocks to the St. Pancras Station."

"Gerald is going to jump on the Eurostar train for the continent," Jack declares. "If we get there in time, we can pick him up before he boards."

I'm on his heels as he heads for the car.

THE TRAFFIC TO ST. PANCRAS IS STOP-AND-GO.

Via the station's CCTV, Arnie has found Gerald buying a ticket to the Paris station—Gare du Nord—so he secures two Business Premier tickets for Jack and me. That way, we can roam through all of the train's cars until we find our target.

"I'll hack the train's security feed as soon as possible in order to loop it for the security wonks," Arnie murmurs in our ears. "At the same time, I'll monitor the live feed. If I spot him first, I'll give you his car number."

"Smart idea," I reply.

Thank goodness the doors are still open on the sleek, bullet-nosed high-speed train. A porter frowns at our tardiness, but still eyes our tickets and nods us on.

Once inside, I murmur, "We should split up. We'll find Gerald more quickly that way."

"Agreed. I'll roam through the Standard Class. You take Business Premier," Jack suggests. "If one of us comes across the target, we'll immediately text the other, but stand down unless backup is needed."

I nod and we part with a kiss.

BECAUSE GERALD KNOWS ME, I'LL NEED TO DISGUISE MYSELF.

The train is only half full. Still, there's enough luggage stored in the alcoves located in the back of the car for me to find something usable.

I start with the most stylish bag in the first car: a classic Louis Vuitton keep-all bandouliére. Its owner is easy to spot since her handbag matches it. She seems about my size.

It takes all of a few seconds for the tiny rod on my specially designed Swiss Army knife to release the bandouliére's lock. It holds some usable items: large Dior cat-eye sunglasses; a cherry scarf and leather gloves the same exact hue; and a chic black Givenchy coatdress that ties with a sash.

Sold.

Okay, really, only borrowed.

I take the keep-all into the adjacent lavatory, locking the door behind me. Four minutes later, I'm a new woman.

After slipping the keep-all back in its cubby in the luggage alcove I begin my hunt for a cold-blooded killer.

I STROLL THROUGH TWO HALF-FILLED BUSINESS CLASS CARS, AVOIDING the owner of my newly acquired disguise. I've just entered the third when Arnie murmurs in my ear, "Donna, Gerald is in there—all the way in the back."

"On my way," Jack replies softly.

At first, I don't see Gerald. The car's other passengers—four in total—have staked claim to two-seat rows near the front of the car.

Finally, I spot him. Gerald sits alone in a large captain's chair facing a four-top table that has its back to the rest of the car. He holds a copy of the *Financial Times*, high, like a shield.

As if *that* will protect him from me.

Not while the vision of Nigel haunts me: flat on his back, stabbed in the heart, the elevator door hitting his extended leg before sliding back.

Not while the memory of Aziza incenses me: the beautiful young woman, taken before her time by being shocked to death—a fatal condition that only a family member, her devious uncle, might have known about. Had Aziza's body been found, the cause of death would have been deemed a freakish heart attack.

Instead, Gerald Morten, a.k.a., Edgar Black, was her angel of death.

And now I am his.

Gerald is surprised when I, a veritable stranger, slips into the seat beside him. "Darling, what an unexpected pleasure," I purr.

I leave him flabbergasted while I raise the armrests between our chairs in order to caress his face with my right hand. By the time I put my left hand behind his head, his primal instincts have kicked in and he turns his body toward mine.

From his stare, I take it that he's more amused than concerned. But just as he starts to say something, my right hand strokes his right cheek. At the same time, I raise my left hand in order to cradle the crown of his head. But before he can pull away, I've slid my right hand to his chin, shoving it high and to the right. At the same time my left hand jerks his head down, to the left.

As his neck and spinal cord break, he releases his life with a grunt.

He slumps in his seat like an oversized rag doll.

I close his lids and leave the paper propped up on his chest, as if he dozed off that way.

I walk out the back door of the car and into the next.

JACK HAS JUST ENTERED THE SAME CAR FROM THE OPPOSITE SIDE. When I give him a thumbs-up, he shows his relief with a grin and a nod toward two empty adjoining seats.

As I sink beside him, I motion to my ill-gotten *femme fatale* accoutrements. "I should change out of these," I lament. "Although, I must admit I could get used to designer duds." Suddenly, it dawns on me: "Hey, since we're on our way to Paris anyway, maybe Ryan will let us fly home from there! That way, I can do a little shopping before we go home. Mary was in tears over her prom dress fiasco. Imagine her surprise if I came home with some adorable little frock from Jean Paul Gaultier, or Thierry Mugler, or Christian Lacroix—"

"And picked up a few pieces for yourself as well?" Jack teases. "Don't tell me you're already missing that Hermès handbag!"

"Maybe just a little," I admit.

"Hey, after you ask for it back, maybe Lucky and Chef Boyardee can put us up for a night. I hear he whips up a mean soufflé."

"Now I *know* you're teasing," I pout. "And besides, if Dominic heard we might visit Lucky, he'd hop the next plane to Paris and track us all down! Lucky would never forgive me."

"Damn it! Now you girls are besties?" He shakes his head, awed. "Tell you what. If you can convince Ryan that we deserve an overnight in the City of Love, I'm in." He hands me his phone. "Of course, you'll also have to call Penelope and tell her where she can stick her prom decorations—"

My kiss tells him I have one very important thing to do first. "Come with me while I change into something less...flashy?"

Jack takes the bait. "Hey, what's the train equivalent of a Mile-High Club?" he wonders out loud.

25

Lucky

*T*raffic had thinned, and Dominic ran through the gears, letting the Lamborghini Huracan gallop. The press of speed pushed me back into the racing bucket. I ran my fingers lightly over the spartan panel, enjoying the feel, the experience of a finely-crafted machine doing what it was designed for. Fast cars made my heart beat accelerate. Fast men, like the one handling the car like an expert, not so much.

Dominic pulled the paddle shifter to downshift, slowing to maneuver around a truck. "You are going to marry this man, this *cook*?"

His inflection made me smile. While the Brits were not known for their food, they were known for their ability to convey disdain in one syllable.

With my thumb I twirled the ring on my finger. "Yes." I said it, though I wasn't sure I believed it. Was Jean-Charles a good man, the way Donna meant it? Yes, he was good at his profession and a good father, but, when it came to me...to his wife...would his inner-patriarch come out? How could I make him appreciate that my job was as much a part of the fabric of me as his was to him? So many men considered a job something a woman played at until she could find a husband. An offensive premise covered in the stink of decaying anachronism.

Time would tell, but I'd better be damn sure before I did the "I do" thing.

"I am not sure you are convinced." Dominic pressed the accelerator. He finessed the machine, each movement subtle and precise.

I stared at the city flashing past and didn't answer. It would only raise the specter of a question: Who was I trying to convince, him or me?

Dominic covered my hand with his. "I need to tell you something."

Amazingly, I didn't jerk back. Instead, I left my hand there, enjoying the connection. We'd both seen death, witnessed it, and he was perhaps responsible for it. A touch would restore our humanity a bit.

But death always exacted a price.

I could feel his nervousness, which surprised me.

He flicked a glance my way. "You have captured my heart."

"What?" That was so not what I was expecting—nor was it a complication I wanted.

"You are so unlike any other woman." He rushed into the awkwardness of my surprise. "I must have you." He squeezed my hand. "You must feel it, too."

Leaning forward I could see planes on short final. The airport wasn't far. "You know where the FBO is?"

He gave me a curt nod but kept his eyes on the road. "You do have feelings for me. Please tell me you do."

I pulled in air, held it then let it out in a calming sigh. "Dominic, you only think you know me. This is your world. Spies and international intrigue. Blowing up helicopters and tapping into security feeds. This is not where I live. It is not who I am."

"But I see how you are."

"Maybe you do. And I appreciate that, I really do." I slipped my hand from under his. "My life is a mess right now. I need to get back to my center, back to who I am, before I can invite anyone in close. Do you understand?"

"But this chef—"

"Is a man I need to deal with right now."

He wheeled into the short drive at the FBO, stopping at the gate. The guard apparently knew him as he waved him through.

"But, if…"

"No ifs."

His face fell.

"I'm sorry."

The gate to the tarmac opened as if by magic. Dominic eased the car to a stop by the stairs to the Babylon's G-650.

One of the pilots rushed to open my door. "We need to hurry, Miss O'Toole."

I turned to Dominic. Leaning over I kissed him on the cheek. "Thank you." I touched his cheek. "You really are something else."

AFTER REACHING OUR CRUISING ALTITUDE, THE PILOT CAME BACK TO check on me. "Oh good, you found the Champagne."

I'd found it all right—half the bottle was gone.

"It's a short flight. We have a helicopter waiting. The traffic is insane."

I threw back the remnants in my flute. "Time for a quick shower."

AS IT TURNED OUT, I HAD MORE THAN ENOUGH TIME SINCE I'D DONE the heavy lifting this morning. All I required was a rinse, a touch up to hair and face, and someone to zip me into the incredible vintage Bob Mackie beaded sheath I'd stumbled upon before I'd left home.

Home.

The young pilot reddened when I enlisted his zipping services, then he left me to sink back into one of the club seats. I grabbed the satellite phone.

Mother actually answered her cell, which was something akin to the second or third sign of the apocalypse. "Lucky! Where are you?"

"Just starting the descent into Paris."

She paused. "You'll know what to do," she said with a soft voice and a very unusual bit of insight.

"If I don't, I won't do anything."

"A good plan, but not one you've used before."

"Always a first time." I stuck the phone between my shoulder and ear, then bent to redo the strap on my sparkly Jimmy Choo stilettos. Jean-Charles may kill me, but the odds were even better I'd kill myself in these shoes. Teddie had taught me to walk in the things.

Teddie.

Why did first loves hurt so much and last so long?

"We're at the hospital, Lucky. Romeo told us you'd shoot him if we didn't let him bring us here, and he was sure your father and I wouldn't want his blood on our hands."

Good for Romeo. I owed him—much more than I could ever repay.

"Thank you," my mother whispered. "Your father is bleeding internally. At least that's what they think. He's weak and they have to open him up again. I'm worried."

"Me, too." At this point hollow assurances wouldn't do either of us any good, so I didn't offer any.

The distance and the fear echoed through the connection—a hollow sound that vibrated with the hollowness I felt inside.

"Any luck with the naming thing?" I asked, knowing there was comfort in the mundane.

"I think I've got them!" Mona's voice brightened.

"Lay them on me." I braced for impact.

"Samantha and Francesca. Frankie and Sammie for short."

"As in Sinatra and Sammy Davis, Jr." It wasn't a question, but more of a verbal thought as I let the names sink in.

"They were good friends of your father's, back in the Rat Pack era. Took him under their wing."

A bit after their heyday, but I didn't correct her. My father wasn't quite that old. "I think you've got it. Totally perfect names. A link to the past. You did it, Mother."

"But the girls will be our future, with a little bit of Lucky, that is."

EVERYTHING WORKED LIKE CLOCKWORK. THE LANDING, THE helicopter, even a car to whisk me a few blocks from the nearest helipad to the Bouclet's flat on Avenue Kleber, between the Etoile and the Trocadero. From the curb, the building looked very much like the London club. Three stories instead of five and no restaurant that I could see on the top but constructed of large blocks of white stone with bay windows starting at a half-level a few feet above the street. Imposing, but in keeping with the neighborhood.

I was curiously calm as the butler helped me up the stairs.

At the elevator, he reached in and pressed a button. "Third floor. The entertainment level."

The entertainment level. To a gal from Vegas that could mean so many different things. I checked my reflection in the polished metal of the doors as I rode up.

The elevator bounced to a stop the way an old lift will do. The doors opened.

Jean-Charles was waiting. Resplendent in a tux with a hand-knotted bow tie—tonight's was blue to match his eyes, he gave me a smile and extended his hand. He pulled me in for a lingering kiss.

I added my heat to his. My heart tripped at the connection. Would the fire go cold?

Time would tell.

I pulled back. "Am I in time?"

"Cocktails are just being served." He hooked my hand through his elbow. "You must've had quite a time." With a forefinger he traced the angry red where a bullet had just grazed me somewhere in the melee before the helicopter had exploded.

Funny, I'd almost forgotten, but the thing stung like hell now.

A frown creased his perfection, then cleared. "I want to hear all about it. But first, let me introduce you to my mother."

26

Donna

"*Y*ou were in Paris over the past twenty-four hours, and you didn't see Lucky O'Toole?" Dominic sputters angrily. "I am livid! Ryan had no right to lie to me about some 'secret assignation' that took you to the Continent!"

Dominic has waited until Acme's private jet—a Bombardier Global 8000—is thirty-nine thousand feet above the Atlantic Ocean before he explodes.

And all this time I thought he was sulking over the fact that Julie wouldn't allow him to switch from his room to the one just vacated by Lucky. No doubt it had something to do with his request that "no housekeeping is needed. Everything must stay just as the last occupant left it."

The thought that he'd be sniffing Lucky's bed sheets must have curdled the poor girl's stomach.

"No, I swear we never saw her!" I point to Jack. "We swear! We were there on a…a strictly *personal* matter."

Dominic's eyes narrow in disbelief. "Pray tell, what was it, then?"

"What part of 'personal' do you not get?" Jack retorts.

Enthralled by Dominic's accusations, Abu and Arnie don't

even pretend to feign interest in a Celtics-Warriors game on the plane's TV monitor.

"I want to believe you, but I'm reticent." Dominic's head drops to his chest. "I've never felt like this. It's as if shards of despair have pierced my heart."

Whereas Arnie is riveted by Dominic's drama, Abu has now opted for earbuds to tune in the game instead of hearing the latest episode of the Dominic Fleming soap opera.

Jack's eye roll evidences his lack of concern.

I'm left with the task of being the sympathetic ear.

I believe in karma. Perhaps if I hold Dominic's hand during this emotional crisis, he'll be there when it's my turn to cry on his shoulder...

Oh hell, who am I kidding?

I'm only doing it because none of us wants to watch him pout for the next ten hours.

I take Dominic's hand and nod toward the plane's only bedroom. "Let's talk, just the two of us."

He eyes Jack warily. "I don't want to put him out."

"He thoroughly understands," I assure him.

Proving my point, Jack waves us away, as if swiping at two pesky gnats.

Dominic shrugs. "Well...okay. I guess I had him all wrong." He raises a brow. "And for that matter, you too."

He allows me to lead the way.

ALTHOUGH I TAKE A SEAT ON THE EDGE OF THE BED, DOMINIC STAYS standing. I guess he's still wary about my agenda.

Patting the comforter, I say, "Why don't you sit?'

He frowns. Finally, he murmurs, "I thought you'd never ask," and does as I ask.

How do you approach a wounded animal? Slowly. Carefully. Gently.

So we sit there for a while. After a couple of minutes go by, I ask, "How were your goodbyes with Lucky?" I ask.

"As you'd expect." Dominic shrugs.

"So, the two of you are…" My voice trails off. No need to rub salt into an already wounded heart.

He nods. "We are indeed."

"Well…I'm sorry for you, Dominic. Truly I am. I hope you know that I'm always here for you." I lay a hand on his wrist. "She's one in a million."

"Irreplaceable." The word rises from the dark depths of his well of sorrow.

"Not necessarily, Dominic." I tilt my head and move it closer, as if willing him to look me in the eye. "Women love you—and you know it. When you're with them, you make them feel special. Alive. Beautiful. Loved." I grin. "Even if it's just for an hour."

He allows himself a tepid smile. "My staying power is much longer than that." He shoos away any doubt with a nonchalant flip of his wrist.

"Duly noted." No doubt there are enough women to take a Gallup Poll on the issue. Still, I'll take him at his word.

Dominic lays all the way back. After a deep sigh, he rolls to one side and props up his head. "I can guess your mission here. I can't say I'm not touched at your…well, shall we call it generosity of spirit?"

I blush. "Thank you for recognizing it."

"Only because we are alike in many ways." He grins slyly. "Like me, you recognize that the act of making love is as easy as it is momentarily satisfying. The terms are acknowledged in advance: flirtation, sensual tension, sexual release. Afterward, the parties go their merry way—until the next time." He smiles ruefully. "On the other hand, love breaks hearts." Gently, he raises my hand to brush my knuckles with his lips. "And that is why, no matter how much you beg me, I will not take you as my lover, Donna. Not here, not now, not ever. You see, Donna dear, I refuse to break *your* heart."

WHAT THE HELL?

I leap off the bed. "I...*beg your pardon?*"

"Of course, I'm flattered," he declares sincerely. "Still, if I'm to be honest, I am very wrong for you. So I beg of you: please don't put your marriage in jeopardy over what would have never been in the first place."

"You are seriously mental!" I sputter.

Dominic sighs. "Oh dear! I was afraid you'd take it badly! Please, Donna, try to understand—"

"Understand? You actually think I don't 'understand'?"

Dominic chuckles. "Well, Ducky, when it comes to love, you've always been a wee dense." He holds his thumb and forefinger an inch apart. "Your first marriage was proof of that."

Noting my glower, he drops his hand before I have a chance to break it.

To his credit, he adds, "Come, now! Gullibility is not necessarily a bad trait in a woman. In fact, many men find it appealing. Jack for instance." He winks. "Then again, he's just as thick."

"How dare you say that about Jack!"

"But it's true, isn't it?" Dominic smirks. "Just a moment ago, your blatant attempt to seduce me went right over his head."

"He didn't react 'thickly' because I did no such thing!"

Incensed, my hands are already curled into fists. As relaxed as Dominic is, they would so easily find their mark—say, pulverize one of his sky-high cheekbones. Or, perhaps, shove that aquiline nose out of joint. The dimple in his chin makes a perfect little bullseye...

"Don't play the coquette," he chides me. "You suggested I follow you here, into the bedroom. How did you put it again?... Oh yes: 'Just the two of us.'" He clucks his tongue. "Then, when I asked if Jack would mind, you replied, 'He understands.'" Dominic waits for that to sink in. "No need to feel ashamed of it. By profession, you're a honey trap. At times, Jack is too. That's proof in and of itself that you both enjoy some extracurricular activity." Dominic shrugs. "But I refuse to be toyed with while I'm in such a vulnerable state."

"I didn't invite you in here for any so-called extracurricular activity,'" I snap. "And I certainly didn't ask you to dissect my relationship!"

"You're right. On the other hand, *you* wished to set me straight on mine." Dominic rolls his eyes. "Did you succeed?"

"Not at all!" I retort. "But now knowing what you think of Jack and me, I no longer give a damn. As far as I'm concerned, you deserve your broken heart!"

His wince is proof I've hit my mark. "Blimey!" he mutters. "It never fails to awe me how women wear their feelings like a second skin! Love, hurt—and in this case, hate—are all felt with such intensity! And yet, men are supposed to feign nonchalance—especially those in the profession of cold-hearted killer. Such rubbish!"

In that instance, the reason for Dominic's little mind game dawns on me:

Even assassins aren't immune to heartbreak.

"I'm sorry, Dom," I say softly. "And you're right. There's no shame in admitting to having that one love who got away."

Dominic hangs his head. "It's the one club I had hoped never to join," he mutters ruefully. "'Lovesick toff' is nowhere in the job description for an 'international man of mystery.'"

Desperate to break through his misery, I make my way to the closet and pull out a garment bag emblazoned with the Valentino couture logo. "This is the reason Jack and I went to Paris."

I unzip it so that he can see the dress inside: a pale pink jewel-neck lace-over crepe ruffle-cuffed party dress.

Dominic whistles appreciatively.

"It's for Mary's prom next weekend," I explain. "She wants to look...well, sophisticated."

"There must be a boy involved," Dominic reasons.

"Our ward, Evan. He's away at college, but he'll be her date."

"I've seen them together around Hilldale," he reminds me.

But of course, he has. Dominic's faux-Tudor castle is just a few blocks over from our house. Having no children of his own, he doesn't qualify as one of Hilldale's highly desirable DILFs (Dad I'd Like To...well, you get the picture).

Except for Penelope's soon-to-be-remarried ex-spouse, Peter,

Dominic is our gated community's only full-fledged bachelor. It certainly plays to his favor that he's tall, blond, and handsome. If his low, silky British accent doesn't turn the heads of Hilldale's yummy mommies, the news that he owns Hilldale's only thirty-four-room Downton Abbey look-alike mansion stops them in their tracks.

I can only imagine how many times a week his doorbell rings for requests to borrow sugar, cup optional.

"With or without the dress, Mary has nothing to worry about," Dominic declares. "Evan is smitten with her. How could he not be? She's positively peng, just like her mother."

I blush. She's gorgeous—like me?

Dominic takes his leave with a wink and a grin.

Not exactly the stoic stiff upper lip. Still, it doesn't hide the sorrow in his eyes.

It must be lonely being you, Dominic Fleming.

"OH MY GOD! MOM! *VALENTINO!* I LOVE, LOVE, LOVE YOU!"

Mary pirouettes around the family room in her new dress for all to see—that is Jack, Aunt Phyllis, Jeff, Trisha, me—

And Evan, whose eyes are as large as saucers at the lean, long-legged vision of loveliness dancing in front of him. Noting my gaze, he stammers, "I guess I wasn't supposed to see her until the big night."

Jack's right brow arches. "She's not a bride, you're not a groom, and that's no wedding dress."

Evan's face turns various shades of red.

"I'll say!" Jeff pipes up. "It's *waaaaay* too short!"

Mary sticks out her tongue at him.

"Can I have a designer dress too?" Trisha asks hopefully.

"Wait until your senior year in high school. Then we'll talk," I promise.

"I wouldn't mind borrowing that hot little number myself,"

Aunt Phyllis exclaims. "What do you say, Mary? Maybe for the upcoming Senior Dance at the Hilldale Community Center?"

Horrified, Mary's mouth drops open.

The cackle of my seventy-going-on-twenty year-old aunt fills the room. "Just kidding, my fabulous little fashionista! I couldn't stand the thought of causing some old codger's heart attack."

Ah, it's great to be home.

I take Evan's hand in mine. "This is a pleasant surprise. We weren't expecting you until next weekend."

His smile fades. "I hadn't planned on coming. However, something came up that may be of interest to you and Jack—really, to Acme. But we should talk in private."

Evan nods toward the window. Beyond it, the backyard beckons.

"Lead the way," Jack says.

EVAN WAITS UNTIL WE'RE SETTLED ON THE PATIO CHAISES BEFORE beginning. "Yesterday I got a call from an old friend. Actually, Jonathan Presley was a friend of my dad's. He's also Vice President of Military Projects at BlackTech, one of my dad's companies."

Before I was a spy, my heart was broken twice. Evan's father, Robert Martin, was the first love of my life. At the tender age of eleven I had a crush on him. I knew him then as Bobby.

I was also lied to, and cheated on, in my first marriage: to Carl Stone.

So yes, I know well that no one—least of all, someone in my profession—is immune to heartbreak. Maybe it's why we spy in the first place.

Ironically, Robert was murdered by Carl.

It happened two years ago, when Evan's mother, Catherine, was running for the office of U.S. President. Catherine won the nation's highest office. But prior to the election, she sanctioned her husband's murder because he threatened to divorce her. He'd discovered her campaign was being funded by a terrorist organization: the Quorum.

I got her to admit to her role in Robert's death. My efforts got me stabbed, but it also got her sent to prison before she could take her oath of office. Instead, that honor went to her Vice President-Elect, Lee Chiffray.

As for my dealings with our current POTUS? Let's just say that it's complicated.

Robert built a conglomerate of technology companies. Someday Evan will inherit them. In the meantime, he is doing all he can to feel worthy of his father's sacrifice and to erase his mother's duplicitous acts.

Jack and I love him as if he were our son.

"What did Jonathan want?" Jack asks.

Evan frowns. "Unfortunately, I was in class and only heard his voice message—something about a very important BlackTech project funded by the U.S.'s Defense Intelligence Agency. He was concerned that it had been compromised by an outside source. He suspected there may have also been an in-house accomplice. When I rang back on his company extension, the call was rerouted to Human Resources. I was told he'd just been involved in a hit-and-run accident." Evan's eyes are ringed with tears. "Jonathan Presley was the victim." He pulls something out of his jeans pocket and hands it to me:

A flash drive.

"This came in the mail to me," Evan explains. "The envelope had Jonathan's initials on it."

"Any return address?" Jack asks.

"Yes. A post office box," Evan replies. "I couldn't tell you if it was his."

I nod. "We can check it out. And if it is—"

The faint buzz of my cell phone is echoed by Jack's.

The text is from Ryan:

Special showing of THE TRUMAN SHOW.

President Harry Truman established the National Defense Agency's predecessor, the National Intelligence Authority. Jack and I aren't being invited to a movie but to Acme headquarters for news on our next mission.

Quite a coincidence. I guess we'll know soon if it has anything to do with BlackTech and Jonathan Presley's death.

Jack and I sigh in unison. So much for a quiet weekend at home.

The backyard's white picket fence separates the cloudless sapphire sky from our emerald green lawn. Sunlight sparkles in the morning dew. Two sparrows dart in and out of the branches of the live oak tree, playing hide and seek.

It's always sunny in Southern California.

It's always tranquil in Hilldale.

Until it's not.

—THE END—

Wanna Get Lucky?

EXCERPT

CHAPTER ONE

AS HER final act on this earth, Lyda Sue Stalnaker plummeted out of a Las Vegas helicopter and landed smack in the middle of the pirates' lagoon in front of the Treasure Island Hotel, disrupting the 8:30 p.m. pirate show.

The video ran as the lead-in for the 11:00 p.m. news. I caught it on a television in the sports bar. Actually, it was amazing I caught it at all. My name is Lucky O'Toole, and I am the chief problem solver at the Babylon, the newest, most over-the-top mega-casino/resort on the Las Vegas Strip. I'd been fighting my way through the crowds packing the casino on my way to Stairwell Fifteen to deal with a naked man asleep under the stairs, when I caught the television feed out of the corner of my eye.

A grainy video of a helicopter with the Babylon's script logo painted on the side appeared on the screen with a small headshot of Lyda Sue in the corner—it was Lyda Sue's sweet smile that actually captured my attention. I leaned over the backs of two guys playing video poker at the bar, a sinking feeling in my stomach. In Vegas, nobody gets their picture on the news unless they've committed some grisly crime or have been a victim of one themselves.

Of course, I couldn't hear what the talking heads on the television were saying. The clamor of excited voices from the casino combined with the pinging from the video machines and the piped-in music to create a cacophony of excitement that made it not only impossible to talk, but to think as well.

Eyes wide, I watched as the station ran the video again—this time the full version as part of their newscast.

Hovering above the lagoon as the show began, the copter began to buck and roll. A body tumbled out, backward or forward —it was hard to tell. Thankfully, the final impact with the water was hidden behind the pirate ship advancing toward the British with cannons belching fire and smoke. The picture tilted, then went dark—a head shot of Lyda Sue taking its place.

"Ms. O'Toole?" My Nextel push-to-talk vibrated at my hip. "Are you coming?"

I grabbed the device and pushed the direct-connect button to shout. "What?"

I pressed the thing to my ear as I tried to hear.

"Ma'am, this is Sergio at the front desk. The doctor's with our naked guy. He's fine—apparently sleeping off a bender. But we got another problem—some guy in Security by the name of Dane is insisting we call the paramedics just to be on the safe side."

I stared at Lyda Sue's picture on the television, my mind unable to process what I saw. The video switched to the police and a body covered with a white cloth, one delicate hand dangling from the stretcher as they loaded it into the back of an ambulance. Nobody was in a hurry.

"Ma'am, are you there?"

The question snapped me back. "Sorry. Naked guy in the stairwell, right. Do *not* call the paramedics unless the doctor wants them. We don't need to cause a scene and have this guy splashed across the pages of the *Review-Journal* in the morning—I'm sure he'd love that." Trying to steady my nerves, I took a deep breath. Instantly, I regretted it. Smoke-filled air assaulted my lungs, bringing tears to my eyes. "I'll be right there, and I'll deal with Dane." I choked the words out as I struggled to catch my breath.

"Yes, Ma'am."

I reclipped the Nextel at my waist.

I fought to not only clear my lungs, but to clear my thoughts as well—a Herculean task as hundreds of questions pinged around inside my head.

Lyda Sue, dead? I'd seen her just last night, holding forth on the end stool at Delilah's Bar. We'd talked for a minute or two; her world had seemed stable enough. Twenty-four hours later, she took a header out of our helicopter, landing smack in the middle of the 8:30 p.m. pirate show. What had I missed?

Damn. Lyda Sue was dead. *Double damn.* She fell out of *our* helicopter. The Babylon would be big news. My job was to keep the Babylon *out* of the news. Or to take the fallout when I failed. The Big Boss was not going to be pleased.

Tonight was shaping up to be a doozie.

I muscled between the two guys intent on their video poker monitors and leaned across the bar so the bartender could hear me. "Get the news off that television. Find a sports feed or something."

The real world had no place in this fantasyland.

My mind clicked into gear. I couldn't wait to get my hands on that pilot. He should have called me right away. Lyda Sue hit the lagoon at 8:30. Damage control was tough enough without giving the newshounds and gossip mongers two and a half hours head start. I had a feeling that nothing short of an overnight nuclear test at Yucca Flats would keep us out of the morning headlines now.

Nevertheless, I grabbed the Nextel, and started in. "Jerry?"

"Yo," our Head of Security answered in his laid-back manner.

"I want our pilot in my office right now—handcuff him and drag him there if you have to. Next, get over to Channel Eight. I want all copies of a tape Marty ran on the eleven o'clock news of a woman falling out of our helicopter. If he refuses, remind him of that awkward little situation at the opening gala—he'll know what you're talking about. Bring the tapes to me when you get them."

"I'm on it."

"Oh, and Jer? I almost forgot. What's the status on the mega-millions winner? Did she actually hit it?"

"We're working on it. I'll have an answer for you in the next half hour—our plate's sorta full."

"Welcome to the club. Thanks."

I disconnected, then scrolled through the stored numbers looking for Dane's as I turned to head toward Stairwell Fifteen. Paramedics! Was the guy nuts?

As fate would have it, his number didn't matter. Two steps with my head down focusing on my phone and I ran smack into the rather solid chest of the man I was looking for—Paxton Dane, the new hire in Security.

At a couple of inches taller than my six feet, Dane was the poster boy for the testosterone-laden, ex-military, jet-jockey set. Square jaw, soft brown hair, green eyes, great ass, and an attitude —which I didn't need right now.

"Did I just hear you tell Jerry to threaten to blackmail the manager of the television station?" His voice held the soft traces of old Texas, yet the sexy timbre of a man confident of his appeal.

"I never threaten. I offered him a deal." I had neither the time nor the patience to educate Dane tonight, but it seemed that was in the cards.

"A rather fine distinction."

"Dane, you'll find those black-and-white lines painted so brightly in the rest of the world blur to a nice shade of gray in Vegas." I put a hand on his chest and pushed him away, since his nearness seemed to affect what rational thought I had left at this time of night. "I was already up to my ass in alligators, and the suicide dive just upped the ante. I really do have to go."

I pushed away the images of Lyda Sue's final moments. If I kept them at a distance, maybe, just maybe, I could make it through the night. If I spoke of her cavalierly, maybe I could hold back my emotions.

"What makes you think she was a suicide?" The soft traces of old Texas disappeared. Dane's voice was hard, flat, and held an edge like tempered steel.

The question and his tone stopped me cold. What did he know that I didn't? "You got any reason to think otherwise?"

Murder, now that would be a real problem.

He waved my question away, arranging his features in an expressionless mask. "I need to talk to you about one of our whales. Apparently, the guy had a mishap in one of the Ferraris. If you want me to handle it, I can, but you'll have to make the call as to what the hotel is willing to do. The whale in question is…" He consulted a folded sheet of paper he had extracted out of his back pocket and gave a low whistle. "A Mr. Fujikara and he seems to be quite a whale—he keeps several million in play during his monthly visits."

"I know Mr. Fujikara well."

Dane glanced up, one eyebrow raised, but he didn't ask the question I saw lurking there, and I felt no need to explain.

"We also have a Pascarelli. Apparently, he wants a hug from you," Dane continued, not missing a beat as he absently rubbed his chest where my hand had been. "And the naked guy…"

"He's all mine as well," I interjected to speed up the conversation. With major problems to solve, I had little time and even less patience. "And, Dane, for the record, never call the paramedics unless it's an all-out emergency or the doctor wants them. Casinos are closed worlds here—we protect our own—and we zealously guard the privacy of our guests. Remember that. Outsiders are allowed in to help with problems only, and I repeat, only when the problem gets out of hand."

Dane's eyes narrowed—his only response. A tic worked in his cheek.

I rolled my head and rubbed the back of my neck. "I need to take Mr. Fujikara as well; this is a game we play. For his millions, he likes some personal attention—apparently I'm the anointed one. You can help me with one thing, though. We had a lady hit the mega-million, but we need to make sure she played the six quarters. Jerry's shut down the machine and is reviewing the tapes. While we're in the process, why don't you offer the Sodom and Gomorrah Suite to the winner and her friends for the night? Make double sure that she understands her winnings have not been confirmed. I'll follow up with her when I get the results of the diagnostics from Jerry."

"And who will authorize the comped suite?"

"I thought I just did." My words sounded harsher than I intended. "Sorry. If Sergio wants confirmation, have him call me."

"Right. Oh, and The Big Boss wants fifteen minutes of your time. He's in his apartment."

"He'll have to get in line."

"He told me now," Dane said, as he rubbed his eyes.

"I said, he'll have to wait." Now that I took a closer look, Danes eyes were bloodshot. The guy looked totally wrung out. I put a hand on his arm. "Are you okay?"

"Fine." Dane shrugged my question off, then shrugged out of my grasp. "You leave The Big Boss hanging, it's your funeral."

"It'll take more than that to put me six feet under."

My relationship with The Big Boss was none of Dane's business. I turned and took off through the casino with more questions than answers bouncing around in my skull: Why the swan dive, why did The Big Boss send Dane to bring me to heel, and why did Dane sidestep my question?

Murder! What made him think Lyda Sue was murdered?

The casino at the Babylon is much like any other. An intimate labyrinth, subtly decorated, windowless and, tonight, jam-packed with people all paying and praying for whatever it was they hoped to get in Vegas. A thin layer of smoke hovered over the crowd, as the slot machines sang their come-on songs and occasional shouts arose from the tables. Cocktail waitresses wearing painted-on smiles and little else darted in and out delivering fresh libations and collecting the empties. Young women paraded around in tight-fitting clothes they wouldn't be caught dead in back home. Pierced and tattooed young men, their jeans hanging precariously across their butts, followed the young women. How the boys kept their jeans from falling straight to the floor was an enduring mystery.

The nightly line of the young and the beautiful snaked from the entrance to Pandora's Box, our popular nightclub and body exchange. Pulses of dance music escaped each time Ralph, our bouncer, opened the door to let one of the hip and trendy in or out. The entrance to the adjacent theatre was empty; the 10:30 show was well underway.

I knew where to find Mr. Pascarelli—thankfully he was on my way to Stairwell Fifteen. Like all serious gamblers, Mr. Pascarelli was a creature of habit and superstition. Dressed in the same shirt, a now-threadbare Hawaiian number his wife, Mildred, "God rest her soul," had given him decades ago when I guessed he weighed forty pounds more than he did now, he always started his night of play at the third slot machine from the end of the third row.

A gnome-like eighty, Mr. Pascarelli was cute as a bug, bald as Michael Jordan, a night owl and, I suspected, a bit lonely. Three was his lucky number, and I was his good-luck charm.

Lucky me.

Truth be told, giving Mr. Pascarelli his hug was usually the high-point of my night, a fact that—had I time to think about it—would probably have concerned me.

"There you are, my dear!" He waved his glass at me. "I was beginning to worry."

"Worry? Don't be silly, but this one will have to be a quickie." I gave him a squeeze, careful to not crush him too tightly.

He laughed at the innuendo. "Hard night?"

"You don't know the half of it."

"Little Lyda taking a header out of the helicopter?"

"Bad news travels fast. You knew Lyda Sue?"

"Sure. When she wasn't busy, she used to pull up a stool and talk to me for a while. Sweet kid, from somewhere in Texas, I think." He shook his head and crinkled his brow. "She'd been sorta jumpy lately."

"Did she say why?"

"If she did, I don't remember."

"Do me a favor—try. When she sailed out of that helicopter, she landed right in my lap. I could use some help on this."

He nodded, his eyes serious.

I patted Mr. Pascarelli's shoulder. "Go easy on us tonight, okay?"

"Sure, honey," he said with a wink.

Mr. Pascarelli was the only man on the planet who could call me "honey," wink at me, and live to tell about it.

I dove into the crowd and wove my way on toward Stairwell Fifteen. I threw my weight against the stairwell door and came face to face with the normally unflappable Sergio Fabiano, our night-shift front-desk manager. Dark hair, olive skin, a face a photographer would love and a body to match, Sergio was the Babylon's resident Greek god. Women were drawn to him like sharks to an injured seal. Thankfully, the women were nowhere in sight. Neither was Security. Apparently, Dane had done as I asked and called off his posse.

"Thank heavens!" A scowl creased Sergio's otherwise flawless face, but his dark eyes danced with merriment. He gestured disdainfully toward the space under the first flight of stairs.

"Good God!" The words escaped before I could stop them.

"But not a merciful God," announced Sergio.

Our naked guest must have weighed four hundred pounds, with pasty white skin and more hair sprouting on his body than his head. Thankfully, he was curled in the fetal position. And he was still out cold. But, judging from the way his ass was twitching, his dreams were good ones.

"We don't know who he is?" I managed to choke out. I kept repeating, *I will not laugh at this* over and over in my head until I felt confident I would do as I told myself.

Sergio shook his head, his jaw clamped tight, his lips compressed together. He didn't laugh, not even a smile, or a smirk. Amazing.

I keyed my Nextel. "Security, any missing-person reports for tonight?"

"Excuse me?" The unmistakable voice of Paxton Dane. Did the

guy ever stop? Like the Energizer bunny, he just kept going and going, handling everything, everywhere.

"Dane, have you guys had any calls from anyone looking for someone who matches the description of our guy in Stairwell Fifteen?"

"Already checked that. And, to answer your question, no."

"Okay, then send four…" I looked at the inert shape again. "Make that five of your strongest guys to Stairwell Fifteen, ground floor."

"On their way—again."

Taking the high road, I ignored the jab. "And, Dane, remember, a bit of discretion here. This man is most likely one of our guests. We wouldn't want to see him on the news, okay?"

"You mean one appearance on the nightly news is enough?"

Did the guy take a class on how to be a jerk or was it something that just came naturally?

"Dane…" I started in on him, then realized I was talking to dead air.

Sergio looked at me, his eyes round black saucers.

I snapped my phone shut. "Sergio, take care of this guy," I said as I reclipped my phone, glad that Dane had retreated. I was too wrung out to do the whole verbal thrust-and-parry thing. "You know, the usual routine."

"Right," Sergio began. "First, get a robe that'll fit him—preferably one with another hotel's logo on it." He paused to flash me a grin, then continued as if he'd memorized it all from the employee handbook and hadn't actually learned it from me. "When Security gets here, have them carry him through the back corridors to the worst room open tonight. Take all the bedsheets, the towels and the robes—anything he can put around himself when he wakes up, so he can't sneak out on us."

"You've got it. But you might see if Security can spare someone to stand outside the door, just in case our friend—" I pointed to the guy on the floor, now snoring loudly. "—has an accomplice to bring him some clothes."

Sergio nodded.

"And the doc is going to check on him?" I asked.

"Every half hour."

"Good work." Another problem down, how many more to go? I'd lost count. "Sergio, another thing…"

Again those black eyes focused on me.

"I need you to alert your staff at the front desk, the bell staff, and the valets. If anyone comes around asking questions about a girl falling out of our helicopter, they are to be directed to my office. That includes the police. Our staff is not to answer any questions or to give any information. Is that clear?"

"Yes, Ma'am." Sergio's eyes grew a fraction wider, but he kept his composure.

"And if anyone is poking around, let me know, okay? Just because you send them to my office doesn't mean they will actually do as you suggest."

I gave one last look around. I couldn't think of anything else. Satisfied Sergio could handle the problem from here, I turned to go—

After all, it's not as if this was our first naked drunk sleeping in a stairwell.

―――――

The elevators lurked just inside the foyer of the Babylon, separating the casino from the hotel. The foyer was the Babylon's showpiece. Designed to draw all passersby inside, the grand ceiling was covered with millions of dollars' worth of Chihuly blown glass. The Bellagio had glass flowers, we had butterflies and hummingbirds—thousands of them. Personally, they made me feel like we all were in a remake of the film *The Birds*, but obviously no one shared my opinion. As usual, a crowd clustered under them, oohing and ahhing.

Numerous walking bridges arched over a lazy river, our interpretation of the Euphrates, which snaked throughout the ground level. Tropical plants and trees grew along its banks, lending shade for the colorful fish, swans and ducks that swam in the clear blue water. Somehow, I doubted whether the birthplace of civilization ever had a river quite like our Euphrates, but The Big Boss wanted it, so there it was.

Off to one side of the lobby, behind a wall of twenty-five-foot windows, an indoor ski slope with real, man-made snow descended from high above. Again, I wasn't sure whether the original Babylonians had ever strapped on a pair of K2s and flown down a snow-covered hillside, but in keeping with the relatively recent adage "If you build it, they will come," The Big Boss had built it and, indeed, they came. Another crowd gathered there, watching the folks who had paid an exorbitant sum to ski indoors on the desert slide down the hill.

The other side of the lobby boasted the entrance to the Bazaar. There one could slide behind the wheel of a Ferrari, buy a six-hundred-thousand-dollar pink diamond ring, a two-thousand-dollar pair of Versace jeans, or load up on five-hundred-dollar Jimmy Choos. A constant line of customers with fat wallets trailed through there like ants bearing gifts for the queen.

The Big Boss was an expert at separating tourists from their money.

Ah yes, The Big Boss—he was next on the list.

I shouldered my way through the crowd, ignoring the man yelling at one of the bellmen—a front-desk clerk was already interceding. Paxton Dane was giving a woman a hug—probably the mega-millions lady. He caught my eye over the lady's shoulder and gave me a discreet thumbs-up. For this brief moment in time, we appeared to have things under control, which, of course, was an illusion. Life in Vegas was never under control; it walked, trotted or galloped, as it chose, and we merely hung on for the ride.

Tomorrow, the Trendmakers would arrive for their annual week of spouse swapping, the stars of the adult movie industry would descend on us for their annual awards ceremony, ElectroniCon started Tuesday, and I would have to deal with the fallout from Lyda Sue's dramatic exit, which would surely hit not only the morning papers but the Internet as well.

Whoever thought up the tagline "What happens in Vegas, stays in Vegas" got it backward—Vegas was always news. Heck, the video of Lyda Sue's final dive was probably playing on YouTube by now.

I was a fool to think I could corral this one.

I rounded the corner, pushed the up button, and pondered the reflection that stared back at me from the mirrored surface of the elevator doors. I looked like a hundred miles of bad road. Barely over thirty, and I could pass for my mother's sister. *Haggard* was the word that leapt to mind. Thankfully, the doors slid open and I was no longer nose to nose with myself. Why people want mirrors everywhere is beyond me.

I stepped inside the empty car, inserted my security card in the slot, and pressed the button marked "private." Self-consciously I patted my bottle-blonde hair, my one concession to the land of the beautiful people. Attractive enough, I guess, I'd never be considered beautiful or buxom—at least not without serious surgical intervention—but I damn well could be tall and blonde. Self-consciously I smoothed my dress, pinched my cheeks to get some color into them, then wiped at the black smudges I had seen under my eyes. I threw back my shoulders and adopted what I thought was an air of confidence.

"Who you trying to fool?" The voice emanating from the ceiling startled me.

I looked up at the "eye in the sky," the small video camera hidden discretely in a plastic bubble partially recessed into the ceiling of the elevator car. Security monitored the video feeds from thousands of similar devices located all over the property. The voice belonged to Vivienne Rainwater, one of our Security team.

"You know what they say, image is everything." I forced a smile for the camera. "I'll be unavailable for a few."

"You go, girl."

"Over the line, Viv."

"I thought there weren't any lines in Vegas, just shades of gray."

"And you shouldn't listen to conversations you're not invited into."

"You'd be amazed at what you see and hear up here."

Not long ago, I had sat where Vivienne now sits, and received a quick lesson into my fellow man, one I assumed Vivienne was now learning. "Titillated? Maybe. Amused? Possibly. But amazed? No. Now, go away and spy on someone else."

The elevator whirred seamlessly to a stop at the fifty-second floor and the doors slid open. Every time I made this ride, I thought of Dorothy leaving Kansas in a tornado and waking up in Oz. Thirty seconds and I was transported from the semi-controlled chaos of the lobby to the quiet, serene living room of The Big Boss's penthouse.

The muted lights cast a warm glow on leather-finished walls. The rich sheen of the hardwood floors framed hand-knotted silk rugs from the Middle East. Each was tastefully arranged and supported a cluster of understated furniture made from the hides of exotic beasts and woods from faraway lands. Lesser works from some of the great Masters graced the walls—sketches by Picasso and smaller works by Van Gogh and Monet. I couldn't identify the others—apparently my high school art history teacher had overlooked them—but I was sure they were all very expensive and "important." The whole effect made a three-thousand-square-foot box of a room cozy.

The Big Boss stood silhouetted against the wall of twenty-foot windows backlit by the lights of the Strip below. He warmed his hands in front of a gas fire dancing merrily in a freestanding fireplace. He explained to me once that he kept the air-conditioning on full blast so he could have his fire. Something about the ambiance.

The Big Boss, Albert Rothstein, was a Vegas legend. He had started as a valet at the Flamingo, caught the Mob's attention—he never would tell me exactly how—and then worked his way to the top of the heap. A short man with a full head of once black, now salt-and-pepper hair, he kept himself trim with thrice-weekly personal training sessions. His smile could light up a room and his manner made you feel like you were the most important person in his world. He had a penchant for stiff whiskey, tall blondes, and big stakes. When I was fifteen, I'd filled out an employment application, stating my age as eighteen. The Big Boss hired me on the spot, even though he had known I was lying.

More than a little peeved at being summoned through the new flunky, I started in as I strode toward him. "Lyda Sue made a helluva splash, but I've got everything under control: Jerry's on his way to get the tape from the station, the front entrance staff has been alerted to direct all inquiries to me, and once I actually make it to my office, I'll work on keeping us off the front page."

I stopped in front of him, but The Big Boss didn't look at me. Instead, he continued staring into the fire, then he reached into his back pocket, extracted his wallet and pulled out what I knew to be a one-hundred-dollar bill. He put his wallet back, then started working with the paper money, smoothing it, lining up the sides, meticulously folding it again and again. The silence stretched between us, then he finally said, "Bring all the copies of the video to me."

"You don't want Security to go over it? May I ask why?"

Now he eyed me over the top of his reading glasses perched on the end of his nose. His eyes were red. He looked like hell. "For once, just do as I say."

"Okay." First Lyda Sue, then Dane, now The Big Boss. Had I suddenly stepped into the Twilight Zone? Nothing about this night added up. "Aren't you interested in what the pilot has to say?"

"The pilot?" he repeated, as if stalling for time.

"The pilot's story should be a doozie."

His hands shook as he folded the bill over and over. "Of course, what did Willie have to say?"

Okay, now I was sure I smelled a rat. "How did you know it was Willie? We haven't found him yet."

The air seemed to go right out of The Big Boss. He closed his eyes, took a deep breath, and let it out slowly. "Lucky, you can truly try a man's soul."

"And you're stonewalling me." I laid a hand on his arm. "Boss, it's my job to solve problems, but I can't do it unless I know what the problems are."

"I was solving problems long before you showed up. This one's mine. I'll solve it myself, my own way." He shrugged out of my grasp.

The second man tonight to do that. Clearly, I was losing my touch.

"Just bring me that tape and keep me in the loop," he growled, looking like a pit bull ready to take a bite out of somebody's ass.

I had no idea how to reason with a pit bull—assuming it could even be done—so I bailed. "You're the boss. Anything else?" If I couldn't go through him, I'd just go around him.

Again the silence stretched between us as he worked, folding and folding. Finished, he took my hand, and closed my fingers around the small shape. He didn't let go. His eyes looked at our hands, then reluctantly met mine. "Trust me on this one."

"Sure." I looked at the shape in my palm. The Big Boss had folded the bill into a small elephant. I extracted my hands from his and dropped the figure into my pocket. "Look. Right now I got more fires than California in the fall and they are spreading by the minute. May I go now?"

"Give that to the first kid you see in the lobby." His voice was tired. His eyes, distracted.

"Boss, it's midnight. If there're any kids around, somebody ought to call Child Services."

"Right." He stepped around me and headed toward the bar. "Tomorrow then." He pulled a bottle of single malt off the shelf and raised it in my direction. I shook my head. He poured himself a drink. He raised the glass to his lips, took a long pull, and then said, "We've got another problem."

That much I knew. In fact, I thought we had several.

"And what might that be?"

"Paxton Dane."

Now *that* I didn't expect.

The Big Boss turned and stared at me, apparently awaiting my response.

If I didn't know better, I'd say he seemed nervous, a little antsy even, as he shifted from foot to foot.

A cold chill went through me. Whatever was bothering him, it must be bad—real bad. I'd only seen The Big Boss this way once before, and we both darn near went down in flames.

"He was your hire. What's the problem?" How I kept my voice even, I don't know.

"I hired Dane so we could keep an eye on him," The Big Boss said, his eyes drifting from mine.

For a moment I was speechless, unable to comprehend what he had just told me, then I found my voice. "Wait, let me get this straight. You put somebody you don't trust in one of the most sensitive positions in the house? Do you think that's wise?" I tried to keep my voice low, my tone smooth, but even I could detect a hint of panic around the edges.

"Probably not, but it was the best I could think of on the fly." The Boss took a slug of scotch. "Jerry knows. He's keeping tabs on Dane, and I want you to help him."

"Why?"

"He asked too many questions and was snooping around like he was trailing after something or someone. It doesn't seem hiring him has put him off the scent. I want to know what he's looking for and who's holding his reins. So, keep him close, okay?"

"Why me? I'm not in Security. I'm the customer relations person, remember?"

"I know it's asking a lot." He turned. His eyes locked onto mine. "But, Lucky, you're the only one I can trust."

The Housewife Assassin's Handbook

EXCERPT

Chapter 1
Please Read and Follow Directions Carefully...

Any woman can be both the perfect housewife and an accomplished assassin, because both functions require the same qualities: creativity; a never-say-die attitude; and an attention to details, no matter how small...

All I really needed to know about being a freelance assassin I learned before my youngest daughter, Trisha, started kindergarten.

I've come to that realization as I lay naked and handcuffed to the bed of my target du jour, a sleazebag by the name of Yuri Petrovich.

Yuri has just downed a couple of Viagra with the last of his Starbucks venti-sized nonfat decaf caramel macchiato. This is to ensure us both that his attempt to mount me will have all the gusto of a broncobuster breaking in the wildest filly in the corral before heading on into the sunset. (In truth, we are in a hillside suite at the Chateau Marmont. But considering Yuri's attitude toward women, the cowboyspeak sums things up quite nicely.)

Believe it or not, everything is going just as I planned, and right on schedule.

At least, that is what I tell myself as I watch him unzip his rock star-tight leather pants and squeeze out of them as quickly as he can because of his erection, which seems to be growing by the nanosecond and has him wincing in pain. (And in Yuri's fantasy if anyone is going to say ouch, it's going to be me.)

Like, say, eighty-eight percent of all my targets, this Russian mafia boss—who came here to unload a cache of AK-103s on some Idaho Neo-Nazis—has an obsessive-compulsive personality. In Yuri's case, that means staying in the same suite at the Marmont every time he hits Los Angeles (although his Slavic accent and pockmarked greaser looks have hardly earned him an iota of the ass-kissing accorded aging rock stars, budding celebutantes, or out-of-town British actors); doing the down-and-dirty with some rent-a-whore, both before and after the arms sale; and drinking macchiatos nonstop, even during his favorite sex act, that Kama Sutra position euphemistically called "the ostrich's tail." (Don't ask, because you really don't want to know.)

I work for Acme Industries, one of the many CIA-sanctioned subcontractors that handle any and all dirty tricks that won't pass a Congressional panel sniff test. My mission is simple:

Take Yuri down.

Here's my to-do list:

First, I was to stall on the sex until the skinheads showed up. Done.

Next, I was to plant a GPS system on one of them, so that ATF can track and apprehend them during the pick-up. Check.

And finally, as a show of tit-for-tat diplomacy with Uncle Sam's publicly acknowledged BFF, Russia, I'm to see to it that Yuri never leaves his hotel room alive.

All in good time, dearie. All in good time.

In fact, all of this is supposed to be accomplished before three o'clock, the time at which I have to pick up my ten-year-old, Jeff, and a carload of his teammates for an after-school baseball game. Otherwise I'd have to face the wrath of two other mothers for having blown the team's shot at taking the county title without a playoff game—

This is why I pray that the 405 isn't a nightmarish backup by the time I head home.

From the moment he landed stateside, Yuri's cell phone calls were monitored. The one to his favorite LA escort service was rerouted to an Acme phone operative, who scheduled Yuri a date with "Precious." (A suitable alias, seeing how I'm trussed up in a push-up bra, a low-cut tank top, and the tight denim micro miniskirt I raided from my twelve-year-old daughter Mary's closet. My gut told me that Yuri would not have appreciated my own Lily Pulitzer twill.)

The fact that I showed up an hour after the appointed time put me just a few minutes ahead of the Neo-Nazis: perfect timing in my book, since it foiled his plan for a little pre-sale foreplay.

Needless to say, Yuri was miffed at me for ruining his timetable. To make this point, he pushed me up against the wall, kicked my legs apart, and frisked me roughly. Really, it was more of a test-the-merchandise fondle.

Anticipating that maneuver, I'd left my trusty 9mm at home. That's okay. In my hooker getup there was no place to hide it anyway, which is why these kinds of close range hits are always tricky. And it's why I get paid the big bucks.

For this job, my weapon of choice was a tiny, serrated dagger that is appropriately called the "street assassin." However, I'm willing to bet that Yuri and I won't be anywhere near asphalt when I strike, but between some very expensive 700-count Egyptian cotton sheets.

What a waste. I wonder if the hotel knows that little trick about using meat tenderizer on bloodstains. Not that I planned on sticking around to find out.

I shrugged off his grope with a giggle. "Yeah, the service warned me how much you love a little foreplay, so I brought these along." Still spread-eagled, I unhooked a pair of handcuffs from the metal belt slung low over my skirt, and jangled them tantalizingly in front of him, in case he needed additional proof that I was his fantasy fuck. That shut him up. It also kept him from noticing my dagger, which hangs as innocuously as any of the buckles on my belt: a great way to fool metal detectors, which, believe it or not, are sometimes used by the bad guys, too.

Then to make sure I had his undivided attention, I rubbed the all too obvious bulge in his jeans with one hand and nodded approvingly, while relieving him of his Starbucks cup with the other. As I took a swig from it, one of his two goons snickered out loud.

Yuri's eyes blazed at my impudence. He lifted his hand to slap me but was stopped by a sharp knock on the door.

The skinheads. Perfect timing.

"Jeez, nobody said it was going to be a party! But hey, I'm open to anything – as long as you cleared it with my service." I handed the cup back to him, sauntered over to the couch, and flopped down as if I owned the place.

While Yuri's goons frisked the two Neo-Nazis, I crossed my legs seductively and leaned over so that my cleavage runneth over in plain view for all to enjoy. No doubt about it, the skinheads were appreciative. The fatter, uglier one even had the balls to ask me if my boobs were real.

"Wanna come over here and find out?" I crooked a finger at Ugly.

It took him all of a second to take me up on the offer. As he pulled me onto his lap, I copped my own feel: under the collar of his military fatigue jacket, where I plant a tiny GPS bug.

Seeing me all over Ugly made Yuri even hotter to be done with the business portion of his trip. He yanked me off his guest and shoved me in the direction of the bedroom.

"No party. You wait in there," he growled.

I pulled him close for a deep kiss. Then, as a reminder of all the fun and games I had in store for us, I handed him the key to the handcuffs. That was all the incentive he needed to get rid of the skinheads *tout de suite*. He closed the door fast, which was fine with me. The tranquilizer I'd slipped into his macchiato before giving it back to him (a time-release version of Rohypnol) was to kick in sometime within fifteen minutes. I was estimating that he'd need about ten to get rid of the boys, which would leave me five to stall before he fell on his face, making it easy to slit his throat before hightailing it out of there.

The minute he shut the door, I set up for the kill. First I snapped on a pair of gloves – black lace from fingertips to the elbows. Sexy, for sure (in fact, they match my G-string) but because they are lined in a microthin flesh-toned latex, I won't be leaving any telltale prints. As I expected, the sliding door to the terrace outside the bungalow was locked and the curtains were pulled, which allowed for complete privacy from the outside. After disabling the alarm with the tiny decoder I keep on my key ring, I went ahead and unlocked the sliding door so that when the time was right I could make a quick getaway.

I wasn't worried about the handcuffs since they were the kind used by magicians and I'd only need a strategic jerk of the wrist to break free. Even if the roofie didn't kick in before Yuri snapped them onto my wrists, I'd be able to get out of them in only a few seconds.

Finally, I slipped the knife under the mattress, near the right side of the headboard. I'd retrieve it when the time was right.

As Minute Eight slipped by, I heard a door close on the other side and guessed rightly that Yuri had said bye-bye to his new skinhead pals. During Minute Nine, Yuri instructed his homeboys not to disturb us no matter how much moaning I was doing – and he planned for me to be doing a lot of it.

Then, as predicted, Yuri opened the door ten minutes after he'd left me. Locking it behind him, he smiled approvingly at my state of total undress: my only attire was my G-string, stilettos, and the lace gloves.

I was somewhat surprised that he wasn't at least yawning by now. Apparently he has the constitution of a rhino. I was hoping that I wouldn't find out if he had the staying power of one as well. It was then that I noticed that the Starbucks cup was still in his hand...

Damn! Hadn't he finished that thing yet? Okay, no big deal. So I'd have to stall for another minute or two.

To put that thought out of my mind, I envisioned the kill instead: watching his eyes grow drowsy from the drug – or if necessary, closed in the ecstatic throes of passion – yanking my hands free, and then reaching under the mattress for the knife...

Yuri wrongly assumed that my sigh was in anticipation of what he pulled from his leather jacket's pocket: my handcuffs. "Okay, bitch. On the bed."

Obediently I dropped onto it and grasped the middle finials on the vine-patterned headboard. As he slapped on the cuffs, he stifled a yawn. (Yes! Yes! Finally!) To keep alert, he took a long sip of his macchiato. Then, as if remembering something, Yuri pulled something out of an inner pocket of his jacket...

Ah yes, the perfect pre-sex appetizer: Viagra.

Humph. I wondered what effect that might have on the roofie...

Now that Yuri's striptease is over, it seems I have my answer: not only does the Rohypnol appear to have been neutralized by his little blue devil, it seems to have accelerated his hard-on–

And from the look of things, it acted as a growth hormone to boot.

Not good. At least, not while I'm in my current position: by that I mean naked, chained to his bed, and about to be mounted like a prize rodeo steer.

But Yuri is in no hurry. Nonchalantly, he ambles over to the built-in armoire and takes a two-foot-long velvet box from the top drawer, which he lays down beside me with a smirk. Then, opening it slowly, he pulls out–

–A riding crop.

Ouch. Seems that the cowboy metaphor is becoming more appropriate by the moment.

Damn it! Acme had implied that Yuri was into bondage, not sadism. There had better be a bonus in this for me.

He runs the whip up my left leg until it catches on the thin silky thread that is my G-string. With one quick twitch of his wrist, it snaps right off.

Damn it, that hurt!

Very slowly he slaps precise little welts onto my belly as he works the whip over to my other thigh, but pauses when it reaches what is left of the G-string, so that I might agonize over the pain yet to come. My wince brings a sick smile to his face. Now I'm feeling a bit queasy, even if he isn't.

Stall! Say anything... Do anything...

"What, you want the dessert before the main course?' I taunt him. "Naughty boy!"

This only provokes him into slapping me all the harder. What is left of the G-string shreds into thin air. With a guffaw, he takes its little lace patch and holds it up like a trophy before flinging it across the room. It lands near the door with a skip.

Suddenly I notice that his eyes are crossing. He sits down on the bed. Falls down, really–

–Onto me. All 174 pounds of him.

And I don't think he's breathing. So, the combination of Rohypnol and Viagra was a toxic trail mix after all.

More like fatal. Still, a hit is a hit is a hit.

I jerk at the trick cuffs, but they won't open. With Yuri on top of me, I'm angled all wrong to break their hold. With my chest, I shove him as hard as I can, but for some strange reason, he's not budging. Then I realize why.

The only thing left standing is his erection, and it has him staked between my legs.

Great. Just great.

As I struggle under his limp-but-where-it-counts-most carcass, I hear muffled noises from the other side of the door. It sounds like a skirmish.

The two faint thumps I hear next tell me that something is terribly wrong.

Someone is trying to break down the door. It gives way, and I see Ugly the Skinhead standing there. As he whips out a 9mm, I realize that the thumps were Yuri's posse being taken out.

And now it's our turn.

Even from the doorway, Ugly's aim is dead on. As the bullet enters the back of Yuri's skull, the Russian jerks forward, and we butt heads. As much as that hurts, it has also saves my life: as my head snaps back, the bullet that just left his frontal lobe whizzes by mine by mere millimeters. Still, that doesn't stop a geyser of Yuri's blood and gray matter from spurting onto my face. I freeze in horror.

"Damn commie. And damn commie-loving whore."

Between my temporary paralysis and my Yuri-spattered countenance, Ugly assumes that I'm dead, too, and turns to leave–

But pauses at the sight of my G-string.

He lumbers over to where it's fallen and squats down to pick it up. After sniffing it, he stuffs it into his pocket. Obviously he feels that is a fitting trophy for his kill. Or, in his mind, two kills.

He stalks out, slamming the door behind him.

Silence.

Shit, I have to get out of here. Now.

But that's almost impossible to do, what with Yuri still on top of me.

Granted, the Marmont is used to strange noises from behind its many closed doors. Still, it's been a while since a dead body was found in one of its suites, let alone three. Of course, I imagine the worst:

That someone heard something, or maybe even saw Ugly the Skinhead leaving Yuri's bungalow, and has called the hotel's staff, which will soon come to investigate;

That, after tapping on the door and getting no response, they will burst in, see Yuri's dead bodyguards, and find Yuri on top of me, then call the police;

That, to my children's horror, I get arrested for prostitution;

That, to Acme's dismay, I will be called as a witness at Yuri's murder trial, which will force them to contract with another assassin to finish the job Ugly started on me.

Worse yet, I imagine my son Jeff's face when he realizes that he'll miss his chance to pitch in today's county title game, which moves his baseball team, the Hilldale Wildcats, one step closer to being the major league state champs–

And that once again it's my fault.

It's that last vision that does the trick for me.

It has been documented that mothers involuntarily demonstrate incredible feats of strength when their children's safety is threatened. I am living proof that this phenomenon also occurs when their kids' championship games are at stake.

Defying Yuri's gravitational pull, I heave myself to a forty-five degree angle, which finally gives me the leverage I need in order to jerk my wrists free from the cuffs. With my hands now free, I can shove Yuri to one side.

At least, what is left of him.

I stumble to the bathroom. Leaving on my gloves, I shove my face under the faucet and wash Yuri's brains and skull off my face and out of my hair, before staggering back out into the bedroom, where I retrieve my handcuffs and my dagger from under the mattress. Then I jump back into my hooker attire, which I had dropped onto the plush chair by the bed. As planned, I leave from the terrace door, grabbing Yuri's cuppa joe with me as I go.

In my now ruined spiked heels, I totter up Monteel, the road that meanders high above the hotel, sprinkling what's left in Yuri's coffee onto a thirsty bougainvillea and burying the cup deep inside a garbage can of a neighbor who has left it curbside for pickup. Besides the fact that a mommy mobile like my Toyota Highlander Hybrid minivan would surely stand out in that sea of Jags, Rolls, and Lamborghinis in the Marmont's lot, in my line of work I can't allow the Marmont's valet the opportunity to ID me.

Just my luck: my van is sporting a ticket that is not even ten minutes old. I do that math: that means that the job took a half hour longer than I anticipated. Aw, hell, I'm going to be late picking up the boys for the ball game. The Highlander would have to be the only car on the road (a fantasy in midday, mid-week Los Angeles), run every traffic light, and break every speed record known to man in order for me to get the boys to the game in time.

I do have another option: call my carpool partner, Penelope Bing, and ask her to cover for me…

Hell no. That would hurt even more than Yuri's whip.

She's bailed me out twice in less than a month: the time I was late getting back after taking out some hothead set on assassinating the Pope while he was here in LA; and then there was that hit I had in Seattle, when I'd booked United on the return flight. (On that one, I should have known better and flown Southwest.) "If I have to hear Penelope's smug barbs again, I'll cry. "Really, Donna, what is it this time? Another tennis lesson? My God, you'd think, after all that time on the court, you'd finally find your backhand. Maybe you're taking lessons from the wrong pro. It's Fernando, right?"

The implication being that I'm lying. Again.

And for the wrong reason: that reason perhaps being that I'm two-timing my husband, Carl, with the local country club's tennis pro. Fernando, with his bulging biceps and swarthy grin, leaves many of the club's female members panting, both on the court and in the bedroom.

Considering the number of times I've disappeared in the middle of the day, the assumption has merit to Penelope and her gossip-mongering clique. As if I would! As if I even could be unfaithful to Carl…

To hell with her.

I hit the road, tossing on a sweatshirt as I drive. At the longest turn-light on Sunset–the one at Beverly–I wrangle on my jeans under Mary's miniskirt before yanking it off. The trucker to my left hoots his horn loudly to show his sincere appreciation.

Miracle of miracles, I pull up only four minutes late! Relief floods Jeff's face. The Terrible Two–his buddies Morton Smith and Cheever Bing, Penelope's little angel–have been giving him a rough time. My tardiness is infamous. But now it's my turn to be smug.

Mary is standing there with them. Usually, you would not catch her anywhere near her little brother and his friends, but Morton's older brother, Trevor, is also hitching a ride to the game, and he's a hottie, what with all that blond curly hair and those soulful eyes. To keep them peeled on her, Mary tosses her long flowing mane whenever he glances in her direction. Watching her, my heart leaps into my throat. At twelve, she's already a first-class flirt.

Just like her mother.

The kids clamor into the back of the van, and we're off. Mary, who, on any given day would have taken the passenger seat up front, chooses the two-seat row in the middle instead, with Trevor.

I maneuver around a Porsche going too slow for my taste, and in the process get honked at by a bus. The driver is miffed because we've killed any chance he has of making the light.

"Cool driving, Mrs. Stone." Trevor's approval wins me a temporary reprieve. Then he smiles shyly at Mary. "So, you and your dad will be at the Parent-Student dance this Friday, right?"

This eighth-grade rite of passage is one of the highlights of the school year. Two years from now, it will be my turn to go with Jeff. Although it's Mary's turn, without Carl there to take her, she will miss out.

Jeff and Mary's father is never there for them, no matter what the occasion.

This is why she retorts, "No way! I wouldn't be caught dead there. It's for dorks."

Certainly not for a girl who hasn't seen her father in years.

But Trevor doesn't know this. Seeing his crestfallen face, Mary falls silent. She is angry with herself.

No really, she is mad at Carl.

I run the last light between the baseball field and us. Yes! Yes! We're only nine minutes late!

I've won Jeff's approval. I know this because he stops to give me a quick kiss on the cheek. "So Mom, you brought my athletic cup, like I asked, right?"

"What? But I ... don't remember!" I rummage through the athletic bag that was packed this morning: uniform, hat, glove, cleats—

But no athletic cup.

"I called and asked you to get it from my underwear drawer, like, four times!"

The caller ID on my cell confirms this.

Aw, heck.

League rules: No one plays without a cup. Not even if you're the team's star pitcher. Because of me, Jeff will be benched for this very important game, which could bring the Wildcats even closer to the Orange County Major League division title.

And there is no way I can make it to the house and back in time. We both know that.

Cheever pumps his fist in the air. He is the team's backup pitcher.

A tear rolls down Jeff's cheek as he staggers to the back of the van.

"Jeff, I'm so sorry," I say. But I know he can't stand to hear my lame excuse.

Why should he? He's heard them all before.

"Hey, Mom, what's my denim skirt doing back here?" Mary holds it up to me, accusingly, before shrieking "Ewwwyuck!"

I glance over and notice that it is sprayed with some sort of white goo. One of the larger chunks is covered in hair follicles.

Yuri's.

But that doesn't seem to bother the Terrible Two. Otherwise, they wouldn't be mimicking Mary's high-pitched squeal as they toss her skirt back and forth like a hot potato.

Once again, I'm back in the doghouse with my kids.

At least, until I outrun a Ferrari or something.

Novels by Deborah Coonts

THE LUCKY O'TOOLE VEGAS ADVENTURE SERIES:

WANNA GET LUCKY?

LUCKY STIFF

SO DAMN LUCKY

LUCKY BASTARD

LUCKY CATCH

LUCKY BREAK

LUCKY THE HARD WAY

LUCKY RIDE

LUCKY SCORE

LUCKY NOVELLAS:

LUCKY IN LOVE

LUCKY BANG

LUCKY NOW AND THEN

LUCKY FLASH

OTHER BOOKS BY DEBORAH COONTS:

AFTER ME

DEEP WATER

CRUSHED

Novels by Josie Brown

About Deborah Coonts

My mother tells me I was born a very long time ago, but I'm not so sure—my mother can't be trusted. These things I do know: I was raised in Texas on barbeque, Mexican food and beer. I am the author of *Wanna Get Lucky?* (A NY Times Notable Crime Novel and double RITA™ Finalist), its seven sequels, four between-the-books novellas; and the following standalone novels: *After Me, Crushed* and *Deep Water*.

If you love stories with heart, a bit of mystery, and perhaps some laugh-out-loud romance, all with a hint of steamy, you've come to the right place!

I'd love to hear from you! I can usually be found at the bar, but also at the following:

www.deborahcoonts.com

deborah@deborahcoonts.com

facebook.com/deborahcoonts

About Josie Brown

I read my first book at the age of three. It was an insightful classic: *Go, Dog! Go!* A thriller if there ever was one. I'm being serious. I didn't know that dogs came in so many colors! And could drive *so fast!* It taught me three lessons about enjoyable novels. First, bring the thrills. Next, a fast car or two doesn't hurt. And finally, I *always* put smart dogs in all my series.

Speaking of which—

I'm the author of *The Housewife Assassin's Handbook* series (16 novels; dogs are Rin Tin Tin and Lassie); the *Totlandia* series (8 novels; the dog is Vsevolod Ivanovich) and the *True Hollywood Lies* series (2 novels; no dogs, but a couple of bitches).

My other novels include:

The Candidate (political thriller); *The Baby Planner* (contemporary women's fiction); and *Secret Lives of Husbands and Wives* (contemporary women's fiction) which was optioned by producer Jerry Bruckheimer for television.

You can reach me via:

www.josiebrown.com

MailFromJosie@gmail.com

facebook.com/josiebrownauthor

twitter.com/JosieBrownCA

Made in the USA
Lexington, KY
21 April 2019